UNLIT SPACES

CAROLINE SHEPARD

The author acknowledges the financial support of the Ontario Arts Council, and The Explorations Programme of the Canada Council.

Also by Caroline Shepard: 'Off Centre' (Oberon Press, 2004)

Author website: http://www.carolineshepardauthor.com

Cover photograph by Parker Duchemin

ISBN
978-1-4602-3382-5 (Paperback)
978-1-4602-3383-2 (eBook)

Produced by:

FriesenPress
Suite 300 – 852 Fort Street
Victoria, BC, Canada V8W 1H8

www.friesenpress.com

Distributed to the trade by The Ingram Book Company

ACKNOWLEDGMENTS

I would like to thank the late H.R. (Bill) Percy for reading an early draft of this novel. Bill's flawless and always twinkling critical eye was invaluable to me. There have been few writers like him in our Canadian literary community. He is sorely missed.

Enthusiastic readers Hillary Nangle, Toby Nangle, Joan Anne Nolan, Gail Starr, and Peggy Neal, kept my spirits high. A special thanks also to Peder Gowenius for the story of the amber, and to Rosa Candia for her guiding questions and advice about Chile and Peru.

Above all, I am deeply grateful to my resident professor, Parker Duchemin, for his constant love, his unwavering encouragement, and his skilled editorial support.

CHAPTER
1

APPROACHING LIGHTS
NORTHERN ONTARIO
AUGUST 1985

Cailey jiggles the spool in the old cash register.

Most mornings it's the same, this easy ritual of jokes and apologies, a few customers waiting in line, offering suggestions while she tries to free up the jammed tape. Today though, her voice is pitched too high, her words drop away, disconnected somehow, from her intended good humour.

She presses the sale button. Nothing. Twice more. No response.

She shakes the machine, is on the verge of calling for Steve, but the ribbon of paper suddenly chatters freely from its slot. She smiles weakly at the round of applause that greets her success.

She tucks her shirt into her jeans, tightens the kerchief that gathers her thick dark hair at the back of her neck. Her brown fingers move swiftly over the keys as she punches in each price. Tent pegs $5.95, Coleman fuel $3.50, toilet paper $1.09 – the routine, mechanical activity restores her privacy – Muskol $2.85, Kraft Dinner 6 x 49 cents... She stops. A few macaroni noodles have spilled from a damaged box. "The box is broken. You can grab another off the shelf." Cailey chucks the broken box under the counter.

"Okay, this one's fine." She glances up at her customer, her eyes resting briefly on the rounded, bulging accusation stretched across his shirt: *Have You Hugged Your Kids Today?*

He misreads her glance, winks, raises his eyebrows. "No kids today, ha ha." The stench of stale cigarettes and beer hangs in the air as the bulge shifts over a sunken belt.

She stares down at the bare wooden floor, takes a long breath. There are always these types, she reminds herself. The beer and yellow finger types. The big engine boat types. Black grease under the nails.

For a moment, she is cheered by the thought that the cabin is almost paid off, that this will be their last summer managing the outfitters store. She drifts into a daydream where there's time in her studio to draw uninterrupted, or to take a break when she feels like it, out on the porch for a cup of tea, or off with Steve and Kim for a swim, or a paddle around the lake before sunset.

The man coughs pointedly, shifts awkwardly from foot to foot. "Miss?"

"Oh sorry." She grins blankly at the money he has put on the counter, tightens her kerchief again, and counts out his change from the cash drawer.

Another wink. "Have a nice day, miss."

She hates that expression, the implied condescension in the man's bloated voice.

"Steve," she peers over the man's shoulder as he turns to leave, "can you check the others through." It is not a question. "I'm going for lunch early. I need some air. I'll check on Kim."

Steve waves to her from the back counter where he is marking canoe routes with one of the guides. He looks up in surprise when she lets the screen door slam.

Outside, the morning mist has cleared, and Cailey has to strain against the brightness of the sun after the dull light of the store. Kim is swimming in the shallow water near the boathouse where a couple of guides are loading up their packs. A small dog is yapping frantically, biting at the water's edge. Kim sends splashes at it with her flat hand, working it into a frenzy of prancing around on the sand. On shore, a young couple is arguing loudly about how to pack the canoe, about where their yappy dog will sit. A car radio sends the CBC news out across the parking lot.

Of course it would be simple enough to wander over there for a quick chat with Kim. She could ask her how the swimming is this morning, or if there are any kids on the trips heading out today. They could laugh at the silly dog,

Cailey drops down onto the end of the dock and slips her feet into the cool water. She eats a few grapes, savours the sweet juice popping into her mouth. It's not that she minds having Kim with them in the summer. It's the interruptions she minds when she's trying to concentrate.

"C'mon Cailey, she's a curious eight-year-old!" Steve had raised his voice at her last night after Kim was asleep. "She only needs a little time. Why not show her what you're doing? Let her try stuff herself, like you've done other years. She won't bother you if you take a couple of minutes, and then explain how busy you are."

"Well," Cailey had countered, mastering her own voice at a whisper, "if Kim would leave me alone in the hours we've agreed on for my work, I might have more patience."

Too often lately, Cailey has hurled her frustration at Steve. "She's your daughter Steve. Just keep an eye on her when I'm working, just stop her from coming into the studio. How hard can that be?"

She knows she's being unfair. Steve is the one managing the sudden increase in outgoing trips so she can continue to progress on drawings for the exhibition.

She sends a disruptive splash at a cluster of water spiders. "There is no progress," she mouths at the scurrying spiders. "None at all."

Every day Cailey's panic rises. So far, she hasn't a single preliminary sketch to show for the time she's spent in her studio. Jennifer, her friend and collaborator, makes light of Cailey's difficulties with Hildegarde, a medieval nun whose life story is the intended theme for the fall exhibition. "Give it time." Jennifer has encouraged her on the phone from Montreal, "It takes a while to enter Hildegarde's medieval world."

Sooner or later though, Jennifer may have to accept that Cailey is not the right person to be illustrating the spiritual and artistic journey of Hildegarde von Bingen. The truth is that Cailey gets no inspiration from Hildegarde's acclaimed liturgical cycle, and even Jennifer's cello interpretations continue to leave her cold. Over and over, she's put on headphones and tuned in expectantly to Jennifer playing her Hildegarde-inspired creations. She's listened hard; she's doodled trees and flowers and cartoons of various characters like that ridiculous fellow at the cash just now. She's doodled and doodled. Anything but Hildegarde.

Steve would surely figure it out, with one quick glimpse at the mountain of crumpled paper under her drawing table up at the cabin, that her work on the exhibition has stalled completely. Most likely, given that he no longer asks to see the drawings she's working on, he knows perfectly well what her predicament is.

Cailey bows her head, moves her legs in slow circles in the water, stares into the current she creates as it bubbles up from the murky depths in the shadow of the dock. She knows her present state of paralysis is unfair to Steve and Kim. She knows, most of all, that it is unfair to friend Jenn, whose enthusiasm for an exhibition already in motion deserves better than what she, Cailey, is able to give. The thought of telling Jenn she's pulling out, if that is indeed her decision, is as agonizing as the paralysis she's allowed herself to fall into.

She wishes the summer were over. She'd love nothing more than to be home in her Montreal studio. She would welcome snow falling for hours onto the street below her window. She would walk out into the cold night air, make fresh marks in new snow with her high boots, find her way down the road to Steve's, surprise him with a bottle of wine, sketchbook under her arm.

Right now, she would prefer that to a warm summer day.

Her thoughts shift back to the earlier events of the morning. She had been half asleep when Beth's call came. She remembers the moment, leaning against the kitchen counter, watching absently as the coffee bubbled its pale beginnings into the glass top of the pot. Steve was in the shower. Through the window over the sink, she could see down the hill where the mist was beginning to rise off the lake. She could see Kim curled up in the swinging bed out on the porch, like an angel.

The phone had startled her, made her jump, even though early calls were not unusual after a rain as heavy as last night's. She had assumed, as she picked up the receiver, that they were being called to take the truck up some logging road or into one of the fishing camps, to pick up canoes and soaked gear and shivering trippers.

"Hello? Beth? Oh my goodness... are you calling from Wood River? You're at Uncle Mickey's... I see. Paul? What about Paul?" She pulled two mugs out of the cupboard as she listened. "What are you talking about Beth? Slow down." The coffee gave its final gurgles. "Paul's gone where? Oh for God's sake, can't you just say?"

She shifted the phone to her other ear so she could pour herself a mug. "Okay, okay, sorry, yes yes, of course I get it. Details when you arrive. Yes Beth, of course I can wait. I was just...what?" She'd sipped her coffee slowly, inhaling the steamy aroma, welcoming the bitter taste even as it was burning her tongue.

"But listen, there's no road up to the cabin. You'll see the sign for the outfitters store on the highway. It's clearly marked." She'd rolled her eyes at the ceiling. "No, we won't miss you, Beth. We'll see the car lights clearly from up here. I'll come straight down to the parking lot." Another sip, another grimace.

"Honestly, you can't miss it, Beth, it's brightly lit, it's where the road ends. I'll be down there before you even open your door…" She'd looked out the window, following the flight of quarreling chickadees . "Sure, okay, Beth, well, wow... right, see you tonight." Click.

Cailey had hung up, staring at the phone as if she needed its physical presence to make the call real.

"Who was that?" Steve had come into the kitchen, still drying his hair with a towel.

She had sensed the rough edges in him, the lingering irritation from the argument the night before. She'd watched him pour his coffee into the large mug on the counter, knowing she needed his closeness, knowing, that at least for now, it wasn't there.

"That was Beth. You're not going to believe this."

"What."

"She's arriving tonight."

"Here? Your sister? You're kidding. Beth's coming here." He'd been amazed. "Just like that?"

"Just like that." Her mind had gone blank as she stared into his face.

"I'll tell you later." And she had turned her back and started slicing away at a loaf of bread, letting the uneven pieces crumble onto the bread-board. He had touched her shoulder lightly, hesitating for a moment before going out onto the porch to wake Kim.

Maybe, Cailey had suggested as they cleaned up after breakfast, she should stay up at the cabin for the day, work on her drawings before her sister arrived with God knows what story to tell about Paul.

Steve had countered that the store was too hectic for one person right now, that he hasn't got anywhere on his work either, hasn't even begun preparing new courses for the fall term. Not that this was something Cailey didn't already know.

And now here she is, lying in the sun on the dock, feeling guilty, and fed up with just about everyone. She turns her face to the warmth, closes her eyes. The clamour of the waterfront recedes, and for a while she hears only the periodic hollow thud of wooden paddles against the sides of aluminum canoes. Beth is there in her mind, released into Cailey's half sleep, tilting her head defiantly, looking straight into Cailey's eyes, just as she had nearly fifteen years ago, the day Cailey left Wood River.

***

Late in the afternoon, with the sun at their backs, Steve and Cailey make their way up the path to the cabin. Cailey inhales deeply on the musky scent of earth and moss and damp decaying wood, the rising warmth of ripening berries. With each breath, she anticipates her accustomed moment of calm after a long day. Today, though, the moment is pushed aside by her own agitation, by her mind's relentless insistence on a release of childhood memories, memories that seem now, with each step up the hill, to be sharpening themselves on the harsh cries of blue jays sounding out from the tall pines.

Perhaps for a while this evening, with Kim caught up in the excitement of canoe trips returning from up north, Cailey will be able to talk things over with Steve. They had left Kim with friends, watching from the top of the boathouse just as the first canoes, paddles gleaming in the distance, rounded the point at the far end of the lake.

Cailey looks back at Steve who is close behind her on the narrow path. His expression is unusually anxious and distracted.

"Steve…" She continues walking.

"Cailey…" She hears the amusement in his voice.

"I can't get my mind off Beth. All those memories."

"Well, why would you expect to?"

"I knew you'd say that."

"What would you prefer that I say?"

She turns to face him. "I'd like you to talk to me about this. I'd like you to say you know this is hard for me." She starts back up the hill.

"Okay. I know this is hard for you. And sorry if I'm just a bit edgy."

"We both are."

"It seems to me, Cailey, that perhaps you're the one who need to be doing the talking. You're the one with the big mystery. All I know is that your mother's still a lush, your father's not a barrel of laughs, and you haven't seen any of your family for nearly fifteen years."

"You know more than that."

"Okay. I know you're haunted by memories, Cailey, particularly of the little cousin who drowned when you were a kid. Perhaps Beth can explain about that. You certainly don't. And perhaps Beth could shed some light on the reason you refuse to go home. Sisters with alcoholic mothers do still see each other you know."

"Beth doesn't know about this."

"Doesn't know about what?"

"About… what happened. Only Gran knew."

"Oh right. Well, I was hoping you might slip up and drop a detail or two. "

Cailey is silent.

"You know, Wendy still believes you're coming to Winnipeg with me for Christmas this year. Even after all those years when you cancelled plans to drive back with her from Montreal, she's never given up on you."

"She never will. She is also fed up with me right now, in her friendly Wendy way."

"Well my mother hasn't given up on you either. She was asking again last week if you're coming home with me this year."

"You told me."

"She won't travel east, Cailey. She's frail. You might never meet her."

"I know that, Steve. How could I possibly go with you to Winnipeg without going up to Wood River to see my folks?"

"You couldn't. That's just the point."

"I guess it is. Could we stop this now, please?"

"Sure."

Cailey's breath quickens. This was not the conversation she needed. Wendy. She'll call Wendy. Maybe while Steve and Kim are out in the garden this evening, she and Wendy could get into one of their riotous hour long phone calls. She'll tell Wendy everything, before Beth arrives.

No, she won't. She knows she won't.

"Steve, I've been wondering… if you might have guessed, I don't know… something…"

"What? How could I?"

"From being with me I suppose. From my drawings."

"Your drawings. The family ones?"

She stops again. "Of course the family ones."

Steve reaches up, turns her around to to face him. "The drawings of your family are haunting, Cailey. But what you draw is shadows. You know that. You draw shadows, with hints you refuse to explain. What is it you want me to guess? Why should I even have to? You hint at what's lurking in those shadows. Isn't that what you intend?"

"I intend the hints." She looks away and they resume walking.

"Hints that go nowhere Cailey. Why not open it right up? Tell it. Not to me necessarily, if you don't want to. Why not tell Beth, since she's coming. Or Wendy as your most trusted friend. Find someone. Anyone. Just tell it."

"I will, Steve." Cailey tenses as soon as he puts his arm around her. "Soon, I will." She feels her shoulders go rigid, feels his arm withdrawn.

By the time they reach the porch steps, she is out of breath. She lingers a minute, leaning against a corner post, gazing back down the hill, out over the lake. Steve waits, impatient to go inside.

"I didn't expect Beth, or any of my family, to come here, Steve."

"Except that you've invited them every year, Cailey. You've also offered to help pay their way to Montreal for Christmas as an excuse for not going home yourself."

"I know." She wishes he'd stop challenging her. "That's my guilt for leaving Beth and Paul to go it alone. I just never intended anyone to actually show up."

"Obviously."

"Obviously." She can feel Steve's eyes on her as she pulls at the fingers on her right hand and bends each one backward, one at a time. This is not an unusual stretch after she's been drawing and her fingers cramp. Right now though, it's frantic. Bending her fingers like this, to make them hurt.

"Don't, Cailey, for God's sake, one of them will fall over the railing." Steve sends her a hopeful grin. She responds with a smile that is really a grimace, and they move together into the cabin.

She watches Steve fills the kettle for tea, then walks out of the kitchen and into her studio.

***

When she enters the small back room, she does not turn on the light, but stands at the screened window that looks out into the darkening forest. Only a few shafts of late afternoon sun filter through the trees. She loves the light at this hour, the shifting patterns on the forest floor, the shadows.

Next to the window is the tapestry – the arpillera – Steve brought her from South America several years ago. Even in this dim light, she can imagine the vibrant scene coming to life, the tiny rag doll women moving about in their village, talking, maybe singing as they work and grieve together, as they look up, over and over again, at the rows of black crosses halfway up the mountainside. They never forget the missing ones, those who have been taken. High in the sky, is the large sun, bright, almost too bright, like the eye of God watching over them, exposing them, revealing to anyone who looks, this one small piece of their truth.

Cailey is in awe of the women who sew these arpilleras. These are women who have had the courage to speak out, to tell the world their stories, the stories of those who have died, those who have disappeared without a trace. More than once she's found herself talking to them while she draws, sharing her story with them, in a whisper.

"You have to choose carefully," Cailey whispers now, as she moves over to her drawing table. "You have to know which stories to put in, which stories to leave out." She gropes around for a box of matches. "Otherwise, people you care about will be hurt." She lights the kerosene lamps on either side of the table.

She is surprised to see the clutter of pencils and paints and markers, the disarray of sketches she'd left scattered about on the table. Usually she is meticulous about keeping everything in place. She pulls her most recent half-finished drawing from one of the shelves next to the table, examines it briefly: oyster mushrooms growing on a log, the slithering tail of a garter snake disappearing off the edge of the sketch pad. Cailey refers to her casual sketches as whittling. Passing-the-time sketches, like Uncle Mickey whittling a piece of wood into something, or nothing at all. She pushes the sketch aside with a smile for the memory, and looks up at the row of photographs tacked on the wall across the room.

These are her favourite artist's proofs, black and white enlargements from a photo study she and a friend had done of Montreal women. The full collection had appeared in their shared gallery exhibition. Several months later, with the assistance of her teacher and mentor, Cailey's photos had been published as a coffee table book. In the end, she'd been disappointed in that book. At least Wendy's lively text had redeemed it somewhat, as had the last minute addition of Cailey's portraits of musicians who'd played for the opening. To everyone's surprise, the book became a bestseller that Christmas, and Cailey and Wendy celebrated a significant increase in income.

Eight years later, Cailey still treasures this small gallery. The faded portraits in front of her now are not the ones the critics had found sentimental and romanticized. One influential, but gleefully nasty reviewer had gone so far as to throw Cailey's own words right back at her, accusing her of participating in the romanticization of women's struggles that her photo study was meant to challenge. At the time, it was cold comfort to

9

have friends and colleagues reject the review as a typical dismissal of any new talent expecting access to the city's rarified arts enclave.

She reaches up now, and selects one of the musician portraits she cherishes. She examines it closely under the light.

Jennifer, tuning her cello.

This portrait was shot in one of those rare moments of perfect lighting, a fleeting instant when the single click of a shutter had captured a transcendent concentration in Jennifer's expression. The intensity of her listening, the profound knowing of sound at its source.

You can hear the bow passing over the strings! That had been Jennifer's own exclamation, as she laughed self-consciously on first seeing the enlargement. Jennifer's reaction was the highest praise. Cailey lingers a moment with the pleasure of that success, then pins the photo back in its place on the wall.

Reluctantly now, with Beth's arrival on her mind, Cailey turns to the wall of sketches just out of view behind her chair. These are the images she creates from childhood memories. For these, she dips as deeply as she dares into that swirling reservoir where currents of truth flow into fiction. Here the shifting patterns can be recreated, adjusted, absorbed.

Of course Steve is right about the play of shadows. Cailey knows all too well how to manage light and dark, no matter what she may be drawing. She likes to nudge her viewer to attend more to what's being concealed than to what is revealed. And yes she hints; she hints at painful childhood memories, prods her viewer to ask the very questions she cannot yet bring herself to answer.

She stares at the sketches for several minutes.

A few of them will have to come down before Beth arrives tonight. Certainly the one of her mother peering stupidly into the river, that deep flowing Wood River, with its ever-shifting currents and shadows. Barely discernible in the background, is the silhouette of Uncle Mickey, his profile unmistakable to anyone who knows him, the beam of his flashlight barely illuminating a small body moving away from the shore just under the surface. Becky his daughter, his only child, drowning.

There is, in Cailey's mind, a companion piece to this scene. More than once, Cailey has drawn it and immediately destroyed it. It's a scene of Uncle Mickey swimming frantically into the darkness as Becky is taken toward the bridge, Auntie Val running, screaming for her daughter, others following her along the flat rocks, Gran and Beth hurrying to the edge of the water where Ellen is swaying back and forth, back and forth. Cailey, frozen in place near the low burning fire.

Beth would have a different memory of that moment. Beth would not have seen what Cailey had seen.

Cailey lifts the sketch of Becky's drowning from the wall, considers what others she does not want Beth to see. There's one of Gran, arms wrapped around Uncle Mickey and Auntie Val at the funeral. Another after the funeral, at Gran's house, with Cailey's mother Ellen holding tight to a bottle of beer, her father's large hands resting firmly on her shoulders.

There is Cailey's treasured drawing of Becky piled on top of Gran and Beth and Cailey, laughing laughing, the hammock threatening to swing off its hooks. She'll leave that one. That will be fun to remember with Beth.

There's one she thought she'd taken down last year, a disturbing one of their mother flaked out on Gran's couch. It had been one of those endless weeks when their father was away, and they all stayed over at Gran's. Cailey scrunches it up in disgust and tosses it into the waste basket.

There are various sketches to the right of the window. Most of them are preliminary outlines and diagrams for an upcoming exhibition telling the magical tale of her grandmother's amber pin and the mysterious *menhirs* that stand outside Gran's home village in Scotland. This is a story full of colour. Cailey is considering illustrations in oil, something she's never tried before.

Under the diagrams are written two possible titles for the exhibition. *The Amber Suite*, would Jennifer's choice, named for the music she's composed; Cailey would prefer *Ancient Passageways*, invoking Gran's words. Perhaps Beth will help them decide which is the appropriate title.

Cailey lingers over the largest sketch on the wall. Beth will realize immediately of course, that something is amiss, and she is bound to ask about Gran's anxious expression, and about the amber pin, which is here fastened at Gran's lace collar. It had taken Cailey weeks to work up the warm golden tones radiating from deep inside the amber, to capture from memory that subtle strength of her grandmother's face. Perhaps the confusion, the sadness that Cailey has illustrated so painstakingly in Gran's eyes, will make no sense to Beth. Perhaps it will.

She lifts the amber pin from the small porcelain dish on her drawing table. Beth will want to know how she ended up with it. She turns it over in her hand, rubbing her thumb over the smooth surface; she feels it grow warm in her palm.

Looking up again, she sees suddenly, that her grandmother's face is her own, her Gran looking at her, peering into Cailey's sadness, into their shared secret.

She shakes her head, willing away tears.

She needs to draw something new, or maybe retrieve one of the old portfolios, put up other sketches to replace the ones she's taken down. She rummages noisily in her closet, finds a portfolio she'd all but forgotten. She unzips it, and spreads the drawings around on the floor in front of the closet.

"Hey, I've been waiting with the tea out on the porch." Steve comes in carrying two cups of tea, a slightly disgruntled tone in his voice. "My God, Cailey," he bursts into laughter, "it looks like a cyclone's just hit." He sits in the armchair across from her, and hands her a cup.

"Look at these, Steve. I haven't taken these out since '74. It's nearly twelve years. Hard to believe. Wasn't that the year you left for Peru?"

"You know it was."

She smiles this time, holding his eyes, wanting connection.

"These are a bit embarrassing. Corny. But Beth will like them. I'll put them up instead of the others. Look what Professor Daniels wrote on this one: 'One Norman Rockwell is already one too many.'"

Steve looks closely. "Well, pardon my corny taste, Cailey, but you can count me in with Beth. I like these."

"You do? Well okay, they're decent snapshots of us little kids I guess. Brownie camera variety. No composition whatsoever." Cailey points to the image of two young girls with lumpy cheeks. "Hey fun! Cute little Beth and cute little me, stealing blackballs at the store. Remember those jaw breakers? They changed colour as they got smaller in your mouth? We'd grab a handful of those from one of the candy bins in Dad's store. Someone would be talking to him up at the cash, and we'd snatch the blackballs when we thought no one was looking. Then if an adult spoke to us, we'd keep the blackballs in our cheeks. One in each cheek. Of course they all knew what we were doing."

"Am I hearing a happy memory?"

"Yes." Cailey picks up another sketch. "That's Paul putting money in the jukebox. What he was really doing was getting the money out. No one else could do it, but he had this ingenious way of moving a paper clip around the slot in just the right place so a few coins would tumble out. He was so good at being an adorable little brat."

"What about this one?"

"That's Beth, and me," she points, "sitting at the bar in Uncle Mickey's tavern."

"His tavern. Right. Aren't you a bit underage? How old are you there? Seven? Eight? Kim's age maybe."

"Something like that. Everyone calls it the tavern, but it's part of the hotel dining room really. Everyone comes and goes. The bush pilots were often around for meals between flights. It's not like beer hall or anything. It's moreore the town's gathering place. All us kids loved dropping in after school. Uncle Mickey spoiled us all. I told you about that."

"No, you didn't." Steve holds the sketch to the light.

"Yes, I did. Anyway, Uncle Mickey favoured Beth and me, particularly after Becky's accident. Everyone called him Uncle Mickey, but he was our real uncle, another dad really. Hot chocolate and Auntie Val's warm blueberry muffins to take home. Made by Mickey even after Auntie Val died. Most nights we'd drop in on him, Beth and I, on our way to the store to get Dad for supper. Mum would send us. She'd say the store phone was busy. We knew she was getting us out so she could tank up and hide her bottles before Dad got home. We'd spy on her; we'd look back in through the kitchen window, and sure enough she'd be pouring Jack Daniels into her beer, hiding the bottle behind the Dutch Cleanser under the counter. We'd run down the hill laughing, although we knew it wasn't funny. Sometimes, before he was old enough to come with us, we'd see Paul through the window. He'd be wandering around unattended, barefoot on the grimy floor, playing with his little trucks, his soggy diapers always hanging down behind him. I have a drawing of that. Did I ever show you?"

"What do you think?" Steve raises his eyebrows.

"Ahh, right. So is Kim back yet?"

"She came running up the path just now, all out of breath with some tale about the mean old trippers throwing their nice guide into the drink while everyone kept cheering and laughing."

Cailey smiles. "The highest honour of course."

"You can't tell Kim that. She likes being outraged. She has her little crushes on most of the guides."

Steve hands a sketch back to Cailey. "So supper, probably we should get supper going."

"Sure," Cailey takes the sketch from him, leaves it out on top of the folder to show Beth. She lowers the wicks in the lamps, blows into the glass chimneys to extinguish the flames.

Out on the porch, with a pot of goulash thawing on the stove, Kim stretches out on the swinging bed. She flips through her favourite comics while Steve and Cailey sit quietly on the steps, finishing their tea. Some inner part of Cailey reaches into Steve's silence; they meet again, as they always do when there has been tension between them. He folds his hand over hers while they watch the shifting colours of the setting sun slide toward them across the wavering surface of the lake.

***

After supper they talk about where everyone will sleep. They decide they'll move to the swinging bed on the porch, and give Beth the bedroom. Kim will be in the hammock next to them on the porch.

"Am I staying up till she comes? Or hey! I know! I'll go to sleep right in front of the fire till she gets here, what do you think about that?" Kim has been chattering about Beth's arrival without stop. "Beth's my sort of my step-aunt, right Cailey?"

"Yes, I guess she is, Kim." Cailey can't help smiling as they clear the table together. She watches Kim. "You know, something tells me you two are going to have some fun together!"

"How come?"

"Well, you're both rascals!"

"I know!" Kim nods, and shoves the last of the chocolate brownie into the bite that already fills her mouth.

"Beth might be hungry," Cailey suggests to Steve as they finish the dishes. "She wasn't even as far as the Sault when she called. Knowing her, she'll only stop for gas or a pee, and feed herself chips and Coke and Joe Louis cream cakes."

"I'll get a bottle of wine from the shed. We might all feel like a glass..." Steve chuckles and runs his hand through his hair, "... or a bottle."

"Beth's a tea granny from way back, but I can help you with the wine." Cailey opens several cupboards, shuts each one with a bang. "Isn't there anything sweet left in this place? Where'd all the brownies go? I better thaw more bread."

Cailey turns and leans against the fridge, finds herself looking up into Steve's warm eyes. "You wouldn't believe my nerves right now."

"Oh yes I would. Hie thee to your studio woman, and leave me in peace. It's got to be more than an hour till Beth arrives."

"I can't work now. I need to do something practical."

"You could clean the bathroom."

"Very clever."

She grins at his back as he goes out to the garden where Kim is busy picking the latest of her ripe tomatoes.

Cailey grabs a loaf of bread from the freezer and lands it with a thump on the cutting board to thaw. She takes out the butter. Pickles.

Mayonnaise. Cheese. Sliced ham. Glasses, cups, plates and knives. What else? She stares blankly at the table full of food. She doesn't know why she is doing all this.

Later, Cailey and Steve watch from the porch as the approaching headlights appear over the last hill. The beams catch the tops of the darkened pine trees, making the forest grow high above them like some great being whose inner life is fleetingly exposed by the light poking at its outer limbs. Cailey stands up slowly and starts the walk down the hill toward the fluorescent glare of the store parking lot. Steve watches her for a few minutes, then goes to the side of the cabin to get an armful of wood for the fire.

CHAPTER

2

TREADING WATER
NORTHERN ONTARIO
AUGUST 1985

A car door slams.

Cailey stops, waits on the path for the next sound. Another door slams. Farther down the hill, almost at the edge of the parking lot, she can see Beth clearly in the floodlights that surround the store. Cailey and Steve have always hated those lights. A sign of the times, the owner had said. Protection, he assured them, from thieves and vandals.

Now the unnatural glare places Beth, unsuspecting and alone, in the middle of an asphalt stage.

Cailey doesn't move as she watches Beth lean into the open trunk of the car. She pulls at suitcases, drops bags helter skelter onto the pavement. A hacking cough rings out into the still cool air, and Cailey finally begins to make her way across the open asphalt.

"Beth?" Her voice comes out as a whisper. Beth continues rummaging in the trunk.

"Beth?"

"Cailey. Oh. Right. Just a sec. Got a helluva mess here."

"What happened?" Cailey feels the blood pounding in her head.

"What?"

"What happened? To make the mess?"

"Raspberry jam."

"That's all raspberry jam?"

Beth straightens up and presses her hands behind her into the arch of her back.

"Raspberry jam," she repeats, looking over at Cailey for the first time, "leaked all over the trunk."

Cailey grins.

"Uncle Mickey and I made up a batch for you and Steve last week." Beth stares blankly at Cailey for a moment, stares down at her feet, a smile spreading over her face. Without looking up, she reaches her hand out.

"Omigod, it's really you."

Cailey takes her hand, wraps her other arm around Beth's shoulders. "It's good to see you, Beth." To her own relief, she means it.

"Why don't we just take the stuff you'll need tonight?" Cailey steps back, suddenly self-conscious in the bright lights. "We'll come back in the morning and clean up the jam."

Beth turns back to the trunk. "Sure. We'll bring our toast." She hands Cailey a suitcase.

***

An hour later, Beth is wrapped in a warm blanket, toweling her hair dry in front of the fire.

Cailey is sprawled on the couch, facing Beth, her legs stretched out before the fire, her bare feet resting on the edge of the long bench that serves as a coffee table. Tonight the bench is laid out as a groaning board, with all the fixings Cailey had prepared for stack high Dagwood sandwiches. There are bowls of pickles and olives; plates of sliced ham, salami, cheddar; jars of mustard, mayo, and chili sauce; a slab of soft butter, slices of tomato, lettuce, spring onion, and a warm loaf of crusty bread awaiting the first cut.

Dagwoods. Their childhood favourite, Beth had remembered as she'd walked in dripping with wet hair. Cailey and Beth laughed at the recollection of Paul stacking his sandwich higher than anyone else around the Sunday night dinner table, knowing his sisters were waiting gleefully for it to topple over, and Paul would collect the dickens from their dad for swearing.

On the floor next to Beth, are her essential travel companions: bottles of Coca Cola, bags of salty potato chips, Joe Louis cream cakes. A giant package of Cheesies she had brought along thinking it would be a treat for Kim. Beth had chuckled when Kim's immediate reaction had been an ungrateful 'ugh'.

While Beth is settling in, Cailey becomes lost for a time, in the movements of the comical marionette that dangles from its place at the far end of the stone mantlepiece. Tonight, from under its hooded black cape, the puppet's spindly arms and legs shift about in the draft, as if attempting a jig. Its plump, red-lipped smile comes to life in the dancing light of the fire; its long silvery gown shoots glimmers around the room. The wide black eyes, as always, flash a certain foreknowledge. "She looks just like you," Steve had teased when Cailey had presented the marionette to him for his birthday, "she's even got that scary flash in her eyes."

Beth glances at Cailey, unsure of the silence. She points a questioning finger at the marionette.

"Brigit." Cailey announces the name without explanation, intending the exclusion she creates.

"What?"

"Brigit. She's our hearth goddess."

"Oh, right."

"Yes, our pagan goddess of the hearth. Also the goddess of poetry."

"Ah-ha!" Beth is is pulling off her socks, rubbing a thumb along the arch of one foot, then the other.

Cailey watches Beth. "Brigit always reminds me of Gran's stories. Especially the ones she told about the standing stones outside her village in Scotland, do you remember those?"

"Standing stones? Nope, can't say I do." Beth pulls her socks back on. "I remember lots of other ones though."

"Okay. So, anyway, Brigit here, she doesn't miss a thing."

"Woo. Scary." Beth giggles as she pours herself a glass of wine.

"This is no laughing matter, Beth." Cailey is aware of her growing hostility to Beth's casual amusement.

"I'm so glad you're still nuts Cailey, I always liked that about you. Everyone did."

"What?" Cailey peers at Beth over the top of her wine glass, needing to keep her at a safe distance. "Really?"

"Yes. Although, I'm thinking perhaps you should get some help. Know what I mean? I hear there are very good people around these days. Like, if someone's losing touch with reality, or whatever." Beth's expression is very serious. "You could get help."

"Oh please, for God's sake Beth…" Cailey stops, stares hard into Beth's face as the once familiar signal passes between them. Years have passed, but there it is! Still. Cailey's been taken in, reeled in by her sister's bait. How could she have forgotten?

Their laughter erupts simultaneously. They recognize it, each of them privately, from opposite sides of a wide space, as the shared laughter of their childhood.

Eventually, Beth leans forward, surveys the tray of food more closely, her expression now completely relaxed. She begins slicing bread.

Two slices for you, Cailey?"

"Okay, sure."

Beth is smiling at the mayonnaise she spreads over her bread; she is smiling at the slices of cheese and ham, at the tomatoes and dills, at everything that is piling up to make her perfect Dagwood.

Cailey can't help drifting in and out of the scene around her, at times absorbed in the patterns of flame and shadow that flicker around them in the darkened room. She is sipping her wine slowly, aware she has already had more than enough.

It's only when Beth clinks the wine bottle against own her glass that Cailey notices she's been talking to her.

"Sorry, what were you saying?"

"I was asking you, hello Cailey, if I could have a smoke in here."

"Oh. Maybe not, Beth. Kim's allergic, like I told you earlier. As for me personally," Cailey closes her eyes, "I'm okay if you have one smoke inside tonight and then not again. Obviously you know about being careful outside? No butts or matches left outside needless to say. You can take a tin can of water and keep it next to the chair by the tool shed out back."

"Okay, thanks." Beth groans with mock sadness. "Banished again."

"Sorry if it sounds fussy." Cailey sits up, begins piling her sandwich with cheese and onions and tomatoes and ham. "Listen Beth, I know it's difficult for you to talk about it, but I really need to know more about what's happened to Paul."

"And I need to let it go for a bit. You know that feeling?" Beth lifts a cigarette from her pack. "It's not much more than I already told you. I mean Paul took off after Dad lit into him. No idea where he's gone. We'll get to the rest tomorrow." Beth lights up, takes a long drag. "I was forgetting about Paul for a minute just now. And honestly Cailey, at the moment, it's forgetting I'm into."

"Like you said, I know the feeling."

Beth turns her head to exhale into the space behind her. "I like Steve, Cailey. Not what I'd expected at all."

"What do you mean?"

"Well, I guess it was Uncle Mickey who figured Steve was this upper crust Montreal guy. We all got that impression from looking at his pictures. Classy, definitely classy. We used to make jokes about…" Beth stops herself. "You never mentioned Steve was from Winnipeg, Cailey. How were we to know he was a good ole hometown boy? Cailey? You asleep, Cailey?"

"No. I'm listening."

"Hey look then, don't stay up for me. I'll sit here for a bit and unwind, if that's okay. The fire's great, so happy to have landed. I'd be fine sleeping right here. I don't feel right taking your room."

"Steve's already asleep on the porch, Beth, and we both love sleeping out there." As Cailey pulls herself to her feet, she wonders if Beth's anger will rise to the surface tomorrow. It's there. Like hers, only different.

"Okay, sounds good."

"Did you notice the swinging bed, Beth? Steve built it the first summer we were here. It's from a drawing I did of the one Granddad built. In fact, I think it's exactly the same as Granddad's. Hanging from the four chains. Remember?"

"The swinging bed? Of course I remember. You and I used to sleep there, on the porch."

Cailey puts another log on the fire. "You want us to wake you when we get up?"

"Me? I'll be up with the birds. I never sleep past six."

Cailey puts her hand on Beth's shoulder. "We usually prop a log against the fire screen when we go to bed. Sometimes the screen tips over."

***

Cailey rolls to the edge of the bed without disturbing Steve. She pulls on her socks and drops Steve's bulky polo sweater over her head. Silently, she moves across the porch, stopping briefly to listen to the rustling of some small animal under the steps. There is still no sign of the rising sun, except, she notices, tiptoeing over to Kim's hammock, that the stars shine out of a lighter sky. The moment of blue, her grandmother used to call it, first light if you're the farmer's wife. She pulls an extra blanket up over Kim's sleeping bag.

Passing by the living room, Cailey sees the fire screen tipped over. She gives the glowing coals a poke, props a log against the screen and gathers up a few remaining dishes. In the kitchen she runs hot water into a dishpan and slips the dishes in to soak.

She hesitates in the doorway of her studio. She's half inclined to go back to bed, to curl up next to Steve, but she startles herself awake by switching on the overhead light. She checks her watch. Five-thirty. She lights the kerosene lamps, turns off the ceiling light and adjusts the wicks to the brightness she likes. Even at home in her Montreal apartment, she prefers to work in this soft subtle light. Often she'll turn the wicks up or down, move the lamps around, to give her the tones and shading she wants, create light and shadow as she sees it.

At the back of her drawing table is a wooden box Uncle Mickey made for her, where she keeps her cassette tapes. She fingers through the box impatiently, looking for the series of cello pieces Jennifer is still composing from Hildegarde's liturgical cycle. One of them is still in the player where she'd left it this afternoon. She does not turn it on. The thought of the exhibition continues to fill her with dread. She pulls a book from the shelf beside her, and flips impatiently through Hildegarde's illuminated manuscripts, slows down to review the story of her life; she hopes perhaps one final review of the material will reveal the opening she's missing to begin drawing. She hopes it won't.

There is something altogether too dreary about this Hildegarde. Her music, inspired as it may be, and as unique as her art is, does not speak to Cailey. As far as Cailey is concerned, any eight–year-old, whether it's Kim or Hildegarde, entering a convent as a wee novice, is grounds for a report to the Human Rights Commission.

"Well then, why not start right there?" Jennifer had suggested jokingly last week on the phone, "Start with your modern woman's weeping, for goodness sake, maybe that will be will be your way into Hildegarde's medieval world, and her brilliant spiritual transformation. It's called historical imagination, Cailey."

Hildegarde's transformation, as far as Cailey understands it, had something to do with the devil doing battle with Christian virtues over the destiny of a female soul.

Cailey rummages in the box for something else. Maybe something she hasn't tried for a while. There's that lovely piece she and Steve had heard at an open air concert last spring. She finds it: *Ancient Airs and Dances* by Respighi. She slips the cassette into the player, turns up the volume, adjusts her headphones.

She is surprised. The opening bars play as a cool stream flowing over her jagged edges. Her mind calms, then comes to life with images of the dance, figures slipping through moonlight. A circle of stones, the great menhirs towering above them. And there it is. Gran's stories. These are Gran's stories.

Once again, she lifts her grandmother's amber pin from the small pottery dish, feels its warmth grow in her hand. She believes in its warmth. She shapes a figure with her pencil. She shapes another, then another and then another, until a circle of opening arms is expanding into the melody.

An imitation of Matisse no doubt. She smiles as she continues. A Hildegarde figure clasped in the middle of the circle. No matter that Matisse didn't do nuns.

Yes. That might work. Get our poor Hildegarde out of the nunnery altogether. Dance her through the moonlight. Jenn might like her as a dancing nun, especially with the filmy gown Cailey is giving her to replace her dreary dark habit.

"Cailey?" Beth pushes the door open just enough to poke her head into the room. Cailey continues her drawing.

"Can I come in?"

"What?" Cailey jumps. She removes her headphones. "Oh Beth, hi, you startled me."

"I'll come back later."

"No no, it's fine, just give me a second here."

Reluctantly, Cailey puts away her pencil, twists her hair into a knot on top of her head as she surveys what she has done. She likes it.

Beth comes up behind Cailey, leans over her shoulder to get a look at the drawing. "Hey, that's cool. How'd you get the arms and legs like that? I could never do arms and legs at school. Is it hard to learn?"

"Well for me yes, it's always difficult. Fingers are the hardest. I have friends who say it's easy. Very annoying. So far, this one's not too bad."

Cailey stands up. She does not want to talk about the drawing. "Okay, coffee time. What time is it anyway?"

"It's a bit after seven. Six in Winnipeg." Beth picks up the amber pin from the porcelain dish. "Hey, where'd you get this?"

"It's Gran's pin."

"I know it's Gran's pin, Cailey."

"I've had it since I left home. Gran had asked Mum to give it to me when I turned sixteen, but of course Mum forgot. There's a sketch I did of Gran, with the pin on her collar, up there on the wall behind you."

"That doesn't look much like Gran." Beth goes over to look at the sketch. "She looks too worried."

"I guess so. I remember her sometimes with a lot on her mind." Cailey lowers the wicks, blows out the lamps. "Come on, I need a coffee."

"Me too." Beth follows, still carrying the amber pin, holding it up to catch the kitchen light that is just beginning to filter in through the trees. "I didn't know Mum gave you Gran's pin, Cailey. Why do you keep it in there?"

"It helps me to draw. I like the connection. It keeps me connected."

"To Gran?"

"Yes, in a way. Other things too of course. Wood River. You. Paul."

Beth goes silent as Cailey fills the pot with water and spoons fresh coffee into the filter. She lights a match, holds it toward the centre of the stove. The pilot flame does its little burst, somehow punctuating her own incendiary feelings. She places the coffee pot on the front burner.

"I'll only be a minute Beth, I'm going for a quick shower." She turns and walks out of the kitchen.

"Sure thing." Beth slips the pin into her shirt pocket and opens the screen door to the porch.

She can see Steve still sound asleep in the swinging bed, and Kim, just this minute, rolling out of the hammock.

"Oh," Kim looks up. "are you Beth? Yes, you are. How come I didn't see you last night?"

Beth smiles. "Because you were asleep. But I saw you."

"They were supposed to wake me up." Kim wraps herself in her blanket, drags herself into the kitchen, and sits down sleepily at the table.

Beth sits across from her and reaches into her pocket for her cigarettes. She stops just in time, remembering her banishment to the tool shed, and her fingers close instead around another small object.

"Oh, now look what I found in my pocket, Kim! I brought this for you, a present from up north on the Winnipeg River where Cailey and I come from." She unwraps the layers of white tissue paper, and hands Kim a small chipped stone that is shaped into a point.

"An old grey stone."

"Look. It's an arrowhead."

"An arrowhead? Oh. Hey, you mean like bows and arrows arrowheads? Like for Indians? Like for shooting cowboys?"

"Sure. Maybe more for hunting. Cailey and I used to find lots of arrowheads up the river near where we lived. We used to have a big collection in an old tin can. But I found this one a couple of months ago when I was out walking with my boyfriend."

"A collection of what in an old tin can?" Cailey comes back into the kitchen just as the coffee has finished brewing.

"Arrowheads," Beth responds without looking at Cailey.

"I remember. Whatever happened to that tin anyway? Those arrowheads could be worth something today."

"Oh, it disappeared long ago. Dad was planning to send the whole collection to the university, but it disappeared. Anyway, Kim, we hardly find arrowheads anywhere these days, so that's a real special treasure for you to keep safe."

"Wow. Indians. Cowboys and Indians. Everyone at home will want one of these. Look Dad! See what she brought me?" Kim holds out her hand to Steve as the screen door slams behind him.

"Lucky girl," Steve nods his appreciation at Beth, "I remember finding them sometimes when I was a kid. Something you and I can learn more about, eh Kim?"

Cailey stares at the arrowhead in Kim's hand, feels it imbedded in her child's heart. She can almost smell the tangle of wood and weed and wet stones, see her own small fingers next to Beth's, scavenging around on the riverbank for the treasure that never failed to call forth the painted spirits they imagined lurking sadly, fiercely, in the woods around them.

"What boyfriend?" Cailey plunks a coffee on the table in front of Beth.

"Andy Mac."

"You're still with Andy Mac? I didn't know."

"Well, you wouldn't would you, Cailey."

"Not if you didn't tell me, Beth."

Steve glances over at Cailey, and raises his eyebrows when he sees the irritation in her face. "I think it's supposed to get warmer today, you guys." His cheeriness only irritates her more. "Might be a good day for you and Beth to take the canoe up to the inn for lunch."

"The store's way too busy for one person right now, Steve. Like you said yesterday." Cailey avoids Beth's eyes.

"Well never mind, I'll keep busy on my own. Or you can put me to work at the store." Beth stirs a heaping spoonful of sugar into her coffee. "Got a mess of jam to clean up."

Cailey pauses, catches Beth's grin.

"Okay, Beth," she returns the grin, "let's you and me clean up the jam together like we said, and then we'll paddle up to the inn. I'd rather take our own lunch with us though."

"Good idea," Steve offers. "There's that little island in behind the inn at the mouth of the creek. Great place to swim."

"I'm coming too." Kim says hopefully to Cailey, who was about to surprise everyone, including herself, by saying yes.

"But I'll need you at the store today, Kim." Steve leans over, ties up his shoelaces. "I'd like you to help me work the cash."

"The cash?" Kim's eyes grow large. "Sure, Dad. I'm really good at the cash."

***

Cailey pulls the canoe up on its keel and turns it over on the flat rock. It will have to be painted soon, she thinks, running her fingers along the deep scratches in the red canvas.

"That's some paddle in the wind, Cailey. For an old broad like me." Beth lies down on the rock, still out of breath, closes her eyes. "Let's have those sandwiches. I'm starving."

"You want a beer? I don't think they're very cold."

"We could cool them off in the river."

"This is a lake, Beth."

"So cool them off in the lake." Beth rolls over to look at Cailey. "Well now. Here we are in our very mature thirties, Cailey, still bickering like we're ten."

"I know. It's kind of reassuring, don't you think?" Cailey finds a shady part of the rock and places two cans of beer in a deep crevice. "That arrowhead was a great hit with Kim, Beth."

"I didn't know I was going to give it to her. I'd been reaching into my pocket for my smokes and came up with that. I'm glad I gave it to her. She's a cutie. How's it been for you, living with Steve's kid?"

"This summer hasn't been as easy as I'd expected. That's because of the pressure for an exhibition I'm working on, not so much because of Kim. She's definitely a neat kid. Annoying but neat. Lately, I'm a total failure as the sometimes summertime mum. I've been feeling guilty about it. She's only with Steve for the summers, and I'd hate for her to go home thinking I've pushed her away. I'd have brought her with me today, but it's better this time with just the two of us."

"Kim's's only with her dad for the summers?"

"She lives with her mum, Anne, in California. I thought I told you that. It's always been that way."

"I think you neglected to mention that in the hundreds of long letters you write home every year."

Cailey ignores the sarcasm. "Not to mention the fact that I don't live with Steve the rest of the year either."

"What, so you guys have a series of one night stands every summer?"

"Exactly. Romance in the woods. Every summer."

"What's the point?"

"Why does there have to be a point? It's what Steve and I figured out a long time ago to make things work for us. Our lives are different. We see each other whenever we want in Montreal, but we keep our own places. I need solitary space for my work; Steve needs sprawling space to hold evening meetings when he gets home from teaching. Those meetings are not quiet! Loud voices. Great guffaws. A lot of his activist friends smoke. Steve is often up late typing a report. His typewriter makes a terrible racket. He's frequently on the phone to Peru after midnight when it's cheaper, and then he'll be talking loudly in Spanish. He doesn't come to bed until he's finished prepping for the next day's classes. So why bother coming to my bed!"

Beth is grinning as she stares out at the lake.

"That's it, Beth. Many quiet evenings are mine; I can count on time for drawing, and for juggling my crazy schedule of school photo shoots, track meets, families at home, business portraits. It makes my head hurt, even without Steve's noisy meetings and the deadly smoke."

"Makes a certain sense, Cailey. Very modern of you. For me, I can't imagine such a thing. I mean living alone when there's someone you love to curl up with? I can hardly wait to move in with Andy Mac. Get married, have kids, our own home, ."

"We always have weekends together, hang out with our friends." Cailey responds defensively. "Steve's place is only two blocks from mine, so we have sleepovers! Even during the week. Surprise visits keep the romance alive!"

"Glad to hear it," Beth laughs. "You know, I was thinking I'd like to head to Montreal if there's no word that Paul's coming up here. I thought he might show up here first. I know he wanted to find you. He has both your phone numbers, the one here, and the one in Montreal. Would I be able to stay at your place if I went?"

"Oh. Sure. There are places I know you could stay, including mine, as long as my friends have left."

"Would your friends know who Paul was if he called?"

"No. Not really. I'll phone them tomorrow though, and find out if anyone's called. Also find out when they're heading home."

"Okay, good.""

"About what's happened, Beth. I must have seemed stunned last night. Not sure what you told me about Paul taking off. I couldn't take it in."

"Probably you didn't want to."

"Maybe I didn't. And you didn't want to tell me." Cailey hands Beth a sandwich and they lie on their backs eating and looking up into an open blue sky. "I need to know everything."

"I know you do. I told you Paul's been drinking more heavily than ever?"

"You did. I had no idea it had gone so far."

"No of course you didn't." Beth leans up on her elbow and looks straight at Cailey. "There's really no way you can have much idea about anything."

"You don't have to bite my head off every time, Beth."

"Yes I do. What do you think I came here for?"

"Well now…" Cailey is about to object, but chuckles instead. "Good thing you haven't changed, Beth. Anything else would be unacceptable."

Beth seems pleased with this response. "Okay good, that's settled. So really the most upsetting thing has been how sick Paul has made himself with his drinking. He stopped taking care of himself months ago. You wouldn't recognize him of course, since you haven't seen him since he was ten."

"I think I could pick him out anywhere. I've seen the pictures you've sent."

"Maybe. You can't tell much from those pictures though. Dad and I would choose ones that made Paul look okay. And he's deteriorated since the last ones we sent. In some ways it seems impossible he's twenty-six, and yet in other ways, he has this amazing wisdom in him, but also too much agony for a young guy. Way too much agony. Drunken." Beth pauses, near tears. "He's one very handsome guy, and forever our cute little bratty brother. But right now I'm scared to death for him, he's so thin and pale, doesn't care about anything, least of all about himself. He's taller than Dad you know, but I think Dad could tip him over with one finger. I'm so scared about him taking off like this. He can't look after himself."

"Was Dad being hard on him as usual?"

"For sure, but for once I don't blame him. This year everyone's been fed up with Paul, even Uncle Mickey. We've all been expecting Dad to blow a gasket."

"Well Dad always seemed that way to me. I mean ready to blow a gasket. I used to watch the muscles in his jaw."

"Of course. Me too. And Paul too. But the thing is, this year when Paul took to living on beer, and not much else, Dad was truly scared. Oh and you won't believe this, Paul does that Jack Daniels trick. Just like Mum. Tops his beer up with whisky. He held down a decent job for a while. Since last spring, he'd been working for hydro repairing the old dam, and sometimes he'd come down the river in this rickety motorboat instead of driving home in the car. About three weeks ago, when there was this really high wind, Paul smashed the boat up, maybe hit the bridge. The police haven't quite sorted that out yet. He was found the next morning, still drunk, washed up just the other side of the bridge."

"At the bridge. Near where Becky's body washed up?" Cailey waits, holding her breath, not wanting to touch the memory. Especially not with Beth.

'Someone will be taken;' she can almost hear her grandmother's voice.

"Yes. Could be the exact spot. That's where the current goes." Beth lights a cigarette. "It was Alex McKnight who found him."

"You're kidding. Little Alex McKnight. Paul wasn't hurt though?"

"Paul wasn't hurt. Little Alex is in law school. Paul threw up on little Alex's nice new tennis shoes. Anyway, when Alex brings Paul back to the house in the afternoon, they're there with Mum for an hour or so before Dad and I arrive. Mum's sloshed. Lipstick smudged onto her chin, you know, the whole bit, hair falling out of curlers and all. You should have heard her. 'Alex 'n I're havin' a chat, aren't we, dear? I was jus' tellin' him how we lost our little Becky, found her right where he found our Paul. Wouldn't never do to have another drowning right at the spot, now would it?'"

Cailey stands up quickly. She cannot look at Beth.

"At that point, Paul disappeared into the front room while Dad was talking to Alex and Mum, trying to sort what had happened. Paul's just sitting there, right? Staring at nothing when I go in to him. I sit on the floor by his chair. Try to talk. He won't even look at me, Cailey, so I give up and leave him there. Within a couple of hours, after Dad tore a strip off him, he's taken off, and we've heard nothing from him since, not for three weeks." Beth crosses her arms tightly over her eyes. "I should have stayed with him."

"You mustn't blame yourself, Beth." Cailey is sitting up, flicking small pebbles into the lake. She goes to the crevice in the rock, and retrieves the beer.

"Let's stop this for a bit now, Beth." She hands Beth a beer, strips down to her T-shirt and underpants and plunges head first from the rock into the cold lake. Under water, she moves with a strong kick, propelling herself forward and upward, until she bursts to the surface several feet from the shore. She is far enough out to see past the inn with its red-roof log cabins, the white sailing tower at the spiffy kids' summer camp, and all the way down to the outfitters store at the far end of the lake. Treading water, she moves around to see Beth watching her from the rock. She turns on to her back and kicks her way slowly to the shore.

"It's not nearly as cold as I thought it would be." She pulls herself up and wraps herself in a towel. "Not like Wood River. You should go in."

"I will in a sec." Beth sits cross-legged, fingering the amber pin she had slipped into her pocket early that morning.

"So then, Cailey, my turn. How about you tell me, now, why it is you won't come back home? No one seems to know but you. And I want you to tell me the reason."

CHAPTER

3

RIGHT ON TIME
WOOD RIVER, MANITOBA
FIFTEEN YEARS EARLIER
SEPTEMBER 1969

"Where's Mum?" Paul slumps down in his chair, his arms squeezed tightly across his chest, his head bent to his shoulder so he can watch his foot tap-tapping against the centre leg of the kitchen table.

Cailey does not look up from the pot of oatmeal she stirs. She pushes the wooden spoon mechanically around the crusting edge of the pot. "Where do you think?" She reaches for the bowls on the top shelf of the cupboard.

"You'll be gone when I come home from school?"

"Beth will be here."

"I could follow you. I know when Franklin drives the turkeys into the city. I know where to hide in the truck. One time I hid there all the way to Brenton and back. He never even noticed."

"Oh great. Well, I don't know where I'm going to be yet, Paul. I won't know which family I'm working for until I get there. Mrs. McKnight still hasn't decided." Cailey looks right at him. "You're not coming to Winnipeg. You're only ten, kiddo. Just forget it."

"How'd you ever get this dumb idea, Cailey? I don't like her anyway."

"Who?"

"Mrs. McKnight. She's all stuck up and fancy about her big cottage by the bridge. She's the one who found Becky, isn't she?"

"What's that got to do with anything?"

"Nothing. I hear you and Beth laughing. You call her Lady Honeymoneybags behind her back whenever she comes into the store. I know you don't like her."

Cailey grins at him. "Well, what if we don't? Maybe she's real nice. We hardly know her."

"Maybe real nice. Maybe real nice." Paul starts up one of his mocking chants.

"Hear that, Beth? Maybe Mrs. McKnight is real nice."

Beth comes in carrying an old cardboard shoebox.

"So what?" Beth puts the box down in the middle of the table and begins searching through its contents. She pulls out a half burnt candle, a couple of tennis balls, a bicycle light, a bag of cat's eyes, an earring with the gold gilt peeling off. "Lots of things in here are yours, Cailey. You want them? I can keep them in my room for you. For when you come back. Your suitcase is crammed full anyway."

"You can have them." Cailey doesn't even look at the items on the table, or notice Beth's shrug as she drops each one back in the box.

"You didn't even look."

"It doesn't matter." Cailey spoons the porridge into the bowls. "Come on, Paul, hurry up with the spoons and milk. You'll be late the first day of school."

Cailey reaches for the sugar bowl in the middle of the table. Its red paint is peeled and chipped, the top cracked and held together with fraying black electric tape. As she stares at it, she represses an urge to throw it, to hurl it across the room, watch it shatter sweet and sticky against the far wall.

She glances at Beth. At Paul. Back at the sugar bowl. She sits very still, holding back the same laughter that had brought such puzzled expressions to her friends' faces at the party last night. She lifts the top, drops two large spoonfuls of sugar onto her porridge, watches closely as the golden granules darken in pools of warm milk.

"Beth," she pushes the words out, "I need to say this. You know Andy Mac's too old for you."

"Yeah." Paul begins edging his chair away from the table over to the warmth of the airtight stove. "No good half-breed."

Beth stands up and drops her bowl with a splash into the sudsy water in the dishpan. "You can just shut your little mouth, Paul. He's been good to you, taking you fishing and everything. He's Métis. How come you have to talk like Dad? I hate it."

Cailey looks down at her hands, picks away the dry skin around her nails. "I'm saying, because he's twenty. Not because he's half-breed."

"Métis."

"Okay, Métis. But five years older is too much."

"So you're my mother now, Cailey? You're two years older than me. Just stop. I'll take care of myself fine, thank you." Beth moves her hands around in the warm water, playing with the suds, her back to Cailey. "I'll look after myself," she repeats in a low voice, a whisper.

Upstairs, a bedroom door opens to the sound of a dry hacking cough, and then the intermittent shuffling of footsteps in the hall. A crash. "Shit! That damn doorstopper. Could have broke my foot. Cailey! You still here, honey?"

"Tea's on, Mum," Cailey yells back. She turns to Beth and Paul. "Someone needs to move that doorstopper. Dad's never stubbed his toe, so you can be sure he won't do it. Just needs a screwdriver."

"What would Mum do if we moved it?" Paul starts giggling. "Well what would she do?" He looks up at Cailey. "How would she wake up?"

The image travels around the table, startling all three of them. Before they know it, they are united by an explosion of laughter. Beth leans against the counter, wiping her eyes with the dishtowel. Cailey lifts Paul onto her lap, rocking back and forth as they laugh, grateful for the excuse to hold him.

"Something funny down here? Where's the tea?"

Ellen Donald appears at the kitchen door holding a tall glass half filled with soaked cigarette butts. An empty Labatt's Blue, inverted and stuck in the top of the glass, rattles to the shaking of her hand. She steadies herself by edging along the wall and holding on to a disconnected radiator piled high with magazines and suppliers' catalogues from the store. She uses both hands to set the glass down on the counter next to the sink.

"Your father left for the store already? He was supposed to leave me money." She lowers herself onto the chair next to Cailey and looks over at

Paul, who is now standing, eyes downcast, at Cailey's shoulder. "And just what is wrong with you, young man. Cat got your tongue?"

"C'mon Beth." His voice is barely audible as he stuffs the lunch Cailey made into his school bag. He tugs on Beth's arm. "Let's go."

"Tea's on the stove, Mum. I'll be right back. I'm just walking Paul and Beth to the gate."

"Think you're not going to school today, young lady? You know I can't be putting up with that nonsense. You're going and that's final."

Cailey's eyes flash at her mother. "Oh for crying out loud, Mum. I leave on the one o'clock bus for Winnipeg."

"Oh yes." Ellen looks away quickly. "I know."

Cailey keeps her eyes fixed on Paul as the three of them walk together along the gravel lane. When they reach the gate, Paul lifts the heavy chain off the spike in the post, and allows the large metal gate frame to swing under its own weight. It gains momentum as it flies open, then shudders to a sudden halt against a concrete block.

Paul begins to walk. The September sun shines brightly and Cailey squints to get a look at the children gathering in the schoolyard down the hill. A few paces past the gate, Paul breaks into a run. Cailey doesn't try to stop him, but turns instead to Beth.

"Beth…"

"Never mind, Cailey, it's okay." Beth turns abruptly and walks away.

Astonished, Cailey stands perfectly still, holding back her tears, knowing they all are.

She wasn't expecting this. She wasn't expecting Beth's anger. She only knows about her own.

It is not until Beth disappears around the corner and the bus to the high school heads up the side road, that Cailey realizes she wants more than anything to be with her sister, to be on that bus, to be going back to the familiar halls of the old school.

As she closes the gate and hooks the chain back onto the spike, she is lost in the memory of the three of them years ago, swinging back and forth, back and forth on the gate, their anxieties shared, but unspoken.

When she reaches the front door, she remembers her clothes are still hanging on the line, and goes around to the side of the house. She pulls the garden hose in from the gravel pile where Paul had left it the night before, and loops it around the faucet next to the basement window. Then, brushing the grit from her blue jeans, she climbs the steps up the stoop and takes her dry clothes off the line: pajamas, underwear, her yellow blouse.

She wishes she wasn't going. Or that she'd already gone. From the stoop, she can see far out past the grain elevators at the edge of town, her eyes travelling unconsciously over the expanse of golden wheat. She leans against the railing, concentrating into the distance as if it might have something to tell her, a parting message.

She thinks of the party last night at Denise's. She knows, in spite of their plans to meet in Winnipeg at Thanksgiving, that Denise won't come, that she would never leave Wood River. She'd known it over this last summer, when she'd watched her riding alone at an easy canter along the railway siding, or when she wouldn't show up to swim at the bridge because she was working for her dad at the wheat pool office. She drops the remaining pegs into the hanging bag on the clothesline.

Slowly, she walks down the steps and in through the side door of the house. In the dimness of the hallway, she can make out the familiar shadowy outlines of muddled pairs of rubber boots, Paul's rusted tricycle, the old woodstove piled high with rags and winter coats, several crusted gallon cans of paint. She'd always thought that one day she'd clean out that hallway and make it into a real cloakroom with hooks and a rack for boots and bags. Like Gran used to have.

Cailey sees that her mother hasn't moved from her chair. A cigarette hangs from her mouth, another still burns on the edge of the table.

"Is that tea ready, Cailey? I'm real tired this morning, hon. Oh and I guess I better have that ashtray. Don't want to burn the old place down, do I? Look, I missed your party last night. I didn't forget you know. Didn't really forget you were leaving today. Look, you wait here a minute, Cailey. Something I have for you upstairs. My God, I'm tired today. Your Dad leave me any money this morning?"

Without answering, Cailey begins to hang her dry clothes over the back of a chair. As her mother shuffles out of the room, she moves across to the stove and pours two cups of tea, sits down at the table. She thinks about her suitcase, packed and locked, sitting upstairs on her bed, and she feels that her whole self, all of her, is now bound up in that case, condensed, compressed, silenced. Barely breathing. She takes a long breath. A few more things to go in the knapsack. Walk down to see Uncle Mickey at the hotel. Audrey at the store. And then Dad. Get on that bus. That's all.

"Well, by God, I found it. If I ever lost this, my dear old mum would turn in her grave, now wouldn't she? Oh thanks for the tea, hon. Well, look here, Cailey. Hand me a cigarette will you? Okay, now look. Look at this. It's amber, you know. Do you remember it?" Ellen's uncombed hair hangs grey and brittle over her face as she leans across the table. She shifts her head sideways just enough to drag long and hard on her cigarette without burning her hair.

"Of course I remember." Cailey stares at her mother in disgust as she places the pin on the table.

"Gran wore it Sundays, on her lace collar. You remember those lace collars, Cailey? How she'd move them from dress to dress? This collar, that collar, always the amber pin. Every Sunday, the same thing. Her mother crocheted those collars you know. I have them somewhere, and Gran brought the whole lot from Scotland. Thing is, Cailey," Ellen takes a slurpy sip of tea, flicks her ash in the saucer, "I was supposed to give the amber pin to you on your sixteenth birthday. Oh dear, I seem to forget things these days. Well one extra year won't matter, will it? Seems to me there was a letter for you about the pin. Or maybe that was for something else. The lace collars maybe. For Beth. Anyway, I'll have a look for that letter."

Cailey picks up the amber pin, holds it to the window to catch the light. She'd held it once before, as a little girl sitting up on Gran's bed one Sunday, watching her fasten a collar to her Sunday dress. The pin is an oval shape, the size of a large brown egg. The front of the stone is highly polished, surrounded by a thin ring of carved ivory, and set in gold. As Cailey gazes up at it in the light, she is sure its golden glow is radiating to her fingers.

"Gran used to tell us," Cailey whispers, placing the amber in the palm of her hand, "about how the old people believed if you opened up to it, you'd feel the amber's healing power whenever you touched it. Granddad laughed so hard when she said that, and Gran could never keep a straight face. 'Oh, what hogwash, Granny,' he'd always say, and then he'd wink at us, at Beth and me. She believed it though. Gran believed about the amber."

"She believed a lot of that stuff. Wish I'd written her stories down, but there may be that letter from her somewhere. That's right, I remember now. I was not to open it she said. She made me promise. It was only for you. Could be there's a story about the amber. Don't suppose it matters so much. As long as you have the pin."

Cailey looks directly into her mother's eyes. She had learned long ago to set the distance between them. She knows how to make her own eyes blind, to dull any light in her mother's. At this moment, she sees nothing in her mother's eyes, nothing at all.

"I'm glad you found the pin, Mum. It means a lot." Cailey stands up abruptly. "I'll do up these dishes, and pack up the rest of my things. And I'll be heading off for the bus. You want another cup of tea?"

"Oh sure, thanks hon, I'll take it upstairs with me. Have a lot to do this morning. I'll have to get dressed for town since your dad didn't leave that money I need to owe for bingo. Come and see me before you go, Cailey."

***

Cailey finds her Uncle Mickey washing up the previous night's beer mugs at the bar, a towel slung over his shoulder, his glasses perched as always, part way down his nose. Even with the windows open out to the porch, and the breeze coming in from the river, there is a lingering odour of stale beer and cigarette smoke that rises up from the bare wooden floor and the worn down tables. Perhaps it isn't such a bad smell, she reflects as she closes the door behind her. Quite possibly, she is going to miss it.

Mickey waves to her from across the bar. He checks his watch. "Well, that took longer than you thought, Cailey girl. Barely time for us to have our coffee. I'll bring us some over there." He points to the table that looks out across the river. The Parcheesi table they always called it, where she and Beth would sit Saturday afternoons playing Parcheesi and drinking cocoa, before they went to help their dad up at the store.

"Remember Gran's amber pin, Uncle Mickey?" Cailey stands at the bar while she unfolds the tissue wrapped around the amber pin. "Mum gave it to me this morning."

"Well I'll be. That was part of your Gran's Sunday best ever since your mum and I were kids. Sometimes she'd unpin it and hand it to Ellen to play with. Trying to keep that little one quiet in the pew was a job I can tell you, and with Dad in the pulpit, she loved to act up for attention. She was one restless kid, that sister of mine." Mickey stirs sugar into two cups of coffee and carries them over to the table by the window. "Still is."

"Did Gran really believe it was magic?" Cailey sits across from him. "The amber, I mean."

"Oh well, I remember those stories. I often wonder if she believed it herself. She was one for mischief and old wives' tales you know. When we were older, Ellen liked to tease that Mum was only trying to get the old man's goat, him being a preacher and all. Well now, isn't that something, Ellen giving you that today, Cailey. It's right for you to have it."

They sit quietly for a few minutes, warming their hands on their coffee mugs, Cailey staring thoughtfully at the amber.

"I didn't say goodbye to Mum, Uncle Mickey. She asked me to come up and see her, but I left. I just left without..." She hadn't meant to say that.

"But she gave you the pin, Cailey. That was her way. That tells you something."

"She was supposed to give it to me when I turned sixteen. That's what Gran had wanted."

"Ellen forgets things. No need to tell you that. Loses whole days sometimes, I'd say."

"She didn't come to my party."

Mickey nods.

"I don't care. It would have been worse if she'd come."

"Maybe." Mickey leans back in his chair, observing Cailey closely. "Maybe."

She looks away. There are some things even Uncle Mickey doesn't know. Must never know.

"Well now, Cailey, I'm to thinking you have a few butterflies fluttering around in there. A bit on edge about heading off alone."

"I'm fine, Uncle Mickey, honest." Suddenly she laughs through her lie, relieved he can see it.

"Well your secret's safe with me. I won't tell a soul about your wobbly knees." He smiles. "Hundreds of butterflies, I'd say."

She smiles back at him, drops her head and scrapes at the table with her fingernail. After a moment she looks up, unafraid of her tears. "No – thousands, there are thousands of butterflies."

"Well now, that's better. Always better to say it right out, don't you think?"

She nods, unable to speak.

"Seems to me you missed a lot of years, Cailey. Years you needed to be a kid." He stands up. "We're very proud of you, you know. We were saying that last night at the party."

"Who was?"

"Oh a lot of people said it. Denise's folks. Your dad and I."

Cailey begins to protest. "I hardly think Dad..."

"Wait now, don't you go looking at me that way. I know your dad well. The way I see it, Cailey, it's just too hard for him to say what he wants to. Can't do it. Too much heartache."

"Okay, maybe." Cailey has a clear picture of her father at the party, leaning against the wall as he talks to Uncle Mickey, looking like he wants to be somewhere else.

Mickey picks up their cups, wipes the towel absently around the table. "Val should have been there last night, to send you off. Well she was there in her way, wasn't she? She hangs around on a lot of important occasions. You know, when Val died so soon after we lost Becky, and then Paul was born soon after," he hesitates, "well, Becky would have been fifteen this year, and well, I don't have to tell you that you three kids are like my own. You were like Val's own." He turns back to the bar.

"Gran used to talk to me about Becky you know. Did I ever tell you about that?"

"Well, no I don't recall your saying…"

"Gran missed Becky a lot." Cailey knows it is a risk to raise this with Uncle Mickey.

"Yes, she did." Mickey stands absolutely still. Listening. Watching Cailey closely.

Cailey feels the old tightness in her chest, her breathing quick and shallow. "It's just that Gran wanted to talk about what happened. Sometimes, she'd take out the amber pin and hold it, seems she needed to feel its healing warmth. And then she'd hand it to me." Cailey waits. "And she'd tell me a story of something that had happened in her village when she was a girl in Scotland. A child drowning. Do you ever remember hearing that story?"

"A child drowning back in Scotland? No, I can't say as I do." Mickey's face was suddenly pale. "Well never mind, she told so many stories, never could keep track of them."

Cailey wraps the pin back in the tissue paper and drops it into her pocket. Through the window, she can see down to the docks where float planes roll slightly in the wake of a passing motorboat. She watches a bush pilot who'd come in yesterday with a group from up north. He is repacking his gear, swinging it, and then himself, up into the cockpit. The single prop sputters to life, revs high as the plane prepares to head into open water for takeoff.

Within minutes, she is walking up the street with Mickey to the store. Nothing more is said about Becky.

Once inside the store, Cailey drops her pack onto the floor next to the window. Just behind her, Mickey comes in carrying the heavy suitcase.

Audrey looks up from the counter where she is refolding an order of boys' sweatshirts.

"Hi, Audrey. Dad out back?"

"Yep, on the phone as usual. So you're all set, Cailey? Hey there, Mickey. All out of breath, eh? I guess those three enormous steps up from the street are getting a bit too much for you." Audrey never lets up teasing Mickey about getting old, especially since she is his senior by at least a year.

Mickey raises an eyebrow in mock outrage.

Too bad they never got together after Auntie Val died, Cailey thinks as she goes through to the back of the store. The whole town always figured they should.

"Hey Dad, it's me."

Jim Donald looks up from the papers on his desk and raises his hand to silence Cailey while he finishes his phone call. He is a big man, thick set, muscular, still youthful with barely a trace of grey in his dark hair. His voice, as he continues his call to a Winnipeg supplier, is filled with the self-assurance that has kept him on top of business even in hard times.

Eventually, he puts the phone down, rearranges his papers in neat piles on the desk, and pulls a file from the centre drawer. "Glad you made it on time, Cailey. A lot to do up at the house I'm guessing. Well, sit you down then, and we'll check things over here. I talked to Janet McKnight earlier this morning and she's already decided you'll work for them. The other folks who wanted you, the Anderson's, had wanted Wendy, the schoolgirl from Brenton. You and Wendy will be at the same school. Just as well you're with the McKnight's, I figure, since we know the family a bit. You won't have to do those interviews with two different families. Janet said she'd be there at the bus station to meet you."

Cailey hears the tightness in her father's voice. It seems to come at her in rapid fire staccato, like an urgent news broadcast. "The bus doesn't get in to Winnipeg till a quarter to eight. It'll still be light when you arrive, so maybe you can see round town a bit. Your ticket and some extra cash, and your scholarship cheque are all in here."

He hands her a brown manila envelope with 'CAILEY DONALD' printed neatly on it. She feels almost like a client, except that she knows his jaw is working, clenching unclenching, a sure sign that the feelings he will never admit to are at the surface.

"In addition," he continues in his business like fashion, "Janet will go with you to open your bank account after school on Friday, so you can deposit your cheque. She'll be putting your monthly pay into the account for your spending money and for saving whatever you can. Should be plenty enough. If you're careful, you might not have to touch much of the scholarship. Earn yourself some interest. Well, let's see now, what else? You already know what you need to about the high school. Everything else you'll discover when you get there. Of course, you get room and board free at McKnight's. Well, not exactly free is it?" he pauses to laugh, "since you'll be working for it, looking after their kid and all. Most schoolgirls get Thursday night and all day Sunday off. You'll work that out with her I'm sure. You must remember Alex, their little boy? A couple years younger than Paul. He comes into the store with Janet whenever they're here in the summer. I'm sure you remember."

Cailey remembers perfectly well, but doesn't trust herself to speak.

"He goes to some posh private school. Quite the little gentleman I gather. God help us. Or you!" He laughs again as he looks at something up on the wall behind Cailey. "Anyway, Janet knows you've been looking after Paul a fair bit, that you've had a lot of responsibility. You should find it easy enough, don't you think?"

"I hope so. I feel weird to be going. Getting on that bus. Leaving Wood River." Cailey knows she will hold back the tears, it will just take a second. She will not cry in front of her father. She concentrates on the CPR calendar in front of her on his desk, the mountains, a train winding along a flowing river. Smiling passengers in a dome car. She measures out her words. "Will I be coming home for Christmas?"

"I sure hope so, Cailey. I'm afraid I forgot to ask Janet what they'll be needing at those various holidays. It's been so busy here. I'll be heading to Saskatoon tomorrow, unexpected problems with a shipment of feed. Just overnight though, so there's no need to worry about Beth and Paul and… well okay, you don't have to worry about that anymore, do you? Anyway, we sure want you back here for the holidays. Wouldn't be the same without my girl."

Cailey is surprised by the sudden softness in her father's voice. He clears his throat and continues.

"Perhaps you'll take the bus home for a weekend this fall, the McKnight's go away weekends I think. We'll see. Depends on the weather too, I suppose. Janet didn't talk about their schedule, so you'll figure it out with her when you're there. Make sure to write Cailey, when you know what's up." He pauses for a minute, turning his pen round and round in his fingers.

"How'd you find your mother this morning?"

"Okay, I guess." Cailey thinks of telling him about the amber, but decides against it.

"She say anything about missing your party?"

"She fell asleep."

"She fell asleep, all right," he mutters more to himself than to Cailey. "She couldn't even walk to the car." He shuffles some papers on his desk. "Well then, Cailey my girl," he smiles with his mouth, but not his eyes, "next year, you'll be choosing which university scholarship to accept! You keep your eye on that. And remember, with your marks in math, you're a natural to do business, and take over the store." With a laugh, he holds up his hand in anticipation of her objection. "Well let's leave that conversation to another time. I know you have some grand ideas about your art, but you'll never find your way with that, I can assure you." He goes on when she doesn't respond. "Right then, my girl. I'll walk you across to Chubb's. Treat you to your favourite cherry coke."

Audrey and Mickey are waiting for them up front at the cash.

"Hey there, Mickey. Audrey. Shall we take our girl out for one more cherry coke? Bus will be along before we know it."

Cailey hangs back as they cross the road to Chubb's. Her dad carries her suitcase in one hand, his other hand rests on Mickey's shoulder as he explains about the fluorescent lights he is putting in the store, and that maybe Mickey should think of them for the hotel. "Save a lot of money in the long run," he says. Mickey nods.

Audrey ducks quickly into the post office next door, waving a letter in Cailey's direction. "Have to get this in the mail, Cailey, be right with you."

Cailey hesitates at the door to Chubb's, looking up the road, her eyes resting easily for a moment in the deep open sky. She searches the horizon for the familiar dust trail of the one o'clock bus. There it is, right on time. She turns and walks into the restaurant.

CHAPTER

4

SHADOWY SHAPES
WINNIPEG
SEPTEMBER 1969

As she closes the door behind her and lifts her suitcase onto the bed, Cailey hears the hollow clacking of Mrs. McKnight's heels descending the wooden stairs to the second floor. Without turning on the light, she makes her way to the window and looks down from the third floor peak into a rolling green back garden. At several points along a cobblestone walk, she sees globes of soft light illuminating flower beds, weeping willows, little groupings of garden chairs.

In the distance beyond the walk is the dark fluid band of the Assiniboine River. Across the river, are intermittent sparkles of lights, and a late summer breeze plays through the trees on the riverbank. As soon as she lifts the tall sash window, she's met by the familiar smell of fresh mown grass, and the muted sound of voices from below. She presses her face close against the screen and peers down the back of the house where she can see a dark green awning covering what she imagines must be an outdoor patio of some sort. Light splays out from the patio over the lawn. A small boy runs out onto the grass carrying a stick. Following the boy is a golden-haired puppy, bounding high and barking with excited anticipation as the stick is hurled into the air.

"Alex! I told you that's enough. Off you go, into your pajamas. The new girl will be down soon to meet you." As the puppy lays down in the grass, wagging and whimpering expectantly at the captured stick, Alex drags himself, head down, back to the patio. The voices become muffled again.

Cailey turns around to face her room. A crack of light shines under the door onto the polished wood floor and spreads itself up onto the shadowy shapes of the furniture in the room. She can just make out the outline of the single four-poster bed, and next to the bed, a square table with a lamp. In the far corner is a dresser and a small armchair. Standing motionless in the semi-darkness, she feels the presence of her own shadowy shape, secret and secure, partially hidden from the light.

When finally she edges her way along the wall and turns on the lamp, bright colours jump to life in the small room. She is startled by them. The slanted attic walls are covered in tiny flowers, coral and white flowers everywhere she looks. Even on the bedspread and curtains. Even the waste basket.

She pulls the bedspread down part way and pushes her hand into the pillow. It is soft and feathery. The pillowcase and the sheets are crispy white, smooth and cool to the touch.

Over on the dresser, painted white to match the bedstead, is a bouquet of purple and yellow pansies arranged in a clear glass vase. An envelope with her name on it is propped up against the vase. Inside, she finds a card printed on one side in formal, old fashioned lettering. Cailey squints to make out the name. "Mrs. John R.D. McKnight Jr." it reads. On the back of the card, is a short message, written in a large, bold hand: "Welcome to our home, Cailey." It is signed "The McKnight Family." She looks up at herself in the mirror over the dresser and forces herself to smile, staring almost fiercely into her blue, watery eyes. Smile on the outside, smile on the inside, Gran used to tell her. It always worked. She mouths silently into the mirror, forming the words with great exaggeration, "Mrs. John R. D. McKnight Jr." And again, "Mrs. John R. D. McKnight Jr." Lady Honeymoneybags. She smiles harder and watches with a young child's wonderment as the tears spill down her cheeks. Then she pulls an abundance of long dark hair over her face, and laughs at the furry beast looking back at her.

"Oh, Cailey? Hello up there?"

Cailey hurriedly brushes away tears and clears her throat. She crosses the room and opens the door only a crack, in case Mrs. McKnight is coming up the stairs.

"Yes, hello. I'm just unpacking my suitcase, Mrs. McKnight."

"Well, of course, dear. That's just fine. But Alex is just about to go to bed and we're having some milk and cookies in the breakfast room, right at the bottom of the back stairs here. Why don't you come down now, dear, and you can finish your unpacking a little later."

"I'll be right there." Dear.

Cailey opens her suitcase, considers putting on a fresh blouse. Then she closes it again, turns and walks down the stairs.

"Oh look Alex, here's Cailey to meet you. Well, don't eat all the cookies, for goodness sake! What about Cailey?" Mrs. McKnight smiles up at Cailey as she enters.

Alex is crumbling the last of the chocolate cookies into a large glass of milk.

"Oh, don't worry about me. I'm really not all that hungry right now."

"Alex! Really! Now look at the mess you're making! Aren't you even going to say hello to Cailey?"

"Hello to Cailey." Alex looks at Cailey gleefully as he rubs his hands together over the milk, spreading cookie crumbs all over the table. "I'm full now, Mummy."

"Oh, I give up," says Mrs. McKnight. "Well, do sit down Cailey. At least I can get you a glass of milk. You must be very tired after such a long bus ride."

"Well, not really, and come to think of it, Alex's milk looks awfully good with all that chocolate floating around in it. Why don't I just have some of that?" And, winking at Alex, she reaches for his glass and drinks down half of it in one gulp. Alex looks quickly at his startled mother, then back at Cailey with large, admiring brown eyes.

"I have a brother a few years older than you," she says. "We both like chocolate cookies in our milk."

Janet McKnight laughs weakly and sends Alex off, still grinning, to brush his teeth and wait for his story.

"Alex loves to joke, Cailey. Well, of course, we all do, don't we. Still, it's important that you set a good example for him. Now let me show you around a little, and I'll explain the household routine. Through here is the dining room. Of course you won't have seen this part of the house because we came in at the garage entrance, didn't we? It can be a bit confusing at first."

Cailey follows Mrs. McKnight from the kitchen into the dining room. As they stand quietly at the doorway, the muted light from several frosted wall lamps seems to magnify the room's stillness. Cailey walks slowly, a little timidly at first, the full length of the dinner table, running her hand over the backs of five high-backed wooden chairs which stand facing their five impassive mates across a broad expanse of glistening red mahogany. She leans over and touches one of the seats. Velvet. Soft. Purple. On an impulse, she sits down in the large armchair at the head of the table and looks up to find Mrs. McKnight observing her with some astonishment.

Cailey jumps up, self-conscious and embarrassed even as she hears her own voice rise unnaturally into the hollow space around her. "I guess lots of people live here."

"Good heavens, no, my dear, it's just the three of us. Well four now, counting you, of course! We do entertain a lot. John's business dinners. And so many old friends and family. It's surprising how often this table fills up."

Then, as if sensing an unwelcome shift in propriety, Mrs. McKnight moves swiftly through the room, and draws open the heavy brocade drapes that cover the entire wall behind Cailey.

"There, now. What a lovely evening. Come and look. See over to the left, Cailey, you can see the patio. There. Do you see? And there's a lovely walk down to the river. Have you looked from your window? We must walk down there this evening, you and I. I've no idea what sorts of things that naughty puppy has dragged into the summer house. In future, I'll want you and Alex to check the summer house each evening before you put him to bed."

***

Cailey hears Wendy call out to her just as she reaches the McKnight's driveway.

"Hey! How come you didn't wait for me after school? I had to run all the way to catch up to you!"

"I did wait. I waited at your locker." Cailey laughs at Wendy's breathless indignation.

"Oh. Sorry. I was talking to Jeff at the gym. I thought you were coming to the gym. Did you find out if you can get off on Friday?"

"No. Not yet. She said I get Thursday night off and every Sunday, but I have to wait and see if they need me for Alex on the other nights."

"Well shit, they can't just leave you hanging like that every weekend, Cailey. The Anderson's always tell me at the beginning of the week."

"I don't know them well enough yet. She's always explaining 'the routine' to me. It's only been three weeks. You've been at the Anderson's' since the middle of August."

"You have to ask tonight. Or they'll just take you for granted. Anyway, call me after supper if you get a chance. Better go. I'm late."

"Okay. See you, Wendy." Cailey turns and walks up the gravel driveway, partly shaded from the warm afternoon sun by a tall pruned cedar hedge. Every day after school, she welcomes its earthy fragrance. Today, she walks with her eyes closed, breathing the memory of evergreen woods on the rocky north bank of Wood River. Today is Wednesday and Mrs. McKnight would be downtown with Alex at his ballet lesson. They would be back at six, she had said. Mr. McKnight plays squash on Wednesdays. So all Cailey will have to do is put in the roast and prepare the vegetables. They will eat at six-thirty. That is the routine. For Wednesdays.

"Mind you don't wander into that flower bed, miss. Most folks walk with their eyes open you know."

"Oh. Mr. Melanchuk, I didn't see you there."

"It's not me you need to see, miss, it's my flowers." Mr. Melanchuk turns back to his gardening.

"Okay, sorry about that." It's a wonder he doesn't tip into the bed of black-eyed susans, Cailey thinks. He must be at least a hundred.

"And don't call me miss," Cailey mutters under her breath, walking past him through the open garage doors. She searches for her key in the pocket of her jacket. It is hard to see the lock in the shade after the bright sun. Most days Mrs. McKnight is home by four and the door is unlocked. Alex's bus drops him off at four-thirty. Except Wednesdays, of course.

She drops her school bag in the back hall. The 'mud room', they call it. It is spotless. No Manitoba gumbo in this mud room. She washes up in the small bathroom just outside the door to the kitchen and then pours herself a glass of milk while she reads the note left by Mrs. McKnight on the fridge. "Cailey. Pre-heat oven to 325°. When red light goes off, put roast in on middle shelf. Wash potatoes, poke with fork and put in with roast at five-thirty. We'll just have frozen peas. Tonight we'll eat in the breakfast room. Alex has some special TV show at seven." It is signed 'J.McK'.

Cailey turns the oven to 325°.

By seven-thirty there is still no sign of Alex and Mrs. McKnight. Mr. Melanchuk had gone home some time ago, bringing Puppy to the door, very hungry. Cailey rummages through the pantry to find the dog biscuits to quiet him down. And now the dinner will be tired and dry at low heat in the oven. She sips a little nervously on a cup of tea. She hasn't eaten.

When the phone rings, she jumps. "McKnight residence, may I help you?" As she's been taught.

"Oh, yes, Mr. McKnight, yes this is Cailey." She listens. "No they're not home yet… oh I see. Well perhaps you'll have some when you come in after your meeting. Oh, oh I see. Certainly, yes, I'll tell her."

At eight o'clock, Cailey hears the car come into the garage. She is doing her homework at the kitchen table.

"Oh dear me, Cailey." Mrs. McKnight comes in breathless and agitated. "I'm afraid we've let you down. Well, never mind. We've already eaten. That roast will make shepherd's pie for tomorrow. I'll teach you the recipe. I hope you went ahead with your meal. Do bring me a glass of sherry in the den. Alex, you can watch TV for half an hour, no more, and then straight to bed. Cailey will make you your cocoa. What an exhausting day we've had, haven't we my little one. Oh Puppy, do get down. Cailey dear, let him out in the back, would you?"

Alex flops into a chair in front of the TV. Cailey puts a disconsolate Puppy outside, and goes to the dining room to pour a sherry for Mrs. McKnight from the crystal decanter on the sideboard. This is the usual evening ritual, performed by Mrs. McKnight herself when she isn't so tired. Mr. McKnight, it turned out, is rarely home for the ritual.

"Mr. McKnight called before you came in." Cailey says, placing the glass of sherry on the table next to Mrs. McKnight's chair. "He said not to wait up for him. Something about a meeting at a club."

"Oh yes, I expect it's the new client from Minneapolis. Well, how are you, Cailey? You seem to be catching on fast. We're very pleased, you know. And Alex seems right at home with you. He was very attached to his nanny, and she just upped and went back to Ireland. It was all so sudden. Four years she'd been with us. And then gone with no explanation."

"Are those her white uniforms in my closet?"

"Why, yes dear. Well, she was a trained nanny, you know. We don't expect you to wear them of course! Except maybe for the odd party. You can put them in one of the other bedrooms up there, if you like. Now, how are you finding school this week?"

"It's fine I guess. I don't know anybody much yet, except Wendy Peterson."

"Oh, yes, the girl from Brenton. I believe she's at the Anderson's. A bit precocious I'm told, although they seem to like her all right. How do you find your classes and the teachers? I told your father I'd be letting him know after a month."

"Oh I like my courses so far. I seem to be a little ahead but I…"

"Well that won't last long. You won't be bored, I guarantee. This is probably just review, you know. The Winnipeg curriculum is always more advanced than the rural schools. But of course you know that. That's why your father sent you here."

"Mrs. McKnight, I'm just wondering if you need me Friday night. Like I mentioned yesterday, there's a party I'm invited to."

"Oh yes. The parents will be there of course. Where is it?"

"At a park somewhere. It's a hotdog roast."

"Well, what fun. Friday you said. I'd better check the book."

Cailey watches as Mrs. McKnight crosses the room in her stockinged feet and picks up her calendar from a large oak desk in the bay window. There is a moment's silence while she looks up the dates.

"Let's see. John will be in Minneapolis again. Perhaps I could take Alex to the gallery picnic after school. They're such a bore, really. Too many children. But Alex will love it. And you'll get your extra night off. Well, good, we're all set then."

"Thanks a lot, Mrs. McKnight. Shall I make Alex his cocoa now?"

"Yes of course. I'll come along with you. I'd like to read to him myself tonight. No dishes for you to do, Cailey, so that turned out well, didn't it? Let's go and see what our boy is up to. I'd like to have these little chats more often, dear, so we get to know each other a better."

Mrs. McKnight pauses at the door to the dining room. "Oh, my, I'd nearly forgotten. We should take a couple of minutes. I've been meaning to show you how the bells work." She points to a diamond shaped brass wall plate with a pearl button at its centre. "Well, the few we use I mean. Mother and Father always had someone to answer their calls from anywhere in the house, if you can you imagine such a thing. Now all we have is Maggie three times a week to clean, and part-time help from you of course."

She leads Cailey toward the large double doors at the other end of the dining room. Alex has already told her that they hardly ever go in there, into the 'great big room'. He told her, with indignation, that he was never, ever allowed to go in there without one of his parents. Not even with his nanny. "Things would break," he said.

"John and I rarely use this room, Cailey. But it's lovely to see. Our life is not so formal now, and I can't say I'm sorry. Certainly not with Alex underfoot. I dare say children aren't so easy to control these days. From time to time we do have large parties however. Catered of course. There will be a couple of cocktail parties for John's firm and clients, and several large gatherings for friends and family at Christmas. You know the sort. Now we don't really expect you to do much for these. We might ask you to serve cocktails, or help the caterers in the kitchen. And of course keep Alex out of mischief! It can be fun, you know. Quite a lot of excitement."

Mrs. McKnight slides open the tall double doors. With a low rolling sound, the doors disappear into the walls.

"Now let's have a look. There are actually four bells in here. I'll show you how the numbers come up in the kitchen, so you can tell which bell to answer. The caterers will know all that for the parties of course. But it's better for you to keep an eye out as well."

In the light from the crystal chandeliers, Cailey stares in amazement at a room that seems to her to be twice the size, at least, of her home in Wood River. A great brass framed mirror hangs over the marble fireplace at the far end of the room, and there are formal portraits all along the walls, and arrangements of wing chairs and sofas and tables, an array of crystal glasses on a long sideboard, a deep red oriental rug that runs the full length of the room.

"Isn't it lovely? Not a bit of it has been changed since I was a child!" Mrs. McKnight speaks proudly, standing very tall, an uncharacteristic glow lighting up her face. "I don't suppose you've ever seen anything like it?"

"No, I haven't," Cailey answers, dumbfounded. Mrs. McKnight peers expectantly at her, and when she receives no further reaction, she switches off the light and leads the way back through the dining room and into the kitchen.

"Well, Alex, did you hope we'd forgotten all about you? Tonight you can watch till nine, I guess. Cailey, why don't you put the milk on for his cocoa, while I explain about the numbers for the bells." She points to a small black rectangular box on the kitchen wall above the sink, which has a glass window in it. In the middle, at the top of the window is a little flag with the number 2 on it. Mrs. McKnight reaches up and pulls a lever on the side of the box and the number 2 disappears.

"Oh Alex, my love, be a dear and go into the dining room and press the bell under the table." Alex lets out a long, enthusiastic "Surrrre" and bolts into the dining room.

Mrs. McKnight laughs. "He's not allowed to play with the bells and that's his favourite one."

As soon as the bell sounds, a little flag with the number 1 on it jumps up in the window.

"There now," Mrs. McKnight says. That's how you know which bell it is. Number 1 is the dining room. That's a different kind from the rest because it's on the floor, under the carpet and I press it with my foot. Just for you to clear the table, or bring the dessert or coffee. It's very convenient. The other numbers are listed here, on this chart." And she points to the side of the black box where Cailey can indeed see the numbers listed next to the names of the rooms.

"Now as I said, we only use a few of these bells. And not very often, Cailey. Don't think we'll be ringing for you all the time! You can stop ringing now, thank you Alex. The dining room bell will only be used at dinner when Mr. McKnight is home. When he's not here, we'll eat together, the three of us, just like we've been doing, here in the breakfast room. I think it's so cozy, don't you?"

"Yes, it is," Cailey is unable to imagine any room in the house being cozy if Mrs. McKnight is in it.

"The only other bells we use, only once in a while, mind you, are the ones in the downstairs den, the one in our bedroom, and the one in Mr. McKnight's study at the east end of the house. Alex, Alex, that's enough now! Well Cailey, I guess you haven't seen our quarters on the second floor. Sometimes John will want a drink served up there if he has to finish some work or make a phone call without interruptions. But that really is quite rare… oh dear, do look Cailey, the milk is boiling over. Alex! Stop that! Stop that right now! One ring was all we needed."

Later that evening, Cailey slides into her bath, exhausted. She can hear the faint but familiar voices of the CBC evening news coming up from Mrs. McKnight's bedroom television. She closes her eyes, imagining a letter to Denise to thank her for the party, and for the foaming bath oil, which now rises around her in a mountain of bubbles as the tub fills nearly to the top. Reaching for the soap, she enjoys the thought of telling Denise about the bells.

CHAPTER

5

HER OWN LiGHTNESS
WiNNiPEG
SEPTEMBER 1969

They follow Wendy single file along a narrow path bordering the river. Cailey recognizes faces from some of her classes; she knows a few first names, has walked to school with a couple of Wendy's friends. At the moment though, she is holding back, preferring, for some reason, to tag along at the end. As the path winds through a stand of the largest oak trees she's ever seen, she is aware of the ground beneath her feet. She stops to pick up acorns, planning to send them home to Paul. Through the trees, up away from the river, Cailey notices an older woman in bright orange rubber gloves pause in the midst of watering plants; she does not return Cailey's wave, but stands with the hose running, waiting for them to leave what is apparently her backyard.

Eventually, on the other side of a high steel frame railway bridge, the path disappears altogether, and Wendy beckons her gang into the tangled brush and brambles along a wide bend in the river.

Cheers erupt when they emerge at last into the grassy clearing Wendy has been promising them all week. She drops her knapsack, stands at the river's edge while she picks burrs from her long denim skirt. She ties a knot at the front of her baggy T-shirt, stretches up, her bare arms raised to the sun, her shiny black hair falls straight down her back.

For a brief moment, there is a stillness in the group. A spell, Cailey wants to believe, cast by a few spindly poplars fluttering in the evening breeze off the river. Except for the faint hum of cars and trucks on a distant highway, there is no sign of city life.

"Where's Steve?" Wendy's boyfriend, intrusive as always, is checking his watch. "He's supposed to be here Wendy, with beer. "

"They're on their way, Jeff, hold on to your hat."

Wendy turns to Cailey. "Help me cut the roasting sticks, Cailey? Oh, wait a minute, who's got the buns? Besides me I mean," she laughs. "Okay, Julia has the hot dog buns. And the fire? Come on you guys. Best place is over on that flat rock. Why's everyone staring at me? Someone's got to get organized around here."

Wendy chatters incessantly as she and Cailey walk back toward the bushes to find enough long green branches for roasting the hot dogs.

Cailey is not listening to Wendy as they walk. She is listening to drowsy flies buzz around her head. Wendy carries on, still talking quite happily to the air around her, not noticing Cailey has dropped down into the tall grass.

Cailey inhales the dusty sweetness of the grasses. She sits cross-legged, facing north, toward Wood River. The same Friday sun will be setting there, friends will be gathering on the rocks by the bridge. Beth, Andy Mac, Denise, the whole gang. She can hear the fire sparking up into the sky. A way up the river, there will be the easy putter of small motors, boats inching through the water, trolling for pickerel. Whole families, perhaps Paul and her dad, out trolling for tomorrow's supper, maybe that old guy who's always out by himself, hoping a muskie's come down from the north, just waiting to be caught.

Wendy reappears, singing her heart out to the song that floats their way from over at the point. *'Oh to live on sugar mountain, with the barkers and the colored balloons'.* Cailey smiles and mouths the words. Neil Young connecting across the miles. Everything so familiar, so foreign.

"Come on Cailey girl, hurry up. Here are the roasting sticks. You sulking or what? Steve and those guys are here. There's beer!" She leads Cailey by the hand to the fire, grabs them each a Molson.

"Just so you know, Cailey, Steve is Jeff's cousin. Everybody's heart-throb. I suppose because he's older. Not my type though. Big thinker kind of guy. That's him over there with his buddies from U of M. Actually, he's at McGill now. Sad thing, his dad died this summer. Sudden. It was awful. That's why he's late heading back to Montreal. His dad left him a neat old car that he's driving back."

Jeff appears behind Wendy, reaches into the cooler, grabs two more bottles. He turns to Cailey. "Hey, where've you been, Cailey? Waiting for me in the bushes, I guess."

"Oh do shut up, Jeff." Cailey stares wide-eyed at Wendy. "Did I say that?"

"I hope so."

Cailey leaves them, and sits down alone on a rock facing the fire. She runs her thumbnail straight down the centre of the beer label, ripping a path through the Molson logo. According to Wood River legend, this means she is still a virgin. A joke of course, but one they all had fun believing. The fun was allowing a beer label to provide proof of purity. It was definitely not acceptable to fail the test. Molson's is a good label. Easy to peel. Some of the other brands have more glue in the middle.

Arms linked with Jeff, Wendy is now singing wildly off key.

It's so noisy at the fair
But all your friends are there
And the candy floss you had
And your mother and your dad.

Oh to live on Sugar Mountain. Cailey stares at the fire, willing the image into the flames. She knows she is drinking too fast, one gulp after another, as she checks out the faces in the flickering circle around her. Julia and Irene are roasting their hot dogs on forked sticks. Two at a time. Like Paul always does. Julia gives a thumbs up when she sees Cailey watching them. Cailey waves and looks away. So that must be Steve over there. The big heartthrob. He catches her eye, smiles and winks. Never trust a guy who winks, Uncle Mickey used to say with a wink. She smiles back at Steve. Like she knows him.

"He's a hunk, eh Cailey?" Wendy pipes up. "Hey Steve!" She points at Cailey. "This is my friend Cailey I was telling you about."

Steve nods. "We already met."

Wendy looks around sharply at Cailey. "What's he talking about?"

"Beats me."

"I see. Did I say he's twenty-three and has a girlfriend in Montreal? Be careful, Cailey girl. He's going to work in South America next year. Too bad, eh?"

***

It's midnight when Steve drops Cailey at the McKnight's driveway. Several kids are still crammed into the back seat of the car. Wendy is asleep on Jeff's lap in the front.

"See you guys at school." Cailey laughs, hesitating before closing the car door. She peers a little drunkenly over at Steve in the driver's seat.

"Next time I'm home, Cailey." Steve is yawning through a smile as the door shuts.

Navigating the driveway is not so easy. The cedar hedge seems to have moved. No, it's there. The house is there. And all lit up at this hour. With the garage door unlocked. Well perhaps that's a good thing. The key in the lock business might have been tricky.

There is music playing. A note from Mrs. McKnight on the fridge.

Cailey takes the note, follows the path of light through the dining room to the den. The music is loud. Not the piano pieces Mrs. McKnight likes. There's a record jacket sitting up on the bookcase. Beethoven. On the table, an open whisky bottle, a glass. Mr. McKnight. Seems he's left everything and gone to bed.

Behind her, a door closes with a click. She turns around fast, and there he is leaning against the door, his arms folded across his chest.

"Well, hello. Hello, Cailey. You found Janet's note, I see. Well, I'll close up, shall I, turn out the lights and all. You go right off to bed." He is not moving away from the door.

"Oh that's fine, Mr. McKnight, thanks, I'll just do that then." Cailey sees his expression, his tie hanging loose, his white shirt unbuttoned. His red eyes.

He is not moving away from the door.

Oh no.

She feels sick to her stomach. Her head is spinning. Too much beer. And the dope. Oh boy.

She stifles a giggle.

Wrong signal.

He moves toward her. "Well yes, I've been hoping to get to know you better, Cailey, if I could just…" His hands reach for her breasts.

The nausea is overwhelming.

Oh.

All over his shirt, his nice white shirt.

He stands back, looks down in astonishment at his shirt and pants.

She darts for the door. And then she flees, she is flying through the house, through the kitchen, and with Olympian speed she is up the back stairs, into the third floor bathroom. Amazing. She sits on the toilet, runs her washcloth under the tap, grabs her towel.

In her room, she locks the door, props a chair under the handle, strips down to her bra and pants. She is shaking all over. Now what to do with her shirt, her jeans, reeking of beery vomit. The window. Out the window. As long as they don't get caught in a tree. Wouldn't that be great. She peers down. Well okay, there they are, right in the midst of Mr. Melanchuk's purple asters. Never mind. He never comes on Saturdays. In the morning I'll recover my clothes before anyone's up. And prop up those poor flowers.

She listens at the door. Seems to be quiet. She wipes her face, runs the washcloth around the back of her neck, and then, not daring to return to the bathroom for a glass of water, she sucks hard on the cloth, clenching it between her teeth. She crawls into bed, pulls the covers up around her and waits for the shaking to stop. She takes out Mrs. McKnight's note.

Cailey dear. Would you believe it! Played baseball at the gallery picnic until 8:30! Alex and I came home exhausted. And my dear, full of wretched hot dogs! Off to bed early. Mr. McK coming in from Minneapolis tonight instead of tomorrow. Could be after midnight. He knows you'll be late at a party so I've asked him to leave lights on for you. Please switch them off. Tomorrow we're off very early to Kenora–Mother McK's 75th birthday–back elevenish–don't wait up. Also dear, we'll need you Sunday noon–just a few people for lunch after church. Nothing fussy. So this week you'll have Saturday off instead of Sunday. Hope that's OK.

Cailey lets the note fall, stares wide-eyed at the ceiling. For a long time, she doesn't move. And then she hears her own laughter. It seems to be rising up from a distance, from some place far away. It is the tears that are so close. She is laughing as they begin to flow. In a torrent, they wash over every moment, every face, over everything she has held in tightly day after day. Faces saying goodbye. Faces saying hello. They are all there, clattering around in her like pebbles under the surface of a fast moving stream. On and on it goes, and the stream keeps running. Until at last, she falls asleep.

***

"Okay Puppy, okay!" Cailey opens the French doors leading out to the patio from the breakfast room. "Off you go!" She watches as Puppy races toward the river.

Beth will be up by now, Cailey is thinking as she follows Puppy out onto the lawn, she will be making tea in a darkened kitchen, maybe tending to Mum's hangover, planning her escape to the hotel to hang out with Uncle Mickey. Paul will be out on his bike, her father at the store.

Cailey, on the other hand, is here on her luxurious estate with her very own first hangover, her very own throbbing head and dry mouth. She has these expanses of rolling green grass, and bright bright sun to hurt her eyes. She lies down on the lawn, her forehead rests on the grass.

Her clothes. She'd forgotten about her clothes in the daisies. She gets up quickly, not good for the head, and walks to the flowerbed under her bedroom window. She lifts her clothes out of the daisies, deciding as she surveys the damage, that it would have to have been Puppy who got in there this morning, naughty dog, he just wouldn't do what she told him.

Back in the kitchen she puts her clothes in the washer. It's then she sees the plastic bag with a note pinned to it, asking Cailey to take a shirt and a suit of Mr. McKnight's to the dry cleaners that's around the corner next to the drug store. Seems he spilled something last night, and tried to wash it off himself.

She can do that. She'll take drop them off this afternoon when she goes out to meet Wendy before Irene's party.

She sips on her tea. So far she has had three large glasses of water, two aspirin she took from a bottle in Mrs. McKnight's bathroom, and half a soda cracker.

She gets her school bag from the mud room, takes out books and scribblers. In one of the scribblers, she finds the letter she began last week.

Dear Mum and Dad, Beth and Paul,

Well, here I am! More than two weeks gone by already. Started two other letters, but I get so busy...

*Hope you saw the one I sent to Denise's folks to thank them
for the party. Denise was going to show you. I asked her to.*

Well, anyway, here goes my third attempt!

*First of all this place is a mansion, as big as Uncle Mickey's
hotel but nicer. No not nicer really, fancier but not nicer,
if you know what I mean.*

Whatever is she talking about? She can't write that. She strokes out
the part about the mansion, and the hotel, slashing her pen up and down
so they can't make it out. That's no good. She'll have to start again.

She puts her pen down, stands up and plugs in the kettle for more tea.
From the window over the sink, she sees Puppy tearing round and round
in wide circles near the summer house. He has something clenched in his
teeth. More likely an old shirt of Alex's, she thinks, than the muskrat he
barks at every day on his ferocious forays into the Assiniboine. She sits
down and tries the letter again.

*Alex—he's the little kid here, you probably remember him
coming into the store—he has a dog named Puppy. Well,
the two of them are the best part of working in this place.
I have a room on the third floor. It's pretty nice really. And
school's pretty good, I guess. Have made a few friends.
Last night we went to a party out on the river. Almost
like home.*

What more to say. A little bit about the party last night. Nothing
about Mr. McKnight.

She puts the letter aside, checks in her bag for her drawing pad. Well,
it's not like they haven't heard from her. Not really. Denise would have
showed them the letter.

She'll work on her homework. Maybe call Wendy in a few minutes,
and find out if Steve has left for Montreal yet. She wants to tell Wendy
about Mr. McKnight. Wendy's likely to have ideas that would be more
practical than vomit. Although that was certainly effective. No, no, she
can't tell Wendy. The thought of telling anyone is too frightening, too
humiliating. She bows her head. How could she have let him touch her.
She is humiliated. She is afraid.

When the kettle boils she drops a teabag in her cup. Not the English
Breakfast tea from the tin. Mrs. McKnight had shown Cailey the Red

Rose tea bags for her use, and had detailed the instructions for making a pot of English Breakfast that Cailey was to bring to her room in the morning. "I'll have English Breakfast again this morning, Cailey dear."

Cailey dear.

Cailey sits down with her tea and flips open her sketchbook. Cailey Donald. She moves the pen carefully across the top of the page. Cailey Donald. Cailey Dear. Cailey at the ceilidh, she writes. Gran used to say that, teaching Cailey the meaning of her name. A gathering of the clan. A celebration. Music. Dance. Stories. She believes in the name Gran gave her. She's always felt it forming her, guiding her on her way.

This week's assignment is caricature. Faces are the hardest. And hands. Copying directly from a photograph is a challenge. She gets the eyes all wrong, starts again. The woman's dress is easy. Long, flowing lines. A bonnet with ribbons. Prissy. Boring.

In the end, she gets the eyes right, and an uppity expression on the woman's face. Her own face. Under a bonnet.

The phone rings. She jumps.

"McKnight residence, may I help you? Who is this?" Cailey stares at the phone. "Certainly not! What?" She rubbed her aching forehead. "Oh for God's sake, Wendy, how do you even think of such things?" She listens and replies, "No, they're away for the day in Kenora. Mr. McKnight's mother lives there."

She laughs. "No she's not an Indian." She groans, "well of course I'm feeling awful… okay, well I have to make the beds, then take in some dry cleaning. I can do that on the way." She looks up at the clock, "Okay, see you at four."

Cailey closes her books and washes up the few dishes in the sink. Once she's finished the beds, she walks down to the river to find Puppy. Her whistles bring him wagging slowly out of the bushes, dragging Alex's nice new jacket. He whimpers over to her feet, eyes pleading against the inevitable.

"Never mind, Puppy, old chum. I have to catch the bus downtown, but you'll have your favourite biscuits in the mud room and before you know it, I'll be back to let you out, and give you your scrummy supper."

***

"I know why Cailey's not coming to the party." Julia freshens her lipstick in the mirror. "She's making a total fool of herself."

Irene laughs. "Well, wouldn't you give up a party for a ride home with Steve Erikson?"

"I don't believe in chasing guys," Julia answers. "It's cheap. Can I borrow your comb, Irene? God this sink is filthy. And there's no paper towel."

"We'd better hurry, Julia. I think Jeff's honking for us out there."

Cailey feels her cheeks burning as she hears them moving to the door. She checks her reflection in the chrome surface of the toilet paper dispenser. Her face comes back at her with giant mutant lips as she mouths insults at their receding voices. She flushes the toilet and goes to the sink to wash her hands.

In the mirror she sees a complexion red and blotchy. She splashes cold water on her face and combs her hair slowly, willing the water to cool her down. She tries out her best expressions. Turn to the right. To the left. The left is better. She brushes her eyebrows up with a damp finger. The way Denise showed her. 'Oh come on Cailey,' she hears Denise's voice say, 'just relax.'

Back in the restaurant, Cailey slides into the booth across from Steve. "How come you moved over here?"

"People watching. I'd rather be by the window."

Cailey watches a group of picketers in front of the department store across the street. A strike that's been on all summer. "Wendy and Jeff and the others have left?"

"Just now. I guess Irene's place has a pool. And no parents, I gather. You would have had fun, you know." He checks his watch. "But you have me instead."

"And now I suppose you're going to wink at me."

"I wouldn't dream of it." They both laugh. "What shall we order, Cailey? I'm starving, and I have to be back at my mum's in," he checks his watch, "two hours." He waits for her to go through the menu. "No doubt I can eat quite a lot in two hours."

Cailey runs her finger down the list of sandwiches. "I think I'll go for the toasted western and fries. And a Coke." She closes the menu. "My first meal of the day. I'm not quite sure how it will all go down."

"So." His eyes linger on hers.

"Is that a question?"

"I'm not sure." He looks out the window. "Those picketers over there." He is fiddling absently with the salt shaker. "Fifty years ago we might have seen thirty thousand people out on this street. You know about that strike?" He doesn't wait for her answer. "The Winnipeg

General Strike. My grandfather was there, he would have marched right past this window."

She knows nothing about it. Absolutely nothing. "Why does it make you sad?"

"You should try not to be so observant." His expression, in spite of a quiet laugh, makes her look away in confusion. It's his eyes. The tenderness that shows, and then clouds over, just as she'd seen it last night. He runs his finger around the rim of his water glass. "My dad died this summer. It was very unexpected."

"Wendy told me. I'm sorry."

"He and I fought a lot. He lived for the union. My grandfather and my father both lived it like a religion. I couldn't see it that way, couldn't make it a religion at least, so we argued. And now, just like that," he snaps his fingers, looks up at the ceiling, "he's gone."

Cailey hopes she is not seeing tears in his eyes. "Do you have a big family for support, Steve?"

"Pretty big. The big part's on my mother's side though. Mum's still living in the house where she was born, where I was born, and there are relatives all over the neighbourhood. Everyone's dropping in these days."

Cailey is relieved when Steve's spaghetti arrives, and her sandwich, piled high with french fries swimming in gravy. She eats ravenously, slows down when she notices his amused scrutiny.

Steve winds the spaghetti round and round on his fork, distracted, still not taking a first bite. "It must be strange for you to be away from home all of a sudden."

"It is, yes. I was trying to write a letter home this morning." Cailey takes a large bite of her sandwich, holds up a finger while she finishes chewing. "I didn't get very far, though. I hardly knew what to say to them."

"Do you have brothers and sisters?"

"What? Oh yes. A sister and a brother. Beth and Paul."

"You're the oldest?"

"Wendy told you?"

"No. Just a guess. You seem older than seventeen."

Cailey tries not to look pleased. "So how old are you?" ·

"You must get homesick, Cailey, not knowing anyone here. I'm twenty-three. Very old."

"I'm surprised how much I miss them. My lush of a mother. My father on the road half the time. I was so used to…" Cailey pokes at her

French fries with her fork, mashes them into the gravy. "Sorry. I don't normally say things like that."

"Easier to say it, maybe, to someone you barely know. They're not going to hear a word of it."

"I have a feeling..." Cailey stops, takes a long drink of her Coke and then absently pushes the fizz around with the end of the straw.

"You have a feeling?"

"That I'm not going back to Wood River. Ever." She is surprised at the tone she hears in her voice. She is surprised that she means it.

"Sounds like a good idea to stay away for awhile. But probably not forever."

"But there are things back home I want to leave forever." She waits for his eyes this time, but he is staring out the window.

He leans back in his seat. "Tell me about working at the McKnight's. What's it like there?"

Cailey finishes the last of her fries. "It's okay. How well do you know them?"

"Well, only through my Uncle Arthur. Jeff's dad."

"Well, they may be important, or rich, or whatever, but—"

"Luck," he interrupts her. "The luck of the draw. Born rich."

"Well, they're not normal." Steve laughs at Cailey's expression. "Well, it's true. I mean, who wouldn't envy them. But I can't relate to their life at all. Except for Alex, the little kid. He's a sweetheart. But they hardly live in that house you know. They just sort of, well, edge around in it. And they talk to each other like they're on the radio. It makes me want to break something."

"I'm not surprised. Do you see much of Mr. McKnight?"

"Well, I've seen a little more of him lately." As soon as the words are out, Cailey puts her head down on her hands and breaks into uncontrollable laughter. When she looks up, still laughing, Steve is staring in astonishment.

"Just a sec... just a sec." She tries to catch her breath. "I'll tell you. I'll tell you."

And she tells him.

"You're kidding, all over his shirt?"

She nods.

Cailey finds it impossible to control her laughter, but mixed in with the laughter, there is alarm, concern, on Steve's face. She knows why of course. It's what she wanted.

He looks at his watch. "I should go. Mum will be wondering where I've got to. Besides, you're making a scene." He grins at her.

"Sorry, but I guess I just had to tell someone." Cailey rests her head against the back of the booth. "It wasn't so funny when I woke up this morning. It's funnier now."

Steve is silent, watching her.

His eyes again. Quickly she picks up her bill, reaches for her wallet, and slides out of the booth.

Outside, they walk in silence to Steve's car. As he guides the car out to the street, Cailey breathes in the familiar old car smell, the leather, the wood, the years of lingering fumes that bring her right to her grandfather's side, sitting next to him on the way to church.

"My mother never learned to drive," Steve tells her. "And my brother Ned is hopeless with cars, hopeless with pretty much everything when you get down to it. Except for betting on the horses. He wins at it sometimes. Gives his take to Mum, borrows it back the next day."

"He's in Winnipeg?"

"He's here for now. He's been staying with Mum since Dad died."

"How do you like Montreal, Steve?" She is thinking up questions, filling in those spaces where sadness takes over. Even an old car seems to bring that on these days.

"Well it's true that Montreal's a great city. I have student digs in an old house east of campus. I share with my friend Anne, plus two other grad students who moved in this fall, and a guy who plays guitar for a living. We never see much of him. He works nights."

"Anne's at McGill with you then." Cailey tries to sound casual.

"We're both in the master's programme, in education. I'll be surprised if she goes on with her degree. She's sort of lost interest this year. I suspect she'd rather be a potter than a teacher; she spent the whole summer on her wheel in our basement. So, things are a bit up in the air for us right now. We've talked about working in South America after I graduate. We'll see. That's a ways down the road." Steve turns to her. "And I suppose you'll be off to university next year? Where do you think you'll go?"

"I have no idea. It seems I'm to take over the family hardware store in Wood River. Can you believe that, a business degree that interests me not one bit? What I know for sure is, I would love to study art."

As soon as the words are out her mouth, they become Cailey's truth.

"Well, why not, you could apply for Fine Arts at McGill, you know. Or at Sir George. Anne already looked into the programmes at Sir George. Of course they'd want samples of your work. You'd have to build up a portfolio, and have a high grade point average. I'm sure Anne could send you some of the bumph she picked up."

"Steve, I'd have to rob a bank to get to McGill."

"Then work for a scholarship, Cailey. Something tells me you could do it." The car slows as he checks the houses looming up in the headlights. "Is this the one?"

"Two more down." Cailey points. "Right there. And it looks like I forgot to leave the garage lights on. Puppy's probably eaten all their boots by now."

"I'll come to the door, Cailey, just to see you get the lights on. When do you expect them back?"

"Soon. Okay, there's the light, thanks Steve. Hey Puppy, okay okay. I'm back."

"One thing, Cailey," Steve laughs at Puppy wagging at Cailey's knees, "about Mr. McKnight. It's not such a joke really."

"I know that. Are you trying to scare me?"

"Well, if it'll make you more alert, yes. You're at a big disadvantage here."

Cailey pours Puppy's dry food into his bowl. "I guess. I'm thinking he won't find me very appealing now, if you know what I mean." She looks up to see his grin. "Seriously. I'm counting on the possibility that I've turned him off forever."

"Well, maybe, but if he's ever around here on his own, I hope you'll get out of the house. Over to Wendy's. Take a long walk. Anywhere. And if he ever touches you again..."

"I know, I know. The thought scares me. Quite a lot. I'm hoping he's just a big dumb wimp. About as scary as Puppy."

"I hope you're right."

"So do I. I'm learning to be watchful." Cailey holds Puppy down by the collar while his tail whacks against the door. "I better let him out back, Steve."

"Okay." He seems reluctant, touches her cheek lightly with his hand. "Maybe when I'm back at Christmas..."

"If I'm here..."

Cailey watches Steve's car pull away, locks the door and follows Puppy's dance through the kitchen, and out onto the patio. The air has turned crisp and cool and she feels suddenly that her own lightness might lift her up into the open prairie sky.

CHAPTER

6

WAITING FOR THE LIGHT TO CHANGE
MONTREAL
MARCH 1974

Cailey stands at the icy curb waiting for the traffic light to change. Across the street, a familiar row of cafés is barely a glimmer through the curtain of blinding snow. A cab skids into the corner, a startled man jumps back, swears in French. The driver honks at him, then spins his wheels furiously in the deeper snow at the curb. Behind her at the bus stop, a student from her art history class stamps his feet and draws frantically on a cigarette. Today of all days, there is no sign of the famous rasta hat. She calls out her hope that big hair will be enough to keep his head warm. He grins and gives her a thumbs up.

The light turns green and she steps off the curb onto the wide thoroughfare; the wind swirls, changes direction, burns her cheeks raw with a sudden assault of ice pellets.

She is looking forward to hearing her friends groan, as they always do, when she informs them, as she always does, that the harshness of the ice cold element exhilarates her.

No matter the weather, Cailey never tires of her solitary walk from the university up to the deli where she'll join the Friday night throng. She's happy Wendy will there be this week, equally happy that Steve will not be. His crowd never shows up until after ten, at which point Cailey expects to be home in bed.

She pulls up her hood as she walks, ties her scarf behind her neck so her nose and her cheeks are covered completely. It reminds her, with the wool growing damp and scratchy at her mouth, of those long walks from school in the relentless blowing cold of Wood River, with the sun gone down, and a single porch light guiding them up the hill.

On the other side of *de Maisonneuve* she struggles against the wind, her head down, her mind buzzing with details of the final issue of the arts journal. Several of the illustrations, and all of the photographs, are hers. Just last week, her work was singled out in a review of the graduating class exhibition at the university art gallery. 'Gifted Graduating Photographer' was the tiny headline in the arts incidentals section at the back of the Saturday newspaper. She had joked in class about being singled out, but the recognition had brought a warm glow to her face.

In many ways, she's sorry this is her last year. She'd love to keep working on that journal. This afternoon, with their close-knit editorial group finishing up the layout, and with Patrick sweeping a mountain of paper cuttings into the corner, Marie-Claude had likened the moment to the closing night of a play. The sets come down. Lights go out. Actors exit the stage for the last time.

Still, she hopes the bonds will survive, that she'll remain friends at least with Patrick, and with Marie-Claude. And surely, after many a punch drunk all-nighter, with the whole crew fully charged on sick humour and coffee and an endless supply of caramels, Professor Daniels is as much a friend as a faculty advisor.

She rounds the next corner a little out of breath, relieved to be in the protection of a narrow street. She hikes up the hill slowly, anticipating the warmth of a delicatessen whose ill-tempered but strangely lovable proprietor only cracks a smile when the right person addresses him as Mr. Grumpy. No doubt he's already serving up smoked meat on rye, the best in town of course, always at half price on Friday, including fries and a pitcher of draft.

Inside the main entrance, Cailey lets her backpack slide to the floor, brushes herself off, steps carefully down the wobbly wooden stairs to the basement. As usual, the place is raucous and smoky and crammed with students.

"What's it like out there?" Wendy reaches a warning hand up to Cailey who stops short as she catches sight of Steve and Anne sitting side by side just two tables away. Wendy had been so sure that Anne was still in hospital.

"It's not too bad on Stanley. Crazy on Maisonneuve though. What the hell's she doing here?"

"Beats me."

Cailey slides onto the bench next to Wendy, returns the waves from a group across the room. She looks away, massages her fingers under the table in a frenzy of frozen confusion until her hands begin to tingle back to life.

Eventually she picks up bits of chatter, cheerful complaints about the 'killer storm' raging outside, woeful tales of another long week at work or at school, growing anxieties about the impending exam schedule. Most critical it would seem, is the passionate speculation about the Habs up against the Leafs at The Forum tomorrow.

From a corner booth at the back, louder voices rise to the pitch of disagreement. Hurled expletives abound. Trudeau and Lévesque, Madame Allende's visit, a sinister CIA conspiracy to invade Canada. As soon as she hears that last bit, she finds it hard not to send a smile in Steve's direction.

Usually, she'd enjoy being challenged by even the most outrageous banter, especially in these last few months, with Steve at her side, with the two of them joining in together, regardless of where the conversation might be headed.

At the moment, though, she is tongue tied. A waiter stands in front of her, waiting for her food order. What she would really like is for him to remain right there, for the rest of the night, blocking her view of Steve and Anne. What she manages is a mute shake of the head.

The waiter shrugs and moves on, and Cailey turns to Wendy, asks a banal question that doesn't fit with anything going on around the table.

Wendy stares hard at Cailey, then at Steve, who for the moment seems unable to take his eyes off Cailey. She nudges Cailey away from his line of vision, and quickly launches into a comic routine about lingerie copy she claims to be writing for a major department store. Apparently, an annoying problem arose this week when her supervisor, a prim little man with a pencil thin mustache, had taken exception to her use of the word 'tits' in the header as a way to promote the advantages of the uplift bra.

All this is Wendy's fiction of course, a truth she acknowledges quite gleefully whenever she's pressed. What Wendy does, in fact, is write creative copy for high-end designer clothes.

Once the laughter subsides, Wendy's boyfriend of the moment holds his hand up to the waiter, checks inquiringly over at Cailey. "Two more pitchers here. What about you, Cailey?"

"I'll stay with coffee, Larry. I need something hot for now."

"Ha ha, I bet you do, Cailey," Larry chuckles, not unkindly. Cailey decides that an annoying idiot may be just the buffer she needs to fill the space between her and Steve. Idiot remains the operative word, however. More often than not, Wendy refers to him as her drunken yogi folk singer. She insists they have 'heavy karma' to work out. Mostly in bed, Cailey has noticed.

Cailey orders a coffee, and then, determined to greet Steve with her most casual and dismissive glance, she looks directly at him.

She fails utterly as soon as she sees the tenderness in his eyes.

***

Early morning sun streams into the apartment. Cailey steps out onto the fire escape, peers down through the metal rungs of the spiral staircase that leads to the street below. Neighbourhood kids are busily constructing snow forts under the steps, hurling snowballs from one war camp to the other, ducking enemy attacks. Their squealing laughter rings out in the crisp air.

Cailey shuts the door on their fun; it only makes her sad. She lies down on the couch under the front window and leafs noisily through the Saturday paper. She considers waking Wendy with a coffee. Larry might be in there. She glances across the room. No sign of his coat in the hall.

As if in response, a bleary-eyed Wendy appears with a wave, and heads straight for the bathroom. When the shower goes on, Cailey goes to the kitchen to make a fresh pot of coffee. She takes a cup to Wendy as she emerges wrapped in a towel.

"No karma with Larry last night?"

"Lay off, Cailey." Wendy gives her the finger on the way to the kitchen for a glass of juice. "He had a late gig at some new club in the city, and I was wiped."

Back in the living room with coffee and juice in hand, and still wrapped in her towel, Wendy pulls the comics section from the pile of Saturday newspapers. She waits, watches knowingly while Cailey holds herself rigid on the arm of the couch, staring out the window.

"Dear God, Cailey, talk about haunted. Same as last night. Like you've just seen a ghost."

"What else would you expect? It's a nightmare."

"Well yeah, but... oh shit, that's the phone." Wendy stretches up, loses her towel as she reaches for the receiver. "House of Doom, may I help you?"

Cailey's smile fades as soon as she realizes who is on the other end of the line.

"Well hello there, Steve. Funny you should call. Hold on a sec." Wendy keeps her hand over the mouthpiece, holds the receiver out to Cailey.

"I'll call him back tomorrow." She sounds decisive, stands up, then sits down again. "No, no, wait. I'd rather talk to him now."

Wendy hands over the phone, and with her towel over her shoulder and the comics tucked under her arm, she takes her coffee and juice back to her bedroom.

"Hi, Steve."

"Cailey. Hi. Listen, I'm hoping you have time to meet me for a coffee."

Silence.

"Cailey?"

"Steve, how could you show up like that last night? You knew I'd be there."

"You don't think I want it to be this way, do you? There was no way to explain to Anne why I didn't want to go. Especially when she was feeling like going out for the first time in days."

"Really." Cailey doesn't even try to stop herself. "Well, she didn't look very sick to me. You haven't called to explain what happened, or about these medical tests, about anything. No explanations for anyone, Steve? It's been more than a week."

"Meet me for a coffee."

"We can talk on the phone."

"It's not that simple, Cailey."

"It's not simple for me to see you, Steve."

"None of this is simple."

She hesitates. "Where."

"Giorgio's? In an hour?"

Giorgio's. It hurts to hear him say it. She hangs up without replying, goes to the kitchen and grabs her cold toast from the toaster.

Wendy reappears in her bathrobe, pours herself a refill of coffee, sits across from Cailey at the kitchen table. "So tell me."

"I'm meeting him for a coffee. Why am I doing this, Wendy?"

"Because you want to see him?"

Cailey smothers her toast with butter and jam. "Did he mention to anyone last night what was wrong with Anne?"

"Nothing that I heard. I have to admit I don't get it, Cailey. But it's good you're meeting him. You deserve straight answers."

Cailey eats slowly; she struggles to swallow every bite.

"Hey, there's something I wanted to mention," Wendy says. "Larry was saying we're nuts to rent a car to go west this spring. He knows a way we can get a new car from Toronto for delivery in Winnipeg. It won't cost us a cent."

"I've heard about those deals."

"Well?"

"Well, what?"

"Well, what do you think? Should we try that?"

"Sure. Why don't you find out more from Larry?"

"Cailey."

"What?" Cailey leaves half her toast, slips it into the garbage, rinses her plate.

"You're not coming, are you? You're going to back out again. I know it in my bones."

"Oh Wendy, I don't know." She hears her voice, its unfamiliar pitch. "Don't lay this one on me right now."

"Lay it on you? It's not just you, Cailey. Every year! It affects my plans. I don't believe this. You're graduating this year. And you're still not going home? This year your parents are so sure you're coming home. Denise has told you that. Uncle Mickey called you just last week about it. What's wrong with you? And, my God , what about Beth and Paul? I don't get it."

"Neither do I. As I've said over and over. But right now Wens, I'm going to get dressed." Cailey hesitates at the kitchen door.

"Fine." Wendy notices the tears in Cailey's eyes, looks away.

"I'm so sorry, Wens. Can we talk about it later?"

"We always do."

***

Steve is waiting for her at their usual table by the window.

"I ordered your coffee."

"A bowl?" She notices how tired he is looking.

"A bowl. So how are you?"

"Fine. We put the journal to bed last night. My last one. It goes to press on Monday."

"And your illustrations?"

"They're good. We used the photo essay." When Steve looks blank, she explains. "From that series I did on row housing down by the market."

"I don't think I saw those ones."

"I thought I showed them to you at my place."

Cailey waits, without looking up, sips thoughtfully on her bowl of hot milky coffee. She is aware of an unfamiliar emptiness filling the space around them, separating them from the reassuring clatter of breakfast dishes coming and going, all around them.

"Okay, Cailey. Now that I'm here," Steve speaks quietly, "I'm thinking you were right."

"Right? About what?"

"About talking this over on the phone, instead of seeing each other."

"Really?" She looks at him in surprise. But even before he speaks, she knows.

"I love you, Cailey. I want so much for this to be a bad dream."

"Just tell me what it's about, please."

"Anne had a miscarriage. She was three months pregnant. She hadn't told me. I didn't know when you and I…"

"She was in hospital for two weeks for a miscarriage?"

"There were complications."

"But I thought you were waiting for test results before you could tell me anything about what was wrong. You've known this all along."

"I needed to wait. There were other tests. Psychiatric tests. She's very unstable, in a deep depression."

"She didn't seem very depressed last night."

"Well, she is." He ignores her insinuation. "She's heavily medicated, an outpatient at the Allan where I've gone with her every day this week. She's suicidal."

"Because of the miscarriage?"

"Not entirely. It seems that after I broke up with her, she was devastated, and when she realized she was pregnant her stress was compounded by the memory of an abortion she had when she was seventeen. Apparently she became quite hysterical and that's when she miscarried. No one knew about the earlier abortion until now. It was a nasty job. Back room stuff. She went through it alone. Stole the money from her mother, checked into a two-bit hotel, never told a soul. She was raised a strict Catholic, something else I never knew until she insisted on going to confession this week. She thinks she's being punished."

"For having an abortion."

"Yes. So at the Allan, she's been admitted," he pauses, "with me as her next of kin. As her spouse I guess. We'd been together a long time Cailey, and I cannot turn my back on her."

"Perfect. Support her with a lie." Cailey shakes her head. "That's enough Steve. No need to explain any more." She picks up her spoon, turns it over and over in her hands, focusing hard on its oval shape. "And what about your thesis? Isn't your deadline soon?"

"I have an extension. But I don't even know if I can finish at this point. If it even means anything to try anymore. Actually it's the farthest thing from my mind. And there's another thing, Cailey."

"Oh good."

Steve raises his hand in protest. "Yesterday we completed applications for teaching positions in Peru. Anne really wants to come with me. As long as she passes the medical, there's the possibility of a placement for her teaching business at a pottery workshop, and setting up marketing contacts for North America. The whole plan seems to be bringing her back to life, and the doctor thinks it will be a…"

"So you're all set then." Cailey pushes her chair back, stands up and grabs her scarf from the back of the chair. "Good plan, Steve. The farther away, the better. Off with your suicidal girlfriend to save Peru."

She drops back into her chair, horrified by her own words. "Shit. Sorry."

"Okay." Steve turns in his chair. "Not quite fair, that one." He raises his hand for the bill. "Anne's sister arrives today. What time is it anyway?"

"I don't know." Cailey stares at her feet.

"I'm late getting back." He hesitates. "Cailey…"

"What?"

"Look at me." He waits. "I can't leave you like this. I need to know."

"Know what."

"What you're feeling."

"Oh for God's sake, Steve. You already know." Cailey stares out the window. "I wish I could stay angry at you. It's so much easier when I'm angry."

She turns to him, regains a steadiness in her voice that surprises her. "I love you even more. How's that? What else would you like to know?"

"Nothing, Cailey, only that… in a couple of years, maybe when…" He looks suddenly stricken, desperate.

"Don't, Steve. Just don't."

Cailey feels herself standing up, slowly this time. She lifts her coat from the hook above their table, wraps her scarf around her neck. Then she leans over to him, kisses him gently on the mouth. For a brief moment, he holds her there, holds her face in his hands.

And then he lets her go.

CHAPTER
7

BITTERSWEET PASSION
MONTREAL
MARCH 1974

Cailey doesn't hear Larry and Wendy come in.

"You sure that's loud enough, Cailey?"

Cailey jumps, waves from her cross-legged position on the floor in front of the stereo.

"I thought you had to be at Professor Daniels' class party at six?" Wendy is yelling over the music.

"I do." Cailey turns down the volume, adjusts the record level, rewinds the tape.

Larry drops onto the couch behind Cailey, leans over her shoulder to see the album jacket. "You recording?"

"Trying to. I need it for some sketches I'm working on."

"Rachmaninoff. You like this stuff, Wendy?" Larry laughs.

"That's my album, smarty pants. Cailey, come on. I'm coming to talk to you while you're changing. Help yourself to a beer, Larry."

Wendy shuts the bedroom door, collapses onto Cailey's bed. "Larry's driving me nuts."

"So why hang out with him?" Cailey opens a dresser drawer. "Where's my red scarf, Wendy?"

"How should I know? I wish you wouldn't ask why I hang out with him every time I complain. Can't you just let me bitch and leave it alone?"

"No. He's such a phony."

"No kidding."

"You amaze me, Wendy. You agree, but you stay with him."

"I don't much care about anything above his waist. Above his neck actually. He's not very bright up there."

"You're disgusting," Cailey laughs.

"That's how guys talk about us."

"And we aspire to be like them."

"I like to shock you. You're such a priss."

"Don't count on it. Anyway, back to the phony part. Remember when Larry said he was working on organizing Madame Allende's speech at The Forum?"

"Not really. Oh wait a minute. Sort of rings a bell."

"Steve was on that committee. Larry has nothing to do with it."

"Well couldn't Larry be in charge of hotdogs or something?"

"Very funny." As she brushes her hair, Cailey watches Wendy in the mirror. "Besides, Larry couldn't do any of that political stuff he says he's into without speaking French."

"His French isn't so bad. You should hear him. *Chiens chauds, patates frites,* Pepsi." Wendy sits up on the bed, eyes wide, an utterly silly grin spreading over her face. "I suppose Steve's got a file on him or something?"

Cailey is pulling on her jeans, picking fluff off her sweater. "I thought you came in to hear about my coffee with Steve."

"Oh." Wendy lies back again. "Yes, I did. That's exactly why I came in here. But I am a jerk you see. Sorry. So tell me."

"Well, Anne's had a miscarriage that's sent her into a deep depression. Some connection to a traumatic event going way back. She's suicidal. I suppose I can see why he has no choice but to stay with her."

"What? He knocked her up while you and he…"

"Wendy."

"What? Well, he could have. He is human you know. Anyway, sorry, go on."

"She's getting better, and now they're applying for those positions in South America which seems a bit nuts to me. Anne's doctor thinks it'll be good for her to get away. Who am I to argue with that?"

"His true love, Cailey, that's who you are to argue with that. He adores you and you know it. Everyone knows it. This is crazy. Anne was miserable before this miscarriage, I promise you. She must know you and Steve have been heading toward each other for the last four years."

Cailey stops. "We were so sure of ourselves." She slips her jeans off, then her sweater. "Just two weeks ago."

"What are you doing?"

"Getting in the tub. I'm not going to the party."

"Oh yes you are. It's just what you need."

Cailey leans against the dresser. "I couldn't ask him to do anything different from what he's doing."

"You're not sure about that, are you?"

"Yes, I am."

"I don't believe you. I'm not one bit sure you shouldn't be fighting like hell to stop this."

Cailey pulls her jeans back on, chooses a different sweater, re-does her hair.

"Maybe someday, Cailey, maybe."

"That's what he said. Don't say it, it doesn't help. Not one bit."

"Okay. Listen, it's supposed to be sunny tomorrow. And warmer. Let's do our hike up the mountain. All the way up to the lookout. Down to the pond. Okay? And then we'll go for spaghetti."

Spaghetti. "Okay, sure." Somehow even spaghetti is about Steve. "What would I do without you, Wendy?"

"Die, I expect."

Cailey checks her watch. "Oops, it's seven-thirty."

"See you tomorrow then." Wendy goes back to the living room. "Hey phony Larry, I sure hope dickie's working late tonight."

"Wendy, you're hopeless!" Cailey grabs her coat, rushes out the door laughing.

***

Cailey props herself against the wall in the long hallway between the living room and the bedroom. Across from her and a bit to the right is the bathroom. Marie-Claude leans against the wall across from Cailey, trying to explain some detail of her final assignment for Professor Daniels. They talk above the melancholy refrains of Leonard Cohen mingling with the crescendo of conversation from down the hall. Someone in the bathroom line lights a joint, passes it along. Cailey takes a long drag, coughs, hands it quickly to Marie-Claude.

There is an eruption of laughter from the bathroom. A flush. A couple emerges.

"Cailey, hi. When did you get here? You missed your favourite pizza."

"Just my luck you guys. I was held up at home."

She wonders, as she takes her turn to perch on the toilet, if it's her own laughter she is hearing, or someone else's. It sounds like hers, but it seems to have stayed out there in the hall. She washes her hands, then manoeuvres her way along the hall toward the kitchen to look for Marie-Claude.

"Hi, Patrick."

"Cailey. Hi. When did you get here?"

"About an hour ago. I've been talking to Marie-Claude."

"Hey listen, come here. Have you seen Daniels' photographs? They're amazing." He pulls her by the hand back down the hall. He opens the bedroom door where Cailey can see a pile of coats on the bed. The light from the bedroom shines into the hallway.

"See? Right along here. There are some in the bedroom too. See here? It's the photo essay he did on rush hour in the subway. Remember he told us about it? They're good, eh? The faces?"

Patrick is watching Cailey's reaction closely.

"Oh yes. For sure. But why is he keeping them hidden in here? Look at this woman, Patrick, and her kid. Don't they look like they've been fighting over breakfast? And the old man watching them? How'd he get that lighting. It's perfect."

"So come in here. These ones are all of his wife. Did you meet her? Jennifer. She's a musician. Plays the cello. Also the fiddle I think – something about Quebec folk music. Wonder if we're supposed to be looking at these."

"Well, we put our coats in here. Are we supposed to keep our eyes closed?"

"Right. So apparently Daniels paints from photographs. Did you know he did that?"

"No. I wish I had though. I mean earlier this year. I wish we could have worked with that idea." Cailey is fascinated by an enlargement of Jennifer Daniels lying asleep on her back in the shade of a tree, naked except for the leaves, her lips parted, her legs slightly open. Innocent.

Sensual. A pre-lapsarian moment. She looks over at Patrick and smiles at his expression.

"Are you serious about going into photography, Patrick?"

"No idea what I'm going to do."

He leads her back to the hall. "I figure I might make it as a commercial photographer, do weddings and stuff, and then do my serious stuff on the side. I don't really know how else to put it together." He sits down on the floor next to the bedroom door. She slides down the wall to sit beside him. She is suddenly very sleepy.

"I know. I've been thinking of doing something like that. I've been wondering about doing portraits. Maybe for schools. Graduations. Big shot executives. Did Marie-Claude tell you she's moving back to Quebec City?"

"I'm not surprised. I never understood why she came to Sir George in the first place. I mean she could have got just as good a degree in Québec."

"But you're glad she came to Sir George, aren't you, Patrick?" She is teasing him about his unrequited love.

He smiles. "I may have to follow her."

"She's too fed up with us."

"With who?"

"Us. *Les maudits Anglais.*"

"That's the others, not us."

"Oh sure." Cailey rests her head against the wall, eyes closed. "Anyway, I'll sure miss her." Her head is swirling. *Just go with it, Cailey,* she tells herself. She stifles a giggle.

"Did you say something?" he asks.

"I don't think so," she says. They look at each other. "You'll always be my buddy, eh Patrick? Promise?"

"Whatever you say, Cailey."

She likes the way his dark hair falls over one side of his face. The way he pushes it back with his hand. She's noticed that. When he paints. Or talks in class.

Patrick reaches for her. She doesn't resist. She knew as they were looking at the photographs.

"Excuse me folks, I need to get something from my room."

"Oh hi, Mrs. Daniels, hi." Patrick leaps to his feet, helping Cailey up with one hand. "Have you met Cailey Donald?"

"Cailey. Hi. Cliff has told me about you. And about Patrick of course." She has green eyes. "I think Cliff has a suggestion for you, Cailey. Talk to him before you go. Have you been in the den yet? I don't think he knows you're here. He's hiding in the den."

"Oh thanks, Mrs. Daniels. I'll find him." Cailey can't quite get her bearings. She squints down the hall.

"Call me Jennifer." She disappears into the bedroom. *Green-eyed goddess*, Cailey thinks.

"Is she a goddess or something?"

"What?"

"Oh nothing. Just her eyes. Patrick?"

"What?"

"I'm quite stoned. Patrick?"

"What?" He is laughing and pushing her down the hall in front of him. She talks at him over her shoulder.

"Did you like kissing me?"

"No. It was terrible."

"So let's go to my place after I talk to Cliff. I mean Professor Daniels." She turns and gazes ecstatically at him. "Wait…did you just say it was terrible?"

"No. I'd never say a thing like that."

"Well, good. There's Daniels over there."

"Where?" He follows her gaze. "Right. Is this a good time to talk to him?"

Someone puts a beer in her hand. She hands it to Patrick. "Hey, I know what. I bet he'll like my kisses."

"You wouldn't dare."

"Well I sure hope not, don't you?" Patrick stands back as Cailey sits on the arm of the couch and waits for a lull in the conversation. Everyone is talking about the October Crisis again. It seems to Cailey that every party ends with the same discussion in raised voices. The War Measures Act. He had to. No he didn't. It wasn't an insurrection. Yes it was. They went too far. No they didn't. Marie-Claude is always quiet for this discussion. She sees Cailey, waves her over.

"What's that music?" Cailey wonders, trying to place the familiar voice.

"*Ça, c'est Pauline Julien.*" Marie-Claude calls out to her. She waves back, smiling a little foolishly.

"Pauline Julien." Professor Daniels repeats, looking up at Cailey. In fact they're all looking up at her. She didn't know she'd asked the question out loud.

"Ah, Cailey," the group shifts as Daniels turns his attention to her, "I'm glad I caught you. I meant to talk to you last night before you left the university. I have a favour to ask. Well, not quite a favour. You'll be paid."

Cailey thinks of the photograph of Jennifer in the bedroom... *oh no*...

"My sister has been asking me since before Christmas to come over and photograph her with the kids. I can't stand that kind of stuff, you know, especially with family. I thought maybe you could come over there with me and Jennifer sometime soon. Maybe for a Sunday lunch. And I'll set you up to shoot the kids." He chuckles to himself, enjoying his own pun.

She hopes she doesn't say what she had been thinking about the photographs in the bedroom. She concentrates very hard.

"Truth is, I have two reasons for asking you, Cailey. I'd love someone to get me off the hook, but also this could be a chance for you to break into a commercial photography network. I'm sure you'd be good with kids. You could build a portfolio with just a few contacts like this one. I've seen this sort of thing work for other students."

"Well, it's not that I don't love the photography, as a hobby, it's just that I want to spend more of my time on my drawing and painting."

"Great Cailey, but do you want to eat? The starving artist in the garret doesn't usually work out you know."

"Sometimes it does. I have friends who have a studio and gallery. A collective. Down in Old Montreal."

"They won't make it, Cailey. It just won't last. Sorry to be discouraging. So are you turning me down?"

"No. Sorry. Of course not. Thank you, I'd be happy do it."

"Good. I'll talk to you after class on Thursday, and we'll set up a time."

"What camera will I use?"

"I guess this time I'll sign the equipment out from school. Student assignment. You do all the work."

Patrick appears at her shoulder. "So when does the kissing start," he whispers in her ear. "Hi, Professor Daniels. Great party."

"Actually, we were just about to go, weren't we Patrick?"

***

Cailey lights two candles on the dresser. She sees herself in the mirror.

She blows them out. Steve. Again. Always.

"What'd you do that for? The candles were nice." Patrick is waiting for her in bed. She is no longer stoned.

"Listen, I need to talk to you about something."

"Come on, Cailey."

"Oh hell. Maybe this was a bad idea."

"Ah. Well, thank you very much."

She crawls into bed beside him fully clothed.

"Okay, so what is it?"

"You remember my friend Steve? When you and Marie came to Giorgio's that night?"

"My night with the Winnipeg mafia? How could I forget?"

"Well, it's about Steve. Don't make jokes, Patrick. It isn't funny. Not for me. It's more like how you feel about Marie-Claude. I can't just jump into bed with you when Steve is on my mind. You're too good a friend."

He pulls her close. "Okay, okay, so tell me the whole story."

***

Cailey wakes up disoriented. She gropes for her clock on the table. Four-thirty, the numbers shine out at her. She remembers. Patrick. What did they do?

Nothing. They talked. They just talked.

She sits up on the edge of the bed. She thinks of working on her drawing, hesitates, knowing the light might wake him.

She gets up and finds her way in the dark to the kitchen. She pours herself a tall glass of cold apple juice, feels it clear and sweet slipping down her throat as she stands in the light of the fridge. In the bathroom she brushes her teeth and washes her face with a cold washcloth.

For a long time she lies on her back in the bed, her eyes open to the darkness around her. She hears Patrick breathing quietly beside her. She is slowly more aware of his presence, the warmth of his body. She reaches out to touch him. Touch his face. He stirs. She runs her hand softly over his chest. Her kisses begin slowly. Against his neck. Along his shoulders. She sculpts him with her hand. Brings him to life. She creates him and he finds her.

CHAPTER

8

DRAWING DOWN THE MOON
MONTREAL
APRIL 1974

"Why are you turning into the driveway, Cliff?"

"Why not? There's no space on the street."

"Why not go farther up? We can walk a couple of blocks."

Cailey catches Cliff's expression in the rearview mirror. He sees her glance, raises his eyebrows.

"Jenn's planning her escape route, Cailey."

"You'll understand when you meet Erica." Jennifer glances over her shoulder. "Last time Cliff parked in the driveway, we couldn't get away until everyone else had left."

Cliff turns into a narrow lane that winds up the mountain behind Erica's house.

"There's a spot, Cliff. That little crescent in there."

"What we'll do, Cailey," Jennifer confides a few minutes later, as she rings the bell of a three story brownstone that fronts onto the road, "is we'll sip Erica's Bristol Cream and let the world slip by. It's the only way, believe me."

The large oak door is opened by a maid in a black uniform with a crisp white collar and cap, and a ruffled apron tied at her waist. The maid greets them shyly, struggling with broken English.

Jennifer looks inquiringly at Cliff.

"Chile," Cliff whispers as the maid steps back to usher them in. "Forgot to tell you. Arrived last week."

"Oh there you are, Clifford." Erica Wilson sweeps into the front hall. "Connie, now you offer to take their coats. Like I showed you. Oh dear, you can see Connie's still getting used to our ways."

"Connie?" Cliff looks blankly at his sister, then at the embarrassed young woman holding her arm out for their coats.

"Well that's our family nickname for Consuela, isn't it, Connie? We agreed it would be easier for the children. It's enough for them to cope with French, let alone Spanish, I mean access to their mother tongue is already restricted *dans La Belle Province*." Erica laughs nervously, her face still. "Now Connie, that's fine, just hang Professor Daniels' coat right there." Erica points to the walk-in closet, shaking her head at Consuela's momentary confusion. "As I explained this morning, the men's coats always go there, in the front hall closet."

Oh dear, Cailey thinks as she sends an empathetic smile in Consuela's direction. Seems there's more than one Mrs. McKnight in this world.

Erica is checking in the hall mirror behind Jennifer, carefully adjusting a wayward strand of streaked blonde in her brown hair. She forms an 'o' with her lips, dabs with her little finger at lipstick that has run red into the creases at the corners of her mouth. She is decorated tastefully, in gold. Earrings, chains, bracelets.

"And so this must be your student photographer. Cailey is it? Unusual name. Scottish? Irish perhaps?" She addresses Cliff, talking right past Cailey's offered response. "Really Clifford, shouldn't you be carrying that equipment for her? Ah, there, that's it Cailey, you can put the equipment down there, until it's time to begin the photographs. Connie will fetch the little ones later. You'll show Cailey upstairs, Jennifer? Oh, and how are you, my dear? You must let me know about your next concert? It's soon I hope. I'm so excited to hear this ambitious composition you're attempting. What will you have, Cliff? The usual whiskey no doubt. Oh, Andrew, here's Clifford. Finally. Do get him his whiskey. Ah," Erica's brightest smile flashes over her brother's shoulder, "here we have the Pritchard's, right behind you, Cliff. I'll introduce you once we're all inside. Longtime patrons of the orchestra, but of course you'd be aware of them, Jennifer. I just know you'll make that audition next year! Third time lucky I always say."

Erica's voice trails off as Jennifer and Cailey reach the top of the stairs.

"She should be sedated." Jennifer drops her coat onto the four-poster in the master bedroom. "Over-sedated perhaps."

"Yes, I can see what you mean," Cailey smiles. "A strange thing though, I feel I know her," Cailey hesitates, "and to be honest, her maid reminds me of me, back in Winnipeg days."

"Really? How so?"

"I had a position for a while, that was pretty much like Consuela's."

"You're kidding. The uniform and the whole bit?"

"Sometimes, when there were parties. Mostly, I was looking after their little boy after school. He was a neat kid, Alex. It was Alex, and having room and board, that got me through my final year of high school." Cailey quickly changes the subject. "What's the concert Erica's asking about?"

"Well, that would be the string quartet." Jennifer pulls her comb through a tangle of knots in her long hair. "The concert will be at St. James Church next month. I've no idea why Erica even bothers to come. Unless it's for the intermissions. She's completely tone deaf. About music. And life."

Cailey is mesmerized watching Jennifer's image in the mirror. A swirl of lines takes shape. Her drawing mind frames the eyes, the startling green eyes. "What instrument do you play, Jennifer?"

"The cello." Jennifer slips her comb back into her purse. "Well, at least with the string quartet, it's the cello. Lately, I've been composing my pieces on the violin, not the cello. I'm thinking I might even brave the violin part for my new composition, if we attempt it at the next concert. Scary. Mostly for the audience! We shall see. Our programme is a bit up in the air right now. We may add a cello player just for this event, turn ourselves into quintet for one night!"

"Will you let me know the date? I'd love to bring my friend Wendy. She's exploring all kinds of music these days."

"Yes, for sure. Tell her it won't be your standard chamber music though. More like jazzy improvisation on a medieval theme I've been having some fun with. Rhythms. Chants. Ancient melodies. I'm told it's a peculiar mix."

"Perfect! Wendy's nothing, if not peculiar."

"Well, good." Jennifer links arms with Cailey at the top of the stairs. "My violin teacher refers to my new composition as a 'right mess'. Which may foretell a coming disaster, or a resounding success. Or nothing at all. My biggest regret is that she seems bored to death, as she insists on saying, by the Quebec folk music I'm weaving into the composition."

At the bottom of the stairs, still talking animatedly, Jennifer and Cailey are only vaguely aware of Cliff leaning against the large door frame into the living room.

"Before we go in there, Cailey," Jennifer continues, "I wanted to sound you out about an idea I have for composing pieces that would accompany an art exhibition. Perhaps Cliff mentioned it in class?"

"I don't believe he did. At least not when I was there."

"Ahh. Well, the idea is for an exhibition that could have a specific theme or subject, and the composer would create from paintings or whatever artwork was going into a show. Or I suppose it could be the other way around." Jennifer goes silent, pensive. "Say you and I were trying such a collaboration, you would draw images evoked by listening to my composition. Or, I'd compose something based on what I see in your paintings."

"Interesting. Like a musical interpretation."

"Yes. Either way. There could be a live performance to open, maybe a couple of live concert evenings we could tape to play for the duration of the exhibition."

Cliff turns to them. "Did someone say live? Maybe you two can help here, because this is deadly." He slips an arm around Jennifer's waist, swirls his whiskey and surveys the gathering. He winks at Cailey. "Noses all powdered, I see."

"Ignore him, Cailey. He's inclined to regress at Erica's gatherings."

Cailey smiles and checks out the unfamiliar setting that is somehow so familiar. The maid appears with glasses of dark sherry on a silver tray. Cailey helps herself, feeling she has somehow got on the wrong side of the tray. She tries without success to catch Consuela's eye.

"Come on, let's sit over there." Jennifer leads Cailey to a large square hassock in front of the fire. Other guests stand in an intimate group near the high expanse of windows overlooking the back garden. The room is bright with late winter sun.

"Tell me, Cailey, what sort of music are you into?"

"I enjoy exploring. I love folk music. I'm interested in hearing about your idea. I often draw to music, and I'm seeing the intersection of music and art all the time." She stops, stares into her glass of sherry. "At the moment, however I seem to be overdoing a Rachmaninoff piece, hopelessly romantic piano."

Jennifer nods with a sympathetic smile. "Oh no, not the great concerto and another broken heart?"

"I'm afraid so," Cailey laughs, with more relief than embarrassment, "and I'm sick to death of it all. The broken heart. And the Rachmaninoff." She looks away. "It's hurtin' country music I grew up on though, and sometimes I think it works just like Rachmaninoff."

Jennifer nods in amusement as she places her empty glass on the tray that has just appeared in front of her. The tray shakes in Consuela's hand. Cailey wishes she could tell Consuela that she once spilled an entire tray of drinks in Mrs. McKnight's lap.

"Interesting. Well, I'm not usually one for country music, but I'm very drawn to authentic folk music. I love Québec folk, old and new. There's a kind of country twang in there I guess. You hear it all around these days, in the coffee houses, *les boites à chansons*."

"Oh yes, I've often been in the old city on Friday nights to hear Jim et Bertrand."

"Yes exactly! The prince of Franglais! They have a super fiddler with them sometimes. I'm trying to learn that fiddle style, but it's not easy to loosen up years of classical training."

When Consuela returns with the offer of another sherry, Cailey looks up to say no, and a trace of a smile passes between them. Consuela's face pales at the sight of Andrew Wilson approaching Jennifer and she moves quickly to the next group.

"Jennifer, my dear. You're looking splendid as usual. And who is this lovely creature? Ah, don't tell me, I saw you at the front door. Cliff's photographer. What a grand idea. He does know how to pick them, doesn't he? So sorry, but I've forgotten your name. Erica did tell me."

He places his hand firmly on Cailey's shoulder. Instinctively she shifts away from his touch. She turns her head to look enquiringly at Jennifer.

"Andrew, this is our friend Cailey Donald. Cailey, this is Erica's husband, Dr. Wilson."

Andrew seems not to have noticed Cailey's dismissive gesture. "Oh for goodness sake, Jennifer, why so formal, she'll call me Andrew, won't you, Cailey? We're delighted you could join us this morning. Well now, there's the bell, and I believe we're just going in for brunch. Smaller group today, so it's sit down this time. I always prefer sit down, don't you? No balancing plates on one's knee. Connie will bring the children in at dessert time, and then you can begin with the photographs."

Jennifer squeezes Cailey's arm reassuringly as they follow Andrew and Erica into the dining room.

***

"You developed the contact sheets without me?" Cailey is outraged.

"Sorry," Patrick says, holding the magnifier to his eye. "But Cailey, these are really good. My God you've a lot of nerve. Ahh, so I see we have a maid? I didn't know Daniels was loaded."

"He's not loaded, Patrick. This was at his sister's place. She's married to some big shot physician who talks with his silver spoon in his mouth."

"Got it. Did they know you were doing these shots? What camera did you use?"

"A Leica."

"Clever. Silent. What Leica? There's no Leica here."

"Cliff had his with him, and then Rolleiflex from here of course. He wanted me to try the Leica. Let me see those, Patrick. Come on. They're my photos. Give me the glass."

"Who are all these silly people anyway?" Patrick ignores her. "Let's see. Okay I can guess some. The kids of course. Being silly. Which is what they're supposed to be. How come you rate Daniels' Leica? That's a stamp of approval, I hope you realize. And what about the formal shots? Portraits. I thought you were supposed to do portraits."

"There are two rolls on the Rolleiflex, but they won't be much good. The kids were hopeless about posing, and their mother was even worse. I used the Leica, even for the portraits. The moments for catching them natural were fleeting. Okay enough, Patrick, give me that." Cailey grabs the magnifier from his hand and puts it to her eye.

She scans the contact sheets. "Hey, you're right, these aren't half bad. There are possibilities here." Cailey hands the glass back to him. "Remember this moment, Patrick, for when I'm famous. Where's the pencil?"

Patrick hands her a grease pencil and she circles several frames and heads to the darkroom.

An hour later, the two of them are examining developed prints that are scattered about on the table.

"So who's this guy?"

"Andrew. The great Dr. Wilson to you."

"And what about these? The maid I guess? Oh, oh, something sad here."

Cailey looks appreciatively at him. "Yes."

"Does she have a name?"

"Consuela."

"She's beautiful. Her face is alive and sad at the same time. This is more a study of her, Cailey, except for a few shots, Daniels' dreadful sister you say, and the kids, and two cozy ones with the dreadful doctor. Okay, let's separate these out."

Cailey succumbs to his direction and together they line up the shots of Consuela, move them around, trying out different sequences. Consuela serving coffee to the guests after lunch. Consuela washing dishes. Consuela standing in front of the fridge listening to Erica Wilson.

"She hardly understands English, but there's Erica yakking away at her. When I took these, the kids were playing in that little breakfast room and I was pretending to try out the lighting for the Rolleiflex."

"Was Consuela alone with the kids in this one?"

"Yes. Yes. That's the one I want to enlarge." Cailey is proud of this one. She is thinking of sending it to Steve.

"Here, put it next to these." Patrick picks up the one of Consuela sitting down with the kids at a small table. She is making them laugh with her hand gestures. The little girl is covering her mouth, her brother is gazing up at Consuela, an ecstatic devilish grin on his face. Consuela's hands seem to be dancing in the air, telling her story, and her eyes are brighter than in the other photographs.

"You know what?" Cailey walks over to the window. "I can't do this right now."

"Can't do what?" Cliff Daniels drops his coat on the desk near the door.

Cailey is staring down at the meandering lines of cars in the street below; her eyes follow the pedestrians as they push their way through the black slush of a late winter thaw.

"Can't do this portrait thing."

"Why not? I thought you were doing great. Let's have a look." Cliff goes through the prints one by one, holding several up at different angles to the light.

"Ah well, yes. I see. And what did you get on the Rolleiflex?"

"I'm not sure. Maybe a few good shots. The kids wouldn't sit still. I haven't developed them yet."

"I see." Daniels is watching Cailey closely. "And exactly what do you propose we do with these gems, Cailey? Perhaps I'll take them to Erica this afternoon. And she can select the ones she wants."

"What…" Cailey looks up at Patrick in disbelief. Patrick sends her a wink as Cliff lights a cigarette and leans over the table. He shuffles again through the prints.

"I don't have to tell you these are really good, Cailey. Exceptional even. I'll go over them carefully with you next week. This one here. A beautiful shot. Foreground could have been lighter." He taps his lighter on the table, draws again on his cigarette. "I think you also know that it's not okay to do this. You can't be doing an unauthorized photo essay when you've been hired to do formal portraits in a private home. You will have to honour the opportunity I've given you here."

"I know." Cailey looks back out the window. "Sorry."

"Thank you. But to be honest, I don't really want you to be sorry. What you've created here is too good. But you must never forget that your clients will have to trust you. And you know the limitations of what you can do with these. You can't ever show them."

"I don't want to show them. I want to draw from them. And there's one there, that one of Consuela with your sister's kids. I'll enlarge that one. But only for my own walls, and for—" Cailey stops.

"For what?" Patrick waits but gets no reply. "Let's develop the Rolleiflex rolls. You might be surprised." He heads for the darkroom. Cailey doesn't follow.

"Patrick?"

"What?"

"I think I'll go now. Sorry, but I mean I'll go home. I've got a wicked headache. I'll develop the rest on Monday." She looks over a little guiltily at Cliff.

"Fine by me. Or you could let Patrick and me develop them for you."

"No way. Please. I want to do them myself. With you two, if you like. But I want to be here."

"Sure, that's fine, but you understand Erica's expecting the proofs of the family photos within a week. You'll be paid based on what she selects."

"Of course."

Daniels turns to Patrick. "Well then, let's work on your new harbour study, starting where we left off last week."

"Right." Patrick pushes Cailey's prints to one side, and pulls out his own portfolio. "Are you coming to the play, Cailey?"

"Maybe. If I get rid of this headache" Cailey slips the prints into her file and slides it back into the rack. "Is Marie-Claude coming?"

"I think so. I'm supposed to call her before supper. Maybe we could come by your place around seven."

"Sure."

"Oh wait, Cailey." Daniels searches in his briefcase. "Jennifer asked me to give you this cassette tape."

Cailey takes the tape, turns it over to read the handwritten title: 'Drawing Down the Moon, Composition for Strings, Jennifer Daniels'.

"Drawing Down the Moon." Cailey looks up at Patrick and Cliff. "I wonder... how amazing. Did I ever tell you about my grandmother's amber pin?" Cliff and Patrick stare blankly at her. "Tell Jennifer I'll call her soon. See you later, Patrick."

Cailey slips the tape into her bag and heads out the door without another word.

***

Cailey slides four more dimes into the coin slot and sits back on the wooden bench as the dryer starts up again.

The woman on the bench next to her lights a cigarette. "*Mon dieu,*" she inhales deeply, "*je suis fatiguée.*" She stares straight ahead, talking into the damp stale air as she exhales. "*Vous n'avez pas des vêtements pour les enfants.*" She points at Cailey's dryer. "*Pas comme moi.*" The woman's laugh quickly turns into a hacking cough. "*Je m'excuse,*" she holds up her hand while the cough subsides.

Cailey nods, her head throbbing as she watches the clothes spin round and round in the dryer. Her blue jeans. Wendy's black bra. Red towels. Zippers and buttons are clinking against the metal cylinder.

"*Non, je n'ai pas d'enfants.*" Cailey attempts a smile. "*Un jour, peut-être.*" She is feeling sick to her stomach.

"Hah! *Anglaise.* Oui, I know you. And your friend, the crazy one with the big hat. Always talking."

"Yes." Cailey laughs then, and takes an interest as she notices the rough warmth in the woman's face. She imagines a life worn too thin. "How many kids do you have?"

"*Cinq.* Five. Five boys. Good boys. Not like some I've seen. What a world for them, eh? My oldest he's ten. Smart in school, like me. But there you are. What's it for, eh? And you? Student I think. At the university?"

"Sir George."

"Ah oui... you come to my café? Everyone comes to Lucie's for poutine. Around the corner. You know it, *je pense. Rue Guy.*"

"For sure, the best poutine ever. So you work there? At Lucie's? Wendy and I go often. I don't think we've seen you there."

"*Mais, je suis Lucie! Lucie c'est moi!*" The woman points at herself with one finger, then nudges Cailey with an elbow. "Next time you look better! Your poutine comes through the little window. That's me, Lucie, on the other side! Or after school, maybe it's my kids."

"Really? You're that Lucie?"

"*Bien sûr. Comme je vous dites. Lucie, c'est moi!*"

Lucie holds Cailey's eyes with an inquiring gaze, and seems to make a decision about her. Immediately she is confiding many worries about the diner closing down, about money for kids' clothes, about waiting for money from Georges, their papa, working at the mill up the north shore.

"Ha!" She turns away, takes a drag on her cigarette. "The money's coming, he's telling me, but maybe not, I am knowing, always maybe not!"

At that moment, Wendy bursts through the door.

"Whoa Cailey girl, there's a mighty wind a blowin' out there!" She drops her floppy hat and her coat on the bench, shakes out the hem of her long skirt, icy and salt-stained from being dragged through downtown streets. "Well, let me tell you, I'm beat."

"Me too."

Wendy bends over to touch her toes. Her voice is muffled as she holds the position, speaking through the long hair that hangs over her face. "Eight rolls of toilet paper on special, you'll be glad to know. The highlight of my day. And," she straightens up, "I even got the groceries put away. You about finished here?"

"There's more folding. Only I've got this splitting headache. Maybe time for a Pepsi." Cailey glances over her shoulder at Lucie. "This is Lucie, Wendy. She remembers us coming here. Either of you want something from the machine?"

"I have my Pepsi." Lucie raises her bottle to greet Wendy.

Wendy waves back and follows Cailey over to the drink machine. "Who's Lucie?"

"Well, in fact, she's Lucie of Lucie's Café, where we go for poutine. She's a neat character. Very interesting face. Reminds me of someone back home."

"Ah, and another face for your gallery no doubt. You could hang her next to Consuela."

"Yeah, maybe. I wish you wouldn't say that."

"Say what."

"That thing you're always saying about faces for my gallery."

"Sorry."

Two bottles of Pepsi clang and bang, finally thudding into the grubby little cavern with the flapping door. Cailey presses one hand against her forehead as she reaches in with the other to retrieve the Pepsi's. "This headache's a killer."

"I may have some Aspirin." Wendy opens her backpack, scratches around in the mess. "What about that Gélinas play tonight Cailey? Are you going?

"No. But Patrick's coming by at seven. With Marie-Claude. You could go with them."

"Here." Wendy ignores the suggestion, drops the bottle of Aspirin onto the table, and begins folding towels. "So you have hero on the brain again."

"Just lay off, Wendy." Cailey stops in the middle of smoothing out the wrinkles in a shirt, and swallows two Aspirin with a long swig of Pepsi. "Why are you on at me today?"

"Hey, I'm not on at you. I just know when you've gone to your Stevie boy place. All that energy wasted on a guy who left you to go and save the downtrodden Peruvians. You know that's your headache, don't you? It's hero on the brain. And it hurts. Like water on the knee."

"Enough, Wendy."

Wendy fills their two laundry bags with the warm folded clothes. They wrap themselves in their winter coats and scarves and prepare to leave.

"*À la prochaine*, Lucie," Cailey calls as she heads for the door.

Lucie answers with a slight smile and a shrug.

Cailey wonders, as she and Wendy trudge along against the wind, why it is she's drawn to knowing Lucie better. Somehow, she'd like to find out more about her, learn her story, photograph her, with her three kids.

What dawns on Cailey, as they round the corner onto their street, is that the sad defeat she glimpsed in Lucie's eyes, is the same sad defeat she has seen in her mother's.

Tomorrow she'll go to Lucie's for poutine.

CHAPTER
9

AT THE WATER'S EDGE
EASTERN TOWNSHIPS, QUEBEC
AUGUST 1977

Cailey lingers at the water's edge listening to the voices of her friends trail off into the woods behind her. She turns with a start when the cabin door slams, then she sinks back gratefully into the slow sway of the hammock. For a time there is only the murmur of water lapping over rocks.

A single jay calls. It's all so familiar, this blue jay's call, with the disquieting energy of darkening water, the intimation of lurking memories, deep down.

Late this afternoon, once they'd unloaded the van, they'd headed single file down the hill to the lake and collapsed happily onto towels spread out on the grass near the shore. They'd waded in and out of the water, picking up pebbles and shells as they swapped stories about the busy afternoon setting up for the exhibition. Every once in a while, they'd stop talking, and join together in an impromptu 'allemande left' as Jennifer hit the tempo on her fiddle.

The unexpected solitude comes as a relief to Cailey now. She looks up, searches the sky hopefully as a few slivers of light tease their way through shifting layers of cloud. Suddenly, the moon, a perfect half moon, bathes the surface of the lake in its ghostly light. A slight breeze shimmers over the water, rustles leaves in the trees overhead; then again, dark and still.

There is a quickening in Cailey, of her grandmother's witchery come to life in that brief shimmer. It would be just like her Gran to travel on some eerie shaft of moonlight, mischievously trying to scare them all into unearthly places of ancient howling wolves, or faeries weaving through standing stones, hiding away in the secret cairns.

'Never try to hide from the faeries,' Gran used to scold Paul in her best raspy voice as he dove under the pillows, 'they'll only come and get you.'

'There's no such thing as faeries!' Paul would scream back, throwing a pillow across the room.

A few days ago, Wendy, at home in Winnipeg for the month, had phoned to say she was bringing the letter Cailey's grandmother had written about the amber pin so many years ago. As Wendy told it, she'd been on the last day of her visit up to Wood River, when Paul and Beth showed up at Uncle Mickey's hotel, their mother in tow, to see Wendy off on the bus back to Winnipeg. Two beers and an untouched tuna sandwich later, Ellen had tearfully placed the letter on the bar in front of Wendy, and left without a word.

Cailey had put the phone down with a heavy heart locked up tight by the absence of a mother; that evening, with the exhibition deadline just days away, she'd spent precious hours trying to capture the elusive light of Gran's amber pin with her camera. She began sketching after that, in hurried rough pencil lines, listening over and over to her cassette of Jennifer's cello. 'Drawing Down the Moon'. The composition haunted her always, transporting her back to her family. She'd sketched her mother's face, her cousin Becky's bright smile. Under water. Then Beth, her dad, Uncle Mickey. She'd ripped the sheets from her sketchbook, and crumpled them into a ball.

Later that night, she lay in bed, escaping to her memory of her grand-mother's vivid tales of growing up in her family village of Kilmartin back in Scotland. As if it were yesterday, Cailey heard the hushed voice, as they sat together out on the front porch at dusk with all their tummies full of pudding. 'Well now, ma wee bairns,' Gran would begin, 'it was back in the old country, and you know, the village was gathering at the stone circle to please the faeries and dance in the next phase of the moon.' Gran would then unwind a rambling tale for them, like a movie, starring the same 'three wee bairns' gleefully frightened by mischievous faerie antics. By the time Gran had tucked them into the big swinging bed on the porch, she would be lamenting that magic was lost forever. 'Lost, lost, lost' she would whisper, shaking her frizzy grey head back and forth. That's when Paul would begin to laugh because, as he told her every time, she looked like a shaggy dog with an old slipper in its teeth. Beth would try not to giggle as she nudged Paul in the ribs to shut him up. Cailey would be silent, hoping with all her might that magic would not be lost forever.

Now she rolls over in her hammock, tucks her feet under her towel, slips her arms into her windbreaker and pulls the hood snug over her head.

Night sounds surround her as soon as she closes her eyes. There is a furtive rustling in the brush behind her, a splash of some small creature at the water's edge. She slips sleepily into the embrace of a soft nocturnal world, waking only briefly to the song of the whippoorwill. A long ago song, she thinks, camping upriver with Dad and Uncle Mickey.

She wakes to the first light in a milky sky, turns her aching body to the glowing ribbon of crimson at the horizon. She checks her watch. Quarter after five. The day of the opening.

Yesterday, she and Marie-Claude, along with the riotous crew still asleep up at the cabin, had finished mounting their exhibition. Much to her surprise, Cailey had come away from the gallery feeling strangely dissatisfied.

'Another face for your gallery.' Wendy's words from a couple of years ago had returned to haunt her as she'd hung each framed image of Lucie. Spotlights streamed onto each photo, onto each interpretive drawing. Lucie at the laundromat. Lucie with the kids, waiting in the line up for Star Wars. Lucie laughing at the camera, pushing Cailey's order of poutine through the serving window.

Cailey had stepped back to take a last critical look. Three long years of work. Until that moment, she'd never doubted that the Lucie series was her best work. Everyone said so, and perhaps it was. Still, in this last disturbing flash of her alert eye, she was caught by her own discomfort, a growing awareness of her art as an intrusion, something stolen from her subject.

Strangely, she'd been hoping Lucie might not come to the opening.

The others didn't seem to notice her confusion as they tinkered with the lighting and the sound system. While Jennifer tested the microphones with a range of notes on her fiddle, her friend Francine was standing behind Cailey, listening intently, a squeeze box in hand, harmonica perched in its metal holder around her neck. Francine nodded as Jennifer shifted from one mic to the other. At the far end of the gallery, Patrick and Marie-Claude were up on ladders, adjusting lights for Marie-Claude's photo essay about the three generations of women in her family.

Jennifer had been peering out the front window, impatient for Cliff and the kids to show up with the van that would deliver them to the Daniels' cottage for the night.

"Okay, finally Jenn! They're here."

Francine handed her instruments to Patrick and fished the keys from her pocket to lock the back door. It seemed only yesterday that Francine and Jennifer had arrived at Cailey's door at midnight, more than a little tipsy, bursting with plans to weave a musical performance into the show Cailey had been preparing with Marie-Claude for most of the last year. The three of them had worked until dawn, pouring over Cailey's drawings and photos, drinking strong coffee, arguing about the women's movement, about their place in the art and music of Montreal. They had lined up enlargements of Lucie photos along the living room wall, and on the windowsill behind the couch. They had sat there on the floor, often silent in Lucie's appealing presence. At last, Jennifer had picked up her fiddle and begun to play. At four in the morning, they had called Marie-Claude in Quebec City to get her agreement for an August opening. At seven, Marie-Claude had called back to check if she'd been dreaming. And somehow Cailey had made it through a formal portrait session she'd booked for nine o'clock that morning.

"And why are you grinning at me like a madwoman?" Francine had laughed at Cailey's distracted smile as they stood waiting to pile into the van.

"I was remembering how insane you were that first night, when you and Jenn invaded my flat."

Francine's reply was a low, easy laugh as she and Cailey climbed into the waiting van.

"Indeed, we were all a bit mad." Cailey smiles as she swings her legs over the edge of the hammock and wraps her towel around her shoulders.

She walks to the end of the dock in her woolly socks and sits down cross-legged to face the rising sun.

Her mind wanders to the recent news she's had of Steve and Anne. She doesn't believe the rumours about their leaving Peru to go back to Winnipeg. Surely Steve would have sent a message before it reached her via the grapevine. She so often holds him in her mind these days, talks to him, engages him in long conversations about the preoccupying issues in her life. She wonders if he would understand her discomfort at observing her Lucie series, Lucie after Lucie, all lined up at the gallery like that, awaiting the scrutiny of well-heeled radicals.

Cailey is aware of the floating dock sinking down behind her. She turns to see Patrick walking toward her in his bathing suit, towel around his neck, shaving kit in hand.

"Wow, Cailey. You're up early. I thought I'd be the first down."

"I never went up. I fell asleep in the hammock."

"Well, I heard your final 'be right there' before we all turned in. You didn't find it too cold?" He drops down beside her, easing his bare feet into the water and putting a casual arm around her shoulders. She rests her head comfortably against his shoulder.

"A bit. By the time I woke up, it was beautiful last night, Patrick. I couldn't bring myself to leave. Where's Marie-Claude and this sunrise swim she was going to join me for?"

"Marie-Claude," Patrick closes his eyes to the warm sun that has just emerged from a layer of low grey cloud, "is still sound asleep in my bed."

"In *your* bed?" Cailey looks at him, a huge grin spreading over her face. "Finally? You two finally…? I don't believe you."

He pretends to be puzzled. "Well. I'm pretty sure it was her. Right there, in my bed."

She laughs. "Wonderful. And about time too."

"I always knew of course. I mean that she was crazy about me. She was just a bit slow on the uptake, that's all." He peers into Cailey's face. "Aren't you even a teensy bit jealous?"

"Well, truth be told, yes, I am. I'll miss the way we've been."

"I know." Patrick looks pleased as he stands up. "Me too."

"I need to ask you something before you jump in."

He turns to her, surprised. "Sure."

"Well this is may sound peculiar to you, but I need to know, and I need you to be honest, no matter what." She pauses. "When you looked at my Lucie series mounted yesterday at the gallery, the lights on, did you see any problem with it overall?"

"Good God, Cailey, where did *that* come from?"

"Well, I felt uneasy. I felt there was a violation of Lucie's space I guess, of who she is really, and my interpretation of her for my own purposes. I mean if you were Lucie, coming into the gallery, seeing yourself up on a wall like that…"

"Cailey, don't intellectualize this. I'll tell you exactly what I thought. I thought 'wow, Cailey has captured something special here, she's uncovered a beauty in Lucie's struggling life that radiates from Lucie herself.' You reveal the light in Lucie. That's a gift, Cailey a real gift. Just the right nuance. Marie- Claude agrees. Her word for it was enchanted."

"Enchanted? Did she really say enchanted Patrick?"

"Yes. She meant something about a light in Lucie's spirit, the light you capture in the photographs, and in the interpretations you offer in your drawings."

Cailey is astonished as she watches Patrick dive in. She follows his powerful strokes cutting through the water, carrying him swiftly to the middle of the bay. She hears her own laugh. He has saved her from herself again. His reassuring words have got her off the hook just in time for the opening.

Still, she is not finished with her unease about the Lucie series. 'If you feel uneasy, listen hard,' Professor Daniels had told them all, 'unease is your teacher.'

For the moment at least, she can afford to feel gratitude for the many hours she spent working with Patrick, supporting and evaluating each other's work, drinking tea at her place, wine and pizza at his, sometimes making love in the warmth of their friendship, quelling their passions for unattainable lovers. He won't be around so much now.

"Well, will you check out our early birds, Marie-Claude!" Jennifer carries a tray of steaming coffee as she navigates her way down the path, followed closely by Marie-Claude.

Cailey grins and raises her eyebrows. "So, Marie, ma chérie. You slept well I hear."

"*Mais oui!*" Marie-Claude hands Cailey a coffee, a warm smile lighting her eyes.

CHAPTER
10

SMILING BACK AT LUCIE
MONTREAL
AUGUST 1977

Dr. Andrew Wilson is humming to himself as he slips in through the back door of the gallery with a case of wine held against each hip.

"Wine delivery, ladies. Where would you like these?"

Jennifer jumps at the sound of her brother-in-law's voice. "Francine's over there, thanks Andrew," she points. "She's the one setting up tables."

"Francine. *Ah oui, la belle Francine.* And the trays of wine glasses in the van?"

"Over there. With the wine…" Jennifer turns away as the word 'obviously' slips out under her breath.

"Francine," she waves across the room, "here's Dr. Wilson. He's brought the wine."

"Please could someone lock that man in the broom closet," Jennifer mumbles as she returns to the tangle of speaker wires she's sorting through with Patrick.

"It would be my pleasure," Patrick chuckles as he winds electrical tape around a frayed cord. "How'd he end up here anyway?"

Jennifer shrugs and shakes her head in disgust. She and Cliff had argued about Andrew all the way into town from the cottage this morning. 'How could you and Erica even dream of handing the liquor order over to the wino doctor?' she'd complained. By the time they'd exited onto Sherbrooke, all Cliff could offer were several expletives diverted to the tailgater behind him.

Jennifer glances up as Andrew steps over the wires she's working on.

"Where's Cliff got to then, Jennifer? Fetching the children no doubt. Ours have their ballet recital today, so here I am instead of Erica, on wine detail for the great event." Andrew's laugh rises, then drops at the sight of Francine's piercing blue eyes staring across at him from her arrangement of crackers and cheese.

"And you would be Francine." Andrew falters as he slides the cases of wine onto the corner of the white tablecloth. "I've heard all about you and your music, my dear. You must call me Andrew. I'm so tired of Dr. Wilson this and that."

"*D'accord,*" Francine smiles. "*Bienvenue,* Andrew."

He bows in mock formality. "Ah, and here's my very own family photographer. You must show me around your exhibition, Cailey; you can tell me all about your art."

"Sure thing, Dr. Wilson." Cailey catches Francine's amused expression and pointedly squirts a long spray of window cleaner across the large front window. "Just let me finish up here." She polishes busily in wide circles where she'd already cleaned.

"What's the time, Jenn?" Cailey stuffs a wad of wet newspapers and the Windex bottle into a yellow pail, then slides it across the floor, and pushes it out of sight under the trestle table.

"Three-thirty. Can you check in that pail, Cailey? Patrick and I are taping the speaker cords down. Is there more black tape in that pail?"

"Maybe. Just a sec." Cailey retrieves the pail, finds the tape, and throws it over to Jennifer. She straightens up and stands watching Andrew organizing bottles of white wine in the ice filled cooler behind the table. With his back to her, he opens a bottle of red, then another, and another. He lines them up in a neat row behind a row of wine glasses, then pours himself a brim full glass.

Andrew Wilson is making Cailey nervous. She turns away from him, holds one hand out in front of her, laughs to herself when she cannot steady it.

"Oh dear," she whispers just as Marie-Claude appears by her side.

"*Ah, mon amie! Je pense tu es un paquet de nerfs comme moi!*" Marie-Claude rests her hand on Cailey's arm. "You worry just like me Patrick says. We are always thinking, thinking, worrying that we steal from the subject we mean to honour, *n'est-ce pas?*"

Cailey laughs with relief, her eyes following Marie-Claude's to the framed print on the wall in front of them.

"See Cailey, my aunt there pulling potatoes from the earth." Marie-Claude holds her head in a mock lament. "*Oh mon Dieu, ma pauvre tante, elle est si fatiguée, si triste.* You see her like that? My camera telling that story? But is it a lie? Is my aunt so tired like that, and sad? What of her defiance, her strength, that crazy laughing I have known all my life. Nothing beats that woman down, nothing." Marie-Claude turns to Cailey. "I don't let the camera say that, do I?"

"No, absolutely, you don't. You do in some others, but this one is poignant. A study of your aunt becomes its own story of women's rural poverty."

"*Exactement!*"

Cailey moves slowly along the line of Marie-Claude's prints. "And what if your camera tells a story of your aunt that she hadn't intended to reveal?"

"*C'est possible.* But I do know my subject. My aunt will be laughing. I can hear it!"

"She could laugh at herself in that image?"

"*Je pense que oui.* Okay she says to me last week, you play with my sexy picture." Marie-Claude grins. "I know it is different for you with the Lucie series."

"Yes, I still have to wonder about my friend Lucie. What she will feel seeing herself."

"Was she okay with the proofs you showed her?"

"Like your aunt, yes, she just laughed." Cailey frowns. "Still, looking around, I'm confused about what I've created here." Cailey and Marie-Claude walk across the gallery to the wall of Cailey's mounted photos. "See in this one, Marie, Lucie at her café. For me, it's my favourite. I love this one of her."

"But of course, it is your best."

"I hope so. Lucie was very quiet when I showed her this one."

"That's okay, Cailey. That could mean she was thoughtful. There's a beauty in her face here, and you engage your viewer so quickly in Lucie's open good humour. There's amusement running through the obvious hardship of her urban life. You can feel it. A part of her seems defeated, *n'est-ce pas?* Also gentle. And knowing. From deep in her eyes. That's a lot to capture in one photo."

"Okay, yes. Thank you, Marie." She squeezes her friend's shoulder. "That's what I was after. I got that expression just as she'd made a joke at my expense." Cailey is warmed by the recollection. "She knows me well!"

"*Bien sûr*, and why wouldn't she? She is smart! And so much time you and Wendy had spent with her family."

Marie-Claude holds up her watch to the light from the window, opens her eyes wide. "*Mais, mon Dieu*, Cailey!" She checks in Patrick's direction, catches his eye. "Only an hour to the opening! Will this gallery really be full of people sipping and nibbling and saying brilliant things about our *vernissage?*"

Arm in arm they move to join the others at the back of the gallery.

"Of course, Marie, we'll stand back in our wisdom, and eavesdrop on artsy nonsense!"

"Ha! The most fun will be ones with beads and long hair and headbands who always check out posters on telephone poles. They'll wander about sipping wine, offering their stoned observations. Can't you just hear them: "Oh look at the weathered face, such pathos in her eyes, such oppression will rise up, blah blah blah blah."

By now, they are enjoying a good laugh. "Oh God, I do hope Lucie doesn't hear stuff like that."

Marie-Claude laughs. "Maybe we should try not to be mad at our guests before they've even walked in the door."

"You're right. It felt good to be mad at something though."

Marie-Claude pulls back on Cailey's arm. "Oh dear, look who's coming our way."

"Well, what a delightful portrait. Is this one of yours, Cailey?" His voice cuts through their conversation, holding his glass of wine, and raising a toast to a portrait of Lucie. "A marvelous face indeed, salt of the earth type. I should know, I have many patients like her, many patients, I know their suffering."

Marie-Claude whispers, "Would you like to see Dr. Andrew Wilson in beads and a headband?"

"What? What's that?" Andrew holds the wine bottle up in their direction. "Anyone else for wine?" He squints at the label. "A Quebec blend from France, I dare say. Well, it will have to do for now."

"Andrew, it's a bit early for that, don't you think?" Jennifer comes up behind him and removes the bottle from his hand. Cailey and

Marie-Claude turn away and make themselves busy arranging the paper plates and napkins.

Andrew lowers his voice to a hostile rasp. "Well, would you listen to Miss Jennifer, sounding like my Erica." Cailey catches him glaring at Jennifer, gesturing with his hand to the rest of the room as he raises his voice. "What about all you lot then? Don't tell me you haven't been smoking something or other by now. Anyone holding out for happy hour? Of course not. Let's raise a toke, raise a glass, each to his own, my friends."

"*Shit la merde, c'est trop chaud.*" Francine passes defiantly in front of Andrew with a stack of empty food containers. "We'll all turn pink like lobster in here, everyone crammed into this small space." She dumps the containers with a clatter outside the back door. "Wasn't there a fan last year, Jenn? Try in there, behind you, Patrick," she points, "in that cupboard. There, right beside you. A tall fan I think. *Ah oui, c'est ça.* Let's hope it works."

While everyone is debating the best placement of the fan, Cailey leaves Marie-Claude, and slips unnoticed out the front door. She inhales deeply on the steamy, exhaust-filled air. The usual Sunday traffic is backed up all the way to Sherbrooke Street; cars honk, jostle with each other on their way to the harbour and the street festivities of Old Montreal.

Cailey welcomes the stifling heat, the sunlight along this narrow street, the possibility of a small café, an espresso, a Sunday paper.

She turns briefly to observe the gallery's display window behind her. There is Lucie of course, watching her from the other side of the glass, her expression amused, her face lit by the flickering blueish light from her television.

Cailey smiles right back at Lucie, then pokes her head in the door, calls out that she's taking a quick walk around the block. Before anyone can object, she is on her way, absorbed in a throng of sun-drenched street life, picking up snatches of lively conversation from outdoor cafés.

At the first corner, she slows her pace, takes the time to peer into shop windows and restaurants. She knows she should be going back, but something is keeping her here, looking at mini-skirted mannequins in a shop window, leaning over to adjust a strap on her sandal, then lingering for no reason in front of plastic sausages hanging over jars of red peppers in a familiar delicatessen.

She checks her waist pouch for change to buy a newspaper, looks up to see a small child turn from her plate of French fries and stick her tongue out at Cailey. Cailey waves at the little girl, startling her into a smile by reciprocating in kind.

She walks on in the recollection of those daring acts of defiance she'd shared with Beth and Paul from the back window of their father's truck.

Turning right, she finds the next street all but deserted. Overhead, she senses the sleeping neon energy that will pulsate from this strip late into the night. A locked down electronics store on the corner has kept its four TV screens going, all on the same channel. Cailey stops to watch. Football. The four identical commentators mouth soundlessly at her. The camera zooms in on a clash of helmeted giants on four green fields. Four paunchy referees in black and white striped shirts, whistles in mouths, red handkerchiefs held up, signal the penalty. The play stops, the crowd jumps silently to its feet. On all four screens. On millions of screens all over North America. Shift to Budweiser. Four times mute bronze men in a speedboat, four times blonde woman waving, skiing in the foaming wake behind the boat. Four bronze men laughing soundlessly into the sun, strong hands gripping sweaty Budweiser bottles.

Cailey leans her back against the window, gazes up the mountain. Perhaps she could walk to the lookout. She would sit on the grass, there's a perfect spot she knows, under a tree, with a clear view of the city and the river beyond. She could eat a foot long hot dog with mustard from the pavilion, watch people, read the newspaper.

Of course she must turn around, head back to the gallery. Whatever is she thinking? At the next intersection she finds herself in front of a cathedral where two drunks lie sleeping on a stone wall at the foot of a well-manicured lawn. An elderly woman in black pulls herself up the railing to the church. Using two hands, she opens the heavy wooden door, hesitates, checking back over her shoulder, then disappears inside.

Cailey takes a minute to rest on the wooden bench across from the cathedral; she stretches her legs out in front of her, stares down at her tanned feet. She feels the sweat running down the back of her neck as she ties her hair in a knot on top of her head.

Why, particularly on a day filled with excitement, would she suddenly feel she might somehow collapse from within? *Simply collapse*, she is thinking, *like a hollow, barely standing tree, deceptively lifelike, propped up only by the growth around it.*

An audible sigh, her own.

She stands abruptly, reties her hair, picks up a newspaper left on the bench. The front page photo catches her eye: Premier Levesque speaking to reporters about a serious labour dispute. Steve would be right in the thick of this one, working side by side with Émile in support of the trade unions.

If only he was. Right here in the thick of it. If only he were here for the opening. She tucks the paper under her arm. Four-thirty. She has made herself late for the opening of her own exhibition.

Halfway up the block approaching the gallery, she realizes that the man walking toward her is Andrew. He carries his glass of wine in one hand, and waves gaily at her with the other.

"Well, there you are, my dear," he calls loudly, his speech slurred, his walk wobbling. "We've all been waiting for you, you know. Someone just came in. Some old friend of yours, lots of hugging and kissing. And now the music's starting."

Cailey hears the music coming from the gallery as she approaches Andrew. He takes her by the elbow and guides her back toward the gallery. Just outside the door he edges her up against a brick wall, holding her arm.

"I have to go in, Andrew. I'm already late." She pushes him away, not quite registering what he is up to. He tightens his grip on both her arms. A few people stare as they go into the gallery.

"Indeed. Indeed. But just one minute, Cailey, I have an invitation for you. I'd like to take you to dinner this evening."

"What? Oh my, I don't think so. Would you let go of my arm now, please."

Andrew lets go but moves quickly into the doorway of the gallery, blocking her entry. "Why are you making a fuss? A simple invitation to dinner." His expression suddenly seems sweet, even vulnerable.

"You mean at your house?" Her voice is barely controlled. "With Jenn and Cliff? Where's Erica by the way?"

"She's can't make it today. But no, I mean just you and me. Erica takes the children to her mother's on Sunday evenings. I have a favourite little restaurant. We can get away alone, I think you've wanted that too. This place is out of the way. Up in the north end. Lovely chef. His wife is a dear."

"No, of course not. I'm going in."

"A business dinner. I mean a business dinner."

"What business?" She tries to walk past him, feels her anger rising. He is pressing his fingers into her arm, hard.

"Well, your portrait business, of course. I can set up many more clients from my contacts. I could make a big difference." He tips the last drop of wine into his mouth while he peers knowingly at her through the curve of the glass. He does not let go of her arm.

"I don't want your help. I'm going in." She wrenches her arm free, resists the urge to strike him across his bleary reddened face.

"The other thing is," he speaks flatly now, as she turns her back, "I could also make things a little difficult. Since most of your portrait business already comes through your first job with Erica and me. And I hear you were taking some snaps of Consuela on the side. Creative photography. Very creative."

Cailey stands frozen on the spot, looking down at the red finger marks on her forearm.

"You bastard." She hardly hears her own voice as she walks into the gallery. "Bastard," she repeats loudly to the surprise of several guests who are craning their necks above the crowd.

"Keep it down, sister." A tall bearded man in a vibrant African shirt glances at her irritably. Beads. Headband.

She edges her way slowly through the crowd until she has Jennifer and Francine in full view. They are already into the music they've been rehearsing to accompany the Lucie series. Jennifer leans into her fiddle, Francine flirts with her audience, moving easily from harmonica to accordion, singing huskily into the microphone. At the chorus, Jennifer lowers her fiddle. Her voice is softer than Francine's. After weeks of practice, their harmonies are effortless, their energy flying. As they move into the next song Francine catches Cailey's eye and smiles.

Cailey knows she's missed the introduction she was supposed to read for the Lucie series. The guests don't seem to need any explanations. Relieved, she looks around the room. A few familiar faces. Wendy chatting with Lucie. Wendy. That can't be Wendy. It is Wendy. Two weeks early. Well good. Those two are whispering and laughing, Lucie is picking something up from the table behind her. Cailey nudges her way in closer to get a better look.

Francine is smiling her consent at Wendy who is now waving inquiringly at her, holding some utensil in her right hand. A spoon. Spoons. Wendy and Lucie both have spoons. Lucie moves her chair in close to Jennifer's mic, right under the portrait of her with her kids in the lineup for Star Wars. Wendy pulls a chair in beside her.

With her eye on Francine, Lucie holds the spoons poised between her left knee and open left palm, chanting comically to Wendy "... *un... et deux... et trois...*" Then she puts her head down and begins to play in time to the music, her large body swaying easily to the complex of rhythms she is creating.

Wendy is finding her way into the beat, doubling over with laughter each time Lucie gives her a sour look. When at last she catches on, Lucie nods with a grin; Francine and Jennifer pick up the tempo.

And so, as the room erupts in cheers and spontaneous clapping, Cailey, in the midst of this crowd of strangers, begins to dance.

CHAPTER
11

BONHOMME GIGUEUR

MONTRÉAL

AUGUST 1977

"Cailey!"

"Aha, could be that Wendy's here." Cailey feels Wendy's weight on the edge of her bed. She rolls over without opening her eyes. "How are you Wens? You saw everyone? Beth? Paul?"

"I can't hear a word Cailey. Try to open your mouth when you talk." Wendy reaches over and lets up the blinds with a sudden clatter that sends them spinning around on their wooden spools at the top of the windows.

"Wendy. Wendy. It's too bright. What are you doing?"

"Waking you up."

"I got that part."

"So. Coffee?"

"Great."

"Eggs, bacon, home fries, OJ?"

"Whoa," Cailey groans and pulls the sheet over her head. "What time is it anyway?"

"Seven-thirty. Beth and Paul were amazing. Not at all like I'd expected. I've a ton of stuff they sent you. A card from Uncle Mickey, a card from Audrey with a bag of your favourite blackballs from the store."

"Blackballs. How perfect."

"Everyone sent you presents. Although I don't know why they're even talking to you at this point."

"And what about Mum and Dad?"

Wendy pauses at the door. "The usual. I didn't see your dad. He was away. Your mum sent along a few things for you, including the letter from your Gran about the amber pin."

"Really? Where is it?"

"In my suitcase with the rest of my life. I'll go find it. Your mum, by the way, was hobbling around on a sprained ankle."

"I didn't know she'd sprained her ankle."

"Well, now, there's likely a lot you don't know. Wouldn't you think?"

"I would think. Yes. What happened?"

"Well, the way she put it, and she was sober the first time I saw her, was that she took off a sweater and threw it down the basement stairs, and she went down with it. She was surprisingly funny in the telling, had us all in stitches."

"Doesn't sound altogether funny to me."

"Uncle Mickey hopes it's maybe scared her sober. Beth told me Mickey made her promise, in front of your dad, that she wouldn't have anything to drink until suppertime, when there were others in the house. You know, if I were younger I'd marry your Uncle Mickey."

Cailey laughs. "You and Audrey, and half the ladies in Wood River."

"Anyway, your father didn't comment, but Beth and Paul thought Mickey was talking into the wind. 'Pissing into the wind' is what Paul said. 'Mum doesn't drink on someone else's schedule,' he said."

"He's right."

"Your little brother, in case you don't remember, is a sweetheart. And very smart. I told him I had a crush on him. He blushes so easily. Very cute."

"I remember. I miss him."

"You're probably missing a little boy who's not there anymore, Cailey."

"Ouch, I know."

"I'm just saying that the guy who blushes is not little."

"Okay Wendy, enough."

"Enough will be when you go to see your family."

"Anything else?"

"Not that I can think of right now." Wendy stands up and goes to the bedroom door. "Oh wait, I forgot. There's a letter from Steve." She shuts the door behind her.

"Wendy?"

Wendy pokes her head back into the room.

"You called? Tea instead of coffee?"

Wendy saunters off toward the kitchen, singing off key as always. "Ah found ma thurrilllll, on Blueberry Hilllll," she croons at the top of her voice, "when ah found youuu…"

"Oh very funny." Cailey mutters with a weary smile swinging her legs over the side of the bed.

Cailey stands silently at the kitchen doorway. Sensing her presence, Wendy looks up from a pan of sizzling bacon to see her bleary eyed friend glaring at her. Cailey's matted hair, tied lopsided on top of her head, brings a huge grin to Wendy's face.

"Love the hairdo!"

"Thank you. If there's a letter from Steve, I'd like to see it."

"In my purse. Beside the coffee table."

"You need a hand here?"

"Not until you read the letter."

"Why didn't you let me know you were coming back early?" Cailey rummages through Wendy's purse. Airmail envelope. Exotic stamps. Birds. Address in capital letters. CAILEY DONALD, C/O JEFF ERIKSON, 10 RALEIGH CRESCENT, WINNIPEG. PLEASE FORWARD.

"Well, I didn't know did I? I flew out at the last minute. Larry's bringing the car. We broke up right after our last visit with your family at Wood River."

In the upper left hand corner, STEVE ERIKSON, LIMA. "You broke up? Again? I thought the last time was for keeps. I didn't even know Larry went to Wood River with you." Cailey collapses into the armchair facing the living room windows.

"Oh."

She stares at the envelope. "Okay, so what happened?"

"I'll tell you after I've had my first coffee. Otherwise I might throw up." Wendy makes a mock retching sound from the kitchen. "Mind if I turn on the radio?"

"Why didn't you give me this yesterday?"

"At the gallery?" Wendy leans into the living room, pointing a spatula at Cailey. "I nearly did. You were having fun with everyone, Cailey. It was your moment. I was afraid prince charming might put you off stride."

"He might have." Cailey fingers the envelope, shakes it, holds it to the light. Four years. She tears a strip down one side and pulls out several sheets written on both sides. She turns sideways lifts her legs over one arm of the chair, closes her eyes, opens them to immediately fall in love with the sight of Steve's handwriting.

Dear Cailey,

I'm not sure how to get this letter to you. I heard you and Wendy had moved up the street, so I asked Mum to find out if Wendy's around this summer. Jeff's written a bit about how you're doing. Wendy complains about you never taking the trip home with her, so I gather you still haven't got back to see your folks. I'm sorry that's so hard for you. Jeff also said your portrait business is picking up. That's great. I have mixed reactions when I hear news of you. Partly it hurts.

It's not easy here, as you might expect. The best part is that so many of my coworkers have become like brothers and sisters to me. I've imagined your camera, Cailey, your sketchbook, capturing these images, events and faces, and the lives of these amazing people! Much needs to be recorded, corrected. Perceptions. Attitudes. We've got things terribly wrong. Recently someone suggested that my place should be home in Canada, where I can advocate for Peru, for workers' rights, and for changes that need to take shape in my own country. I'm trying to decide about coming back. Not sure I could face teaching in Canada. I might ask my old friend Émile—remember him?—about solidarity work with the unions. I'd have to improve my French! My language brain has gone Spanish.

Is there much coverage in Quebec of the general strikes in Peru? I bet not. Almost nothing in the Winnipeg press. My dad would have been ashamed I think. Of Canada.

He's on my mind a lot these days, so's my grandfather, and those early days of organizing in Winnipeg. I tell my campañeros about the Winnipeg strike, and they seem sceptical that such a thing would happen up there. Have made a couple of trips home to Winnipeg. Spent Christmas with Mum two years back. Believe it or not, I miss the snow! The crunchy blue sky snow! Anne was in Pointe Claire for her grandmother's funeral. Neither of us felt like contacting anyone.

Truth be told Cailey, I've started this letter a dozen times in the past week. I expect you must have moved on by now, at least from what you and I had together. Sometimes though, I like to imagine you know how often I think of you. In my more practical moments, I know I'm deluded, that it's only my longing for you that's created the constant feeling we're still connected. There are lots of ways of saying this I guess, but the simplest is just that I love you... always... how can that be? You may have heard that Anne and I have gone our separate ways. She is very angry. It's mostly my fault I'm afraid. Some of it I don't understand. I've been dishonest with her about my feelings for you, and she says I've been emotionally absent. She's right. This has hurt her. I've handled it badly. Got it wrong in the first place. And I am left with my anger at losing you.

My decision about returning to Canada doesn't depend on whether there is still a chance for us. But I would like to see you. To know you're still real. Well, much more than that if there's a chance. But I would accept just that! To see you.

Yours, Steve

"Here we are, a feast to behold! Let's eat in the living room. It's so sunny." Wendy carries a tray of cups, plates, a mountain of toast, a pot of coffee. "The rest is coming." She puts the tray down on the coffee table and glances over at Cailey.

"Cailey? Oh Cailey? Hey breathe for God's sake. You look like you just fell out of a plane."

"Unbelievable." Cailey shakes her head, slowly folds the pages, slips them back into the envelope. "Too bloody unbelievable." She stands up abruptly. "Okay, you need to give me a minute here. I'm not talking about this yet." She stares hard at Wendy. "Come on then, I'm famished. I'll help you with the food."

Cailey laughs as she enters the kitchen. "Hey this is great! The kitchen hasn't looked like this for a month!" She surveys the line up of greasy pots and pans covering every surface; there are eggshells, orange peels, crumbs, bits of paper towel. She'd forgotten.

"I will never marry you, Wendy."

"Oh darn." Wendy hands Cailey a platter piled high with scrambled eggs and bacon.

"Is this Monday?" Cailey lowers herself to the floor in front of the coffee table. Wendy sits on the couch, pours them each a glass of orange juice.

"Monday. Yes. You have stuff on today?" Wendy spoons out the eggs.

"Not much today. Tomorrow. I'm doing photos at a day camp on the West Island."

"A day camp? How'd you get into that?"

"A client from my Christmas card business. Tell me about you and Larry."

"Well, I've had it this time. Really. I told him. Please don't smirk at me like that. This was the last straw."

"What was the last straw?"

"He borrowed money from my sister and made her promise not to tell me. Only she told. I think he was coming on to her. Bastard. So I took off. He can pay for the car rental. For everything." Wendy shakes the ketchup bottle until a startled crimson trail splatters out over her eggs. She looks down at it with satisfaction and begins to eat.

"Well yes, that would certainly qualify as a last straw. Can't say I'm sorry. As long as you're okay with it. I won't be missing his presence around here, as you know."

"Well me neither." Wendy looks up sheepishly. "I might miss his body."

"That was the problem wasn't it? The body."

"Yes indeedie," Wendy chuckles, "that is some body."

"Such good nosh, Wens. This joint is definitely my favourite greasy spoon."

"Mine too," Wendy agrees, constructing a tall bacon and ketchup sandwich.

For a few minutes, they eat in silence. A comfortable silence, Cailey thinks, with the two of them retreating easily into their own worlds. Cailey's thoughts swirl around Steve's letter. She picks at the last of the eggs, puts her fork down. "So. It sounds like Steve's coming home."

"I figured as much. What did he have to say?"

"He said..." Cailey pulls the letter from her pocket and hands it to Wendy.

Wendy opens the letter and reads. "Ah, seems he wants you back."

Wendy speaks more softly as she looks up into Cailey's tear-filled eyes. "That's what Jeff was guessing when he dropped off the letter."

Cailey takes her coffee over to the window. In the street below she watches Madame Bedard sitting on the steps talking to the neighbours. Her kids are rummaging through the Steinberg's bags in her shopping cart and she hollers half-heartedly at them as they run up the street tossing a bag of potato chips triumphantly in the air.

"So Cailey, here we are. Me on the loose, Your Prince Charming coming home, a brilliant opening of your exhibition, and we can..."

"Oh my God. The exhibition!" Cailey swigs the last of her coffee. "The reviews, Wendy! I forgot about checking for reviews. We have to get the papers. Come on. Finish your eggs. We'll go to Giorgio's. I'll buy you a cappuccino and we'll read the reviews."

"Giorgio's? You want to go to Giorgio's? You haven't been there since Steve left."

"Exactly." Cailey covers her face with her napkin as she walks to the bathroom to wash up.

***

Cailey stares at the phone for several minutes. When she finally picks up the receiver, she rotates the dial slowly, hangs up before it rings. She knows Wendy is watching her from the living room. She dials again and this time she lets the call go through.

"Hello? Hello? Is that you, Mum? It's Cailey... No... It's me Cailey. I'm calling to find out how your ankle is. What? I can't hear you... okay that's better. It was Wendy who told me. My friend Wendy. She was just visiting you. She told me you'd broken your ankle."

She peeks into the living room where Wendy is reading a book. "What? No, I don't know where Dad is. I'm calling from Montreal." "Oh, I see. I see. Are you getting out for bingo?"

Cailey reaches up a hand and massages her neck. "Mrs. Larson? No I didn't know. I'm sorry, Mum. I know she was your good friend. Can't someone else take you to bingo?" She rolls her eyes. "No, Mum, I'm in Montreal. Where are Paul and Beth? I wanted to talk to them too, thank them for the presents."

She shakes her head slowly. "Oh, I see. Tell them I called okay?" She paces back and forth, stretching the coiled phone cord to its limit. "No, I can't make it this year, Mum. I had to change my plans."

She stops pacing. "Yes, I know I say that every year. I'm sorry. But, about Gran's letter. Why did you open it?" She lets out a sigh. "The part about Becky? What do you mean?"

Cailey raises her shoulders, trying to release some tension. "No, I have no idea what she was referring to. I don't think it meant anything." Wendy looks up and raises her eyebrows.

"Right. Yes, okay, yes, I'll write soon, Mum. Tell Dad okay?"

Cailey shrugs in answer to Wendy's unspoken question. "And Denise? Of course I wrote her. I wrote her as soon as I got the birth notice. I know she got it, Mum, because she sent back a picture of herself with the baby." Cailey sighs again. "How's Uncle Mickey doing?"

Cailey listens with concern. "What do you mean at the hotel today? Maybe you did have too much."

She resumes her pacing. "Okay, Mum, okay. Of course he's on your side, Mum." Still massaging her neck, she adds, "Sure. You take care, Mum. Okay, okay, bye." Cailey hangs up the receiver.

"Not so good?" Wendy looks up from her book.

"Not so good." Cailey slides onto the couch. "When you saw her, did she mention anything particular about Gran's letter?"

"No."

"Well it seems she opened it. She certainly knew what was in it, and she was nervous."

"Why would she be nervous?"

"There were references to the day Becky drowned."

"Why would that make her nervous?"

"No idea." Cailey tries without success to push away the dreaded churning in her stomach, the tightening of her breath. She changes the subject, "She said Paul and Beth were working down at the store, and she was mumbling something about Dad that I didn't understand. I guess he's away again."

"You're a master at changing the subject, you know."

"Yes." Cailey glances at her watch. "I should get over to the gallery now, Wendy, then out to Jennifer's. You sure you don't want to come to the concert with us? There's that extra ticket of Cliff's."

"I don't think so this time. I need a night to read, and go to bed early."

"What're you reading?"

"*Fear of Flying*. Did you ever read it?"

"Only the dog-eared pages that were being passed around."

"If memory serves that was my copy going around our whole school. I always did like my reading with heavy breathing, and I used to think that's all that book was about. Maybe Erica's a bit too pleased with herself but really you have to admire her writing, not to mention her courage. I mean it's a tad better than my very best lingerie ads."

"You should be writing something besides lingerie ad copy, Wendy. You know you have a real talent there."

"I have been writing something."

"Really? Will you show me?"

"Are you crazy? It's restricted."

"Hard core?"

"Totally."

"So what are you really writing?"

"A play. About pigs."

"Pigs."

"Yes, pigs. My mother's family raised pigs during the war. She talked about it while I was out there this summer. The women brought in the only income for an extended family of more than thirty. Today Mum breaks out in hives if she sees so much as a pork chop. It's a pretty funny story, the way she tells it."

"So it's a comedy."

"I guess. Maybe more like your Shakespearean tragic comedy."

"What's it called?"

"The Pig Play."

"Of course. I want to read it."

"It's still cooking." Wendy waves as Cailey heads out the door.

***

"Sorry about the mess, Cailey. The kids have been wild today. You want some wine? There's some open in the fridge."

"I'll grab a glass of water thanks. That was a longer walk than I thought."

"You walked from your place?"

"No, from the gallery, but my feet are killing me." Cailey turns on the tap, lets it run cold and fills her glass. "I must be getting old, Jenn."

Jennifer calls out to Rob and Trisha to come for supper. "Wait till you're my age, and two kids down the line! So what were you doing at the gallery? Rob, put that down! How many times do I have to tell you kids not to bring toys to the table. God, would you believe the mess in this room!"

"I didn't bring a toy, Mummy."

"Okay, Trisha." Jennifer looks back at Cailey. "So how come you were at the gallery?"

"I needed time alone there. With the photos and the sketches together, to see them up on the wall when everything was quiet. It's been too hectic."

"And what did you see?"

"Well I did see that the reviewer in The Star made good points. She liked the exhibit, both Marie-Claude's work, and mine. But she noted that my treatment of oppressed women was on the verge of reinforcing stereotypes. Of course that stung since I mean to be doing the opposite. The thing is, she's right about some of the photos of Lucie. I'll re-hang the sketches, I think, and place each one closer to the accompanying photograph. The reviewer might have seen that I push past cliché with the sketches. She didn't mention the sketches."

"It's true that the sketches weren't well enough identified; they were a bit lost in the show. Still, I doubt it would make a difference if you moved them, Cailey. Critics will always try to outsmart the artist in some way, even if in a good review. If I remember correctly The Star review was very positive. Time to work on growing a thicker skin, I'd say."

"That's what Wendy said. I do want to continue experimenting with interpretive drawings of my photographs though. I'm thinking I'll practice on my candid shots of Consuela. I had them out the other day."

"Why work on those ones? You know you can't use them."

"I know. I'd be experimenting."

"Right." Jennifer turns to the kids, pushes Trisha's peas to the front of her plate and points.

"I'm not eating peas this week, Mummy. Maybe next week."

"Well then, how about counting them? I need to know how many are on your plate."

"Okay watch. I count way faster than Robbie." Trisha's head dips down over her plate. In a flash, she and Rob are counting their peas out loud.

"Just be careful not to eat any," Cailey laughs.

"Okay, where were we?" Jenn continues, more annoyed than amused.

"The photos of Consuela. Of course I won't show them publicly, Jenn. I'm playing with an idea. There's something that inspires me there. In Consuela's story. Steve left behind a few LP's of Andean flute music. Somehow I can imagine Consuela's story in that music. I'll draw her to musical themes, the play of the rhythms, different combinations, interpretations of her expressions as she talks about Chile."

Jenn nods hesitantly. "Still, you don't know Consuela all that well, Cailey, or much about her story. So you'd be making most of it up."

"Exactly. It's imagined. That's how I work."

"Why not go with the story of the amber pin now that Wendy's brought the letter from your grandmother? It might be easier to experiment with something familiar. Besides, it sounds fascinating from a musical perspective, and I'd love to work on it with you. You could try it with the 'Drawing Down the Moon' composition. You have an intimacy with that. You can go deeper. Did you bring the letter?"

"I did. I read it just now at the gallery. In a way, though, the story of the amber is more challenging for me personally, than a study of Consuela would ever be. The letter refers to Becky's drowning."

Jenn is thoughtful as she pours milk for Trisha and Rob who are now racing to see who can finish their peas fastest with their fingers.

"Becky?"

"My cousin who drowned. I think I told you about her."

"Someone drowneded?" Trisha looks up in alarm and Robbie races to the end of his peas.

"Hey! No fair, Mummy. He cheated."

Exasperated, Jennifer clears both their plates and ignores the bickering.

"You did tell me. Yes, a while ago."

"Well, it's an eerie connection Gran's making with what happened eons ago in her village in Scotland."

"And the amber figures in that? And your cousin?"

"Seems so." Cailey lowers her voice. "The story of the amber pin, and my little cousin floating down the river." She drops her head into her hands. "That's not a story I'm comfortable working with right now, Jenn. Wendy says I keep half my life hidden away in the shadows."

"Don't mind me, Cailey, but I think Wendy's right. Why not shine light into those shadows. Makes for better art, you know. Dark to light sort of thing, you know? Same with music, lighting up dark often makes brilliant music." Jennifer pauses, waits for Cailey to look up at her. "What if you started by drawing Becky's face. What did she look like?"

"Draw Becky?"

"Is there music that makes you think of Becky? From when you were kids?"

"'Mockingbird Hill.'" It comes to Cailey's mind in a flash. "Becky sang it everywhere she went. 'Tralala twiddledeedee,'" Cailey laughs softly. "'...it gives me a thrill, to wake up in the morning to the Mockingbird's trill.' Now how's that for a dreadful song? Patti Page. We all loved it. Gran sang it with us, and she turned the radio up every time it came on. Becky used every dime she could get her hands on to play it on the jukebox in town."

"There, you see, Cailey? I rest my case. You could find a recording, and see if the music brings Becky's image to life in a positive way. You could draw your gran with Becky." Jennifer stops and turns her attention to Rob as he slips off his stool.

"I don't think so, Jenn. This is sounding like therapy."

Jennifer grins. "It is therapy."

"I'm finished, Mum, okay? Hey! Okay, Mum?" Rob yells, "I din't like that s'getti."

"Finish it later then. If you want ice cream. Consuela will be here in a few minutes, and you'll have to finish before you have ice cream."

"Consuela?" Cailey is surprised.

"Oh, I forgot to say. The sitter cancelled, and Consuela agreed at the last minute."

"Can I have ice cream too, Mummy?" Trisha's face is covered in tomato sauce.

"Of course, but wipe your face, and we'll wait for Consuela."

Rob zooms and swerves his way over to Cailey with his Lego spaceship. He climbs up on the rung of her stool.

"Are you staying too?" Robbie asks, his eyes hopeful.

"Maybe next time, Robbie."

Robbie leans against her and flies his spaceship into her face. She holds his hands down in her lap.

"Hey, no fair." He wriggles free and jumps down.

"When does Cliff get back, Jenn?"

"Okay, you kids can have TV till Consuela gets here, then off it goes. Cliff will be home in three very long days, Cailey. I doubt I'll get near my cello or my fiddle. Francine's already wanting to rehearse her new tune for the closing of the exhibition. We were both going to have something new in time." Jennifer wipes off the counter. "I thought," she pauses, shaking her head at the mess, "that I might be able to work late at night while Cliff's away. At this rate, I doubt I'll keep my eyes open after nine-thirty."

"I'm not surprised."

"Cliff's so much better at bedtime routines. He gets it running so smoothly. I have no patience left by the time he gets home, but for him, when he's been contained in that cerebral world at the university all day, he loves nothing more than his escape into the fun of the kids' baths and reading stories before they fall asleep." She turns back to the kids. "Hey guys, there's the bell. Turn off the TV, please."

Jennifer dumps the dishes into the sink. She puts her hands over her ears as Trisha and Robbie leave the TV on and run screeching to the door to let Consuela in.

"Ice cream. Ice cream. Ice cream!"

"When you're tempted to have kids, Cailey, remember this moment."

"They are adorable little devils, Jenn." Cailey smiles as she grabs her bag from the counter. "Hi there, Consuela."

Consuela waves happily at Cailey with her free hand, pretending to resist as Trisha and Rob pull her into the kitchen.

"Okay Mum, get the ice cream. Hey where's my s'ghetti? How'm I asposed to eat it if it's not here?"

"I chucked it. Never mind, Robbie, have your ice cream anyway. They're wild, Consuela. Sorry about the mess. Dishes and everything. I'll do them when I get in. You know they'll be perfect for you. As soon as I walk out the door."

Consuela looks around the room and nods. "I'm someone new to play with. You go. Have fun!"

Jennifer fishes in her bag for the car keys. "My keys must be upstairs. Just a sec, Cailey."

"You're looking so well, Consuela. How's Gaetan?"

"He's very fine." Consuela replies as she reaches into the freezer for the tub of ice cream.

Cailey is trying to remember when they last saw each other. They'd had coffee downtown just after Consuela quit her job at the Wilson's and was starting night school to learn French. Cailey had shown her the photos she'd taken at the Wilson's brunch, and Consuela had talked nervously when she saw them. Cailey had sensed her trying to hide her fear. Consuela had told her about fleeing from Chile, about the position she had held in government before the coup, the hopes they'd all had for her country when Allende was elected. Several of her friends had died in the stadium, and Victor Jara had sung their agony until they took all his fingers so he couldn't play his guitar. Later, they shot him. Cailey hadn't mentioned to Consuela about her friend Steve in Peru, or his solidarity work with Émile for Madame Allende's visit to Montreal. Somehow his involvement shrank in the face of Consuela's.

And then a month ago they'd waved at each other on the metro, and made their way to each other through the crowd. Consuela talked excitedly about living with her friend Gaetan, about her part time job in the airport coffee shop that was paying for her French course. Her eyes seemed less guarded.

"Okay kids, ice cream. Ice cream." Consuela smiles brightly. "Yes, Gaetan is fine. We have a nice place now, in Dorval. You should come and see us."

"I'd love to."

"Do you still have those pictures of me, Cailey? Your 'Connie pictures?'" Consuela's laugh is self-conscious.

"Yes I do. Do you still want copies?"

"Maybe yes. Gaetan, he thinks I'm teasing him. He says I would not dress up in a little white hat and a little white apron. I can show you I tell him, while he's laughing at me. I have a friend with pictures!"

The hesitation that so often makes Consuela seem vulnerable, vanishes when she speaks of Gaetan. There is a sureness in her now that Cailey suspects was hiding on the other side of language.

"Found them." Jennifer returns holding up her keys. "The neighbour's phone number is here on the fridge, Consuela, in case you need anything. The kids will be angels now. Look at that. Halos already. I can't stand it. Will Gaetan pick you up?"

"He'll come at ten. There's a movie on TV we want to see, so don't worry about the time."

"Well, I'm so grateful to both of you for coming in at the last minute." Jennifer plants a kiss on a cheek of each ice cream covered face in front of her.

"Really, no problem, it's fun to meet here after he gets off work."

Consuela goes with them to the door.

"I'll copy those photos for you, Consuela." Cailey taps Consuela's arm. "I'll call you."

Consuela waves to them as Jennifer slides into the driver's seat and turns on the ignition.

"What was all that about?"

"All what?"

"The photos you were talking about." Jennifer backs the car out of the drive and heads down the hill.

"Oh, Gaetan doesn't believe she ever worked as a maid. I said I'd give her the photos. You remember, she saw the file a couple of years ago. Cliff gave me hell."

"I remember."

Cailey looks over at Jennifer who is concentrating on the traffic at a busy intersection. "Andrew made a pass at me, Jenn, at the opening, quite a nasty come on in fact."

"Shit. Why didn't you tell me?"

"I just did."

"This is exactly what had been going on with Consuela at the Wilson's. Shit shit shit!" Jennifer hits the steering wheel with her hand. "I knew we should have done something at the time, Cailey. Cliff was too anxious about Erica. I should have done something." Jennifer pulls out into the traffic. "Tell me what happened."

"He was insisting I go out for dinner with him. Some special place he knew. It was a threatening invitation. There were people in front of the gallery, so he couldn't really do any harm. But he scared me. Grabbed my arm hard. He was a bit like the husband in the house I worked at in Winnipeg."

"Erica and Andrew have been having horrendous shouting matches lately. The kids keep telling Cliff about it, sometimes tearfully. And we know from Erica that Andrew's drinking more and more, even when he's on duty. Surely something has to be done about that. There's no doubt Erica's become quite afraid of him."

"I think she should be. I think he could be violent. He left marked bruises on my arms."

"How did he threaten you?"

"He would damage my photography business, he said, if I didn't come along. So many of my contacts had come through their friends."

"How disgusting." Jennifer is thoughtful while she shifts lanes. "Cliff has to face up to this. We both have to."

"Did you know Andrew threatened to have Consuela's immigration challenged if she told anyone about his advances to her? She was terrified that he could do something that would get her sent back to Chile."

"I'm afraid we did know that, but we didn't think Andrew would dare, or that he could ever succeed if he tried."

"I don't agree. I think with the position he holds in this town, he could have done it." Cailey is watching out for a parking space on their third time around the block. "There, that guy's leaving, Jenn." She points. "Do you think we should talk to Cliff about this?"

"I'm not sure, Cailey. Oh what am I saying? Of course we should." Jennifer is frowning as she angles the car into the space. "Can you grab my purse from behind the seat?" She rolls up her window.

Cailey checks her watch. "We better run, we're almost late."

They get to their seats just as the house lights are dimmed and the long wispy figure of Gilles Vigneault dances onto the stage like some *bonhomme gigueur* brought to life.

Jennifer leans over and whispers, "Have you answered Steve's letter?"

Cailey looks straight into Jennifer's knowing green eyes. "No, I haven't."

"What the hell are you waiting for?"

Cailey grimaces and lifts both hands, palms up, in a gesture toward the stage.

They turn together as Gilles Vigneault raises his arms over his head, his laughter tumbling out into the hall.

"*Tout le monde est malheureux,*" he sings to an eruption of thunderous applause. "*Tam ti de la dé te li la té te l lé de l la ti tam…*"

Well, exactly, Cailey thinks as the bittersweet music dances through her heart.

"*Tam ti de la dé de lam… Tout le monde est malheureux.*"

CHAPTER
12

DO NOT RUN FROM MAGIC
THE MARITIMES
AUGUST 1977

Cailey drives to the coast by herself, leaving a surprised and outraged Jennifer sitting on her front porch nibbling soda crackers to quiet her morning sickness. "The least you could do is take over the morning sickness," she moans to Cliff as he helps Cailey load up the last of the camping gear.

Finally, feeling somewhat bewildered, and offering too many thank you's, and too many regrets that Jenn wasn't coming, Cailey steers their old Plymouth out of the drive and heads east to the autoroute.

Now, after two days on the road and very little sleep, she strains impatiently to read the highway signs through a relentless downpour. She would be quite happy if she were warm in her own bed right now, or up having tea with Wendy, nestled into her corner of the couch with a good book.

It had been Wendy really, who had pushed her to do this trip alone. Their friends joined her in the chorus. "You're in a rut, Cailey. You need to get out of here. You haven't drawn a single line since the show opened. You're quite boring really," Wendy contributed with her best sardonic grin. "The trip will be good for you, and besides I'm planning a month of all night parties, motorcycle gangs rolling off the couch for breakfast, you know the sort." Jennifer had managed a pale smile and nodded her agreement with Wendy. "She's right Cailey. Don't worry, you'll be fine alone. Cliff's got the car all tuned up for you."

They ganged up on me, that's what they did, Cailey reflects with wry appreciation, as she pulls off the highway to wait for the rain to let up. She'd been about to back out, and they ganged up on her. Patrick had come over with a mountain of maps and guidebooks from his mother in New Brunswick. He'd said something lyrical about sacred places by the sea, and she allowed herself to imagine sitting alone in the sun, going for long walks along the beach, drawing and reading, listening to music while a few little fishing boats bobbed casually on the horizon.

But really, Cailey wonders as the rain blows more furiously against the windshield, *why the hell am I doing this?*

At the moment, she can barely make out the flashing taillights of the other cars pulling onto the shoulder in front of her. On the opposite side of the highway, there is a line-up of blurred headlights at the side of the road. Even the eighteen-wheelers that have terrorized her for the last two days now sit immobilized, flickering and panting like defeated steel giants.

Cailey shivers in the damp sea air and tries to remember where she packed her sweater. She reaches up and switches on the overhead light. She groans. The backseat is a jumble of bags and books and a partially spilled box of blueberries she'd picked up at a roadside stand. A sweater and socks. That's what she needs. Socks. Where are they? She stretches back and lifts her knapsack into her lap. It is the same knapsack she'd carried to the bus in Wood River years ago. Here they are, warm socks, the old sweater. That's better. She tries the radio. Nothing but static. She turns off the light and waits, welcomes the spreading warmth of wool socks, the comfort of her sweater; her muscles relax as she sinks down in the seat.

She is reassured by the circle of lights around her, the transient close-ness of a silent community bound together by the shared storm. She is sorry when the rain finally lets up and she must join the now anonymous line of cars pulling back onto the highway. She picks up speed, and settles into the last forty miles of her journey. On the dashboard, she reads the relentless rotation of the odometer, measuring her progress, apparently in inches. She imagines setting up her tent in what will be a dark and unfamiliar space. Her anxiety returns.

"That park is magical," Patrick had told her, excited to be sharing his home province with her, and with Marie-Claude, who leaned into his shoulder as the three of them poured over his maps. "You could try for one of the sites up here on this rocky cliff," he points. "My two favourites are here," he circles them on a campsite map with a red marker.

As she steers the car through the log gates of the park, she is mentally pitching her tent. Cliff had twice demonstrated how to set it up, but she's sure she'll forget which pole goes where.

In the end, with an uneasy sense relief, she locks her doors, and sleeps in the car under the dark blowing pine trees just inside the gate, where a sign swaying back and forth on the chain across the gravel road tells her the park will open again at seven the next morning.

***

In the morning, an attendant guides Cailey to her campsite. She considers the possibility of turning around and heading back, finding a motel somewhere. Instead, she unravels her very stiff limbs from the driver's seat, opens the trunk, and spreads the green nylon tent, along with its confusion of poles and pegs, in a circle around her on the soggy ground. She lines the poles up as best she can remember from Cliff's instructions. To her surprise, within half an hour, she is standing before a perfectly pitched tent. She shifts its position once, thinking to set it at a better angle to the wind, but it quickly becomes apparent that she has made it more precarious, not less. With some annoyance, she places rocks on the corner pegs, and shrugs at her little green house while it shimmies and clangs in rebellious fits and starts as if thwarted from its intention to lift off.

That first night in her tent, she sits cross-legged on her sleeping bag, drinking tepid tea. A small Coleman lantern swings from the tent bars overhead, casting its glow around emerald walls.

With her journal balanced on her knee, she jots down random reflections from her drive; her first sight of the north shore of the St. Lawrence; the tattooed trucker and his white poodle sitting on separate stools at a Drummondville stop; the best bacon and eggs ever at Irving's; the cleanest toilet ever at the Welcome to New Brunswick; the ponytail blonde who tailgated her from Edmunston to Grand Falls; the rain, the rain, the relentless rain for the entire last leg of her journey.

She is becoming aware, as she writes, that every word, every reflection, is for Steve. She is writing to Steve.

She closes the journal, tucks it away with her pen in a side pocket of her knapsack, and lies back on the pile of clothes she has rolled up as a pillow. Tomorrow she will buy a real pillow. Somewhere. Patrick was wrong about not needing a pillow.

She watches, mesmerized, as a disturbingly plump spider descends toward her on a single silky thread hanging from the roof of the tent. "I'm afraid you'll have to go, spider." She tears a piece from the newspaper lying next to her. "It's just that I don't want you crawling across my face while I sleep. Although I'm sure you have friends to replace you. Or avenge your death. Oh yuck, you are a squishy one, aren't you?"

What's that? She sits up again, stares at the zippered tent door. *A small animal? Rustling around out there. Probably a chipmunk. Or a bear. A sweet little bear. With claws and...*

There it is again. Rustling nearby. Only now there's a voice.

A man's voice. Maybe two voices. There must be two of them. Moving closer. She turns down the lantern and tries to remember where she put the hatchet. Outside of course. By the tree.

The voices become hushed, and urgent.

"Come on, get a move on, Jackie." Cailey remains absolutely still, barely breathing, listening intently to the thrashing movements in the underbrush right outside her tent.

"What are you doing?"

Cailey cringes at the controlled sharpness in the man's voice.

"It's number two, Daddy. I have to do my number two."

"Oh I don't believe this. Okay, okay, let me get the toilet paper from Mummy. Jesus. What next?"

Cailey drops her head in relief, and with a sort of silly euphoric laugh, she turns the lantern back up. *Well, Jackie whoever-you-are, thank you for not being a bear.* She fishes her pajamas out of the backpack. It's liberating to get out of damp clothing and slip into soft dry flannel. Warm. She pulls on a second pair of wooly socks, pumps up the air mattress, lays out her sleeping bag and crawls in.

For a while, she lies on her back, wide awake, mulling over the unfamiliar realization that no one knows where she is, except perhaps a park attendant, and maybe Jackie whoever-you-are and his daddy. Or her daddy. She rolls onto her side trying to find a niche in the uneven contours of a leaky air mattress. Cliff had warned it might be flat by morning. She may have to reinflate it each night he'd added helpfully, sorry to say he'd never figured out the source of that darn leak.

She stares up into the darkness. The language of the sea is astonishing to her; she waits in each expectant hush between the intermittent crash of waves, haunted by the voice of a foghorn. She is alone, the foghorn tells her. She is sound asleep as soon as she closes her eyes.

She awakes with a jolt to the sound of loud squabbling voices. Jackie has spilled his orange juice in the scrambled eggs. A request, a woman's voice, desperate, to please get the weather forecast on the car radio. Please. They'll be going home if this fog doesn't lift today. If the kids don't pipe down. And that's final. Silence.

Cailey looks around the floor of the tent. In the absence of the glowing lantern light of the night before, everything appears as an unfriendly jumble of shoes and clothes and papers.

A maid. That's what she needs. A solitary escape into nature. And a maid. Thanks, Neil Young, but it's not just a man needs a maid.

She finds her towel, wonders if she should go to the showers in her pajamas. Everyone must do that. As she attempts to reorder the mess in her tent, she hears the clanking of tent poles being dismantled, car doors slamming, and then the unmistakable sound of automobile tires crunching slowly down the winding gravel road. *Goodbye. Jackie my old pal. May you land at the nearest greasy spoon for a plate of sizzling eggs and bacon.* All at once, Cailey is ravenous. As soon as she unzips the tent flaps, she sees that she is still completely enveloped in fog. She cannot see the picnic table six feet in front of her. Forget the showers. She'll use the water tap down the path.

She stands half naked and shivering at the tap, rubbing her skin with icy cold water, hoping there are no campers about to emerge through the curtain of fog. Back at the tent, she towels herself down until her skin tingles. She piles on layers of T-shirts, sweaters, sweatpants; combs out her hair, ties it in a scarf at the back of her neck.

In the trunk of the car she finds the two burner camp stove and sets it up on the picnic table with the small billy pots filled with water. One for tea. One for oatmeal. Oatmeal, Cliff had insisted, is mandatory when camping in maritime weather.

While she's waiting for the pots to boil, she steps over to the trees behind the campsite and runs her hand tentatively along wet bark, over lumps of sticky spruce gum. She pulls off a piece of gum, rolls it in her hand, holds it to her nose. She needs to touch, to feel what is around her and is fascinated and unnerved by a total absence of familiar reference points. She has no idea who might be camping a few feet away, or how far down the sea is, or how to find her way to the showers. The spruce fragrance lingers on her fingers, hangs redolent, captured, like herself, in the dense salty fog.

Eventually she inches her way over to the row of trees near the cliff. She grabs onto two of them, peers down toward the thunder of waves she's been listening to all night. She can see nothing beyond her extended hand except a straggly shrub with one leafy branch.

Back at the picnic table, she drops four tea bags into one boiling billy pot and stirs the oatmeal already bubbling in the other; when the oatmeal is done, she douses it in sweetened canned milk, spoons it hungrily into her mouth directly from the pot. She wanders around the campsite as she eats, speaking out loud from time to time, about what she might do for the rest of the day.

She keeps moving, running on the spot, stretching up, stretching down. She unloads the car, reorganizes the tent, rinses dishes and pots at the tap down the path.

By lunchtime, she suspects she may be having a good time.

She settles in with one of her drawing boxes open on the table. She stares into it, considering the array of pencils, charcoal, tubes of oils, various brushes. She looks up, stares out into the fog, watches a bush beginning to reveal its branches. She listens to foghorns, picks up a ship's answer sounding out nearby, not far from the cliff.

She opens the cooler on the bench beside her, reaches in and breaks chunks of cheddar from the block of old cheddar Wendy had packed for her. She presses the chunks onto an oval slice of pumpernickel bread that she's laid out on a tea cloth; she bites into an overripe beefsteak tomato, squashes it in a mess all over the cheese, and sprinkles it with salt. She folds the bread into something resembling a sandwich. A most satisfying sandwich, it turns out. She is grateful for uncluttered flavour, for the simple textures, the sensation of hearty nourishment.

The damp softness of sea air on her face.

She pulls out her sketchbook, begins working up a few shapes in black charcoal. Her own hand with chipped fingernails. Her palm, its wandering lifeline, one crooked little finger. She attempts to draw fog; how to draw what isn't quite there? She sketches in the emerging bush, and there is the fog.

She is surprised. She likes what she's captured of the light, or perhaps it's an absence of light. She seems to have drawn the absence of light.

The letter and the pin. Gran's pin. Cailey swings her legs out from the bench and returns to the car. She pushes around some maps and papers in the glove compartment until she finds the package she's looking for. Back at the table, she places the amber pin at the top corner of a blank page in her sketchbook, takes out the letter, and rereads it.

My Dear Cailey,

I've asked your mother to give you the amber pin on your sixteenth birthday and I've sealed this package carefully and told her that you must be the one to open it. You are too young for it now, but soon enough you will be.

This afternoon, you sat here at the end of my bed, as you have almost every day in these long months since I fell ill, and you were all a-light with your stories from school tumbling out one right after the other. You do have a special way of seeing the world. It is a quick clear eye you have, and an intuition that came into the world with you. There will be times, though, when this gift will seem a burden.

What you were so quick to see that day, when Becky was taken back by the river, will be with you for your life. I do believe it was right not to tell your Uncle Mickey at the time. He could not have borne such knowledge on top of everything else. And even now, if it should be known, it would tear the town apart, and your family most of all. Perhaps, when you came to me, I was wrong to commit us both to silence. I have never been sure. I will take that confusion with me to my grave. I have often told my old village stories to you and Beth and Paul. You may remember something of this one. As you read about how the amber came into our hands, you will understand that this is not the first time that one of ours has been taken by the river. I know it's easy to hear the old beliefs as mischief and old wives tales, as Granddad loved to say, and keep us all laughing in the telling. But who's to say what's true and what isn't? At my age I see more things unexplained than explained.

If you keep the amber close to you Cailey, its healing power will find you. Whenever you hold it in the palm of your hand, know that you are holding the ancient wisdom of the great forests. It comes to your hand through many hands. Its warmth is the healing power of the sun.

Love always, Gran

For a moment, she can hear it: her Gran's pen scratching slowly across the page. A strong sure hand rolling the white blotter over wet ink. She feels her presence as if she were sitting across from her, her dry fingers reaching over, brushing lightly over Cailey's forehead. And then a memory, Gran's face appearing behind her at the low dresser, reading a backwards message appearing on the blotter as it turned frontwards in the mirror. 'Time for tea', it would say, or 'today I will wallop you at checkers.' Gran's teasing reflection over Cailey's shoulder. A soft fragrance as they sit at the kitchen table with the checkerboard. Roses. Small drops of rose glycerine on the back of Cailey's hand.

Cailey picks up the rest of the letter and begins to read the story she had barely dared to skim when she'd read it at the gallery last week.

The Story of the Amber
for Cailey from her Gran

In the village where I was raised in the north of Scotland, there is a ring of standing stones that can be seen across the river from the top of the church steps. As children we were told that the church was built in that spot to subdue the power of the ring after a group of travellers had made a complaint to the local magistrate. The story is that they had seen a circle of women, naked save for the garments flowing around their arms, singing and dancing them- selves into a frenzy inside the ring. And I can remember our poor red-faced preacher roaring out the true gospel from the pulpit each time a farmer would take his sick cattle over the river bridge to rub against the stones. Or when the old women would walk a child three times round to cure an illness.

My own grandfather, a good Christian all his life, and an educated man, still believed the magic would be given to anyone who played the fiddle within the circle of standing stones. And each year before the ceilidh, he and a few others would cross over before sunset and play for an hour inside the ring. They had the magic. You'd know it if you'd ever heard them play.

Now you can make of this what you will, but I can tell you that when we were young, we were often drawn by the power, like those before us, to sneak over the bridge just before midnight, when the moon was high, and to wait, crouched down in the tall grass, our hearts pounding, listening for the sound of the cuckoo, watching for the turning of the restless stones, for the dance of the faeries. We knew the old legends well, and we could not afford to disbelieve them, for it was said that if you entered the circle at the time of the dance you would be pulled in by the faeries and you would be danced to your death or led along the stone avenues and taken back by the river.

Taken back by the river. Cailey puts the letter down. That was the way Gran spoke of Becky's death. That little life going back to the source. She reads on.

Well we never did see the stones turn, though we liked to think we did, but we saw the faeries dance, and we heard them sing as they went round and round the sacred well at the centre of the circle. Afterwards, someone would say that we had seen them, naked, or in filmy white robes, linking arms and, just as the cuckoo called at midnight, beginning the dance. And we would all agree, because it gave us the magic to believe it, filled us with enchanted terror that this was what we had seen. And so we had seen it, just as we thought.

We only ever heard of one person who dared to enter the sacred ring of the faerie dance. And that was my own mother's sister. She was Elisabeth, like your sister. The story was, although my mother would not speak of it herself for many years, that she and Elisabeth and their friends were watching at midnight just outside the circle of stones. And suddenly, right at the sound of the cuckoo's call, Elisabeth jumped from the shadows and ran across the field and into the centre of the ring. My mother leapt up immediately, as if she would run after her sister, but she stopped suddenly outside the circle of standing stones and did not enter. The others did not move from their hiding place, so paralyzed they were by the thrill and the terror of what these sisters had done. Something surely must have come over Elisabeth, for she turned abruptly from the dance and with a great cry she ran out toward the river.

The others ran after her then, and cried out for her, calling her name. One in the group turned around just in time to see my mother, as if in a trance, moving slowly toward the well in the centre of the ring. She was reaching out to a lone figure who appeared from behind the tallest stone. My mother said afterwards that the old woman had touched her face, and had spoken to her for a long time in a way that she understood. She had lifted my mother's hand in hers, and placed the amber in her palm. And when she turned and walked away, my mother fainted, right there in the centre of the ring.

When the others saw my mother fall like that, and could find no trace of her sister at the riverbank, they ran in terror back across the bridge. All of the village was roused and they lit torches and searched up and down the river, calling out for Elisabeth. It was my grandmother, who lay down beside my mother in the centre of the ring and stroked her forehead until she knew there was no chance of finding Elisabeth that night. Then she picked my mother up in her arms and carried her poor limp body home. She laid her down on a cot and tried to revive her, though the life seemed to have gone completely from her. My grandmother held her hand and tried with all her strength to pull open the fingers clenched tight, but she could not.

In the morning, after Elizabeth's body was found far down the river, and brought home, my grandfather came into my mother's room. He was said to have known something of the power from his time playing the old tunes within the circle, and when his strong hands finally removed the amber from her palm, he studied it closely in the light, and he saw the markings on it. My mother could do nothing, she watched as he put the amber away in his pocket.

Years later, when my mother was married, my grandfather had the amber polished on one side, and mounted into a pin by a goldsmith, and he gave it back to her the morning of her wedding, saying he knew it was more precious than any possession she would ever have. She said to him then that he should never have taken it from her, and that her reasons for having it could never be spoken. He said that he knew that well enough. He had been protecting her from the wrath of the village. For he had heard what such wrath could do to one who had a power about them, and would not renounce it for the true gospel.

After her wedding, my mother taught in the village school. It was said she had an uncanny way about her, and not even the preacher would dare to stop her from teaching the old ways. There was always a magic woven into her stories, and she could read the sacred signs in the earth and the sky and the flowing water.

It was not until just before I came out to Canada that she called me to her room. She unclasped the pin from her own collar and put it in my hand. Turn it over, she said, and look closely at the markings under the setting, where it has not been polished. You see these brush strokes, she pointed with her finger, they are worn down by the centuries, but they do not lose their meaning.

Cailey examines the pin again, turns it over. At first she sees only the rough surface on the underside, but when she looks closely, a pattern of crisscrossing lines is discernible.

When my mother closed my fingers around the pin, she told me that the markings were an ancient symbol of energy, and they signified the healing power given to the amber by the heat of the sun. She told me that when she heard the cuckoo call that night, it was calling her sister's name, and a foreknowledge came upon her of what was about to happen. When the cuckoo called a second time, it was calling my mother's name. She knew immediately to walk to the edge of the standing stones. When the old woman came to her, she was not frightened. She could see her clearly in the light of the full moon.

Do not run from magic, the old woman spoke those very words, her voice soft and young with music. Already many passageways have been sealed forever, and those that remain are fewer and more difficult to find.

And then she opened her hand to show my mother the amber glowing in her palm. She placed the amber in my mother's hand, and turned and walked away.

Cailey orders and reorders the pages, folds the letter carefully, once, twice, opens it again, reads it one more time.

It is the child Cailey, back in Wood River, who sits so still in this present moment, on a picnic bench by the sea, trying to absorb a grandmother's message.

Do not run from magic.

It is the older Cailey who places the letter in its envelope, who wonders what magic, what wisdom has come to rest just now, in the palm of her hand, charged, if she would believe it, with the ancient healing power of the sun.

Had Gran hoped to counter the truth of their shared horror by turning to some fateful mystical foretelling?

But that wouldn't be at all like Gran. She was never one to look away from truth. It had to be a deeper wisdom Gran intended for her in the gift of a storied amber pin. Cailey has no idea why the amber's energy is so reassuring to her; it is her Gran's embrace, her magical ways of knowing. It is Cailey's own longing that now warms her palm, her own longing for ancient passageways to open once again.

Taken by the river. A passageway to the unknown. Faith in mystery.

Cailey closes her fingers over the amber, picks up her charcoal and begins to draw.

There was a full moon the night of Becky's drowning, she is sure of it. She sketches the wide river, the outline of the bridge, a powerful current churning around its piers, figures at the fire, kids with hotdogs on sticks, little ones grabbing marshmallows from an open bag. Her father, Uncle Mickey, Auntie Val. They had stood talking, their backs to the bridge. Cailey sketches Beth next to her father, and then herself, just at the edge of the gathering around the bonfire keeping an eye on her mother, counting how many beers she's had. Then a partial sketch of that lone figure in the shadows by the rocky ledge. Gran is there in her lawn chair, facing the others with their backs to the river. She is singing softly 'oh give me a home, where the buffalo roam…' There is beer. Lemonade. Potato chips. The talk is excited.

Cailey smudges the charcoal image with her fingers, stops drawing. She remembers.

Becky. Alive again in her mind.

Becky is running around the fire. Wanting marshmallows, right now, she calls out. Not now honey, they're for later. Becky hangs around her father then, pulling on his hand. You heard your mother, Uncle Mickey is saying, lifting her up in his arms, holding her there, laughing at her. Becky's face golden and sulky in the light from the fire. That auburn in her hair. The look on Uncle Mickey's face. He is setting her down. She is leaning into his legs. Uncle Mickey is saying something to Cailey's father, Cailey can hear him clearly. "She's had enough Jim," Mickey says to Cailey's father, glancing over his shoulder at Ellen, "Someone should take that beer from her." Her father is not bothering to look, "You know it won't do any good, Mickey, she'll just take another." Gran's old songs pick up speed, the others join in, the moonlight on the river behind them. It is only a moment later that Cailey looks back at her mother. It is only for that one second, that Becky is standing there, grabbing at the beer bottle in Ellen's hand.

Cailey's breath tightens. To have seen that. To have known for so long.

She turns the page in her sketchbook and opens a box of coloured pencils. She tries drawing her grandmother's face from memory. Gran dressed for church, eyes bright, thin lips set in proper repose but still revealing such mischief, a delicate light playing into the golden amber at her collar. Over and over, Cailey tries to work up that area of deeper glow in the amber. If only she'd brought the good pencils, the right paper. A final drawing will have to wait till she's home.

She is remembering, as she plays with colours, how at first, Gran's grief would not allow her to hear what Cailey was telling her.

"I couldn't say it to Dad, Gran," Cailey had sobbed. "Mum didn't remember."

"A blackout," Gran had answered Cailey helplessly, holding her close. "Your mother's life is one long blackout."

Cailey drops her head on the sketch of her Gran and weeps.

***

The fog lifts late in the afternoon. Cailey does not look up from her book until the mist is rolling out over the sea. And then it is not the sea itself, revealed to her for the first time that surprises her. It is the burst of sunlight in an ever-expanding sky – the sky, resting there on the unfamiliar sea. She walks to the edge of the cliff, thinking that such an infinite expanse of sky would surely be more at home resting on the wide open prairie.

She checks her watch for the first time that day. Six o'clock. She will try the path down the cliff to the shore. She peels off two heavy sweaters, kicks off her rubber boots, and grabs a shirt and her running shoes from inside the tent. She takes her camera from the front seat of the car, and finds her way down the first few feet of a crumbly path. There are already other campers out on the crescent of beach just below her, and several fishing boats are chugging into the wharf on the other side of the bay. She sits down on a gnarled root protruding from the cliff and removes the lens cap from her camera. She tries several angles of the bay through the viewfinder and then lets the camera rest on the strap around her neck. She replaces the lens cap. It is magical to look at, she decides, but right now it is not a photograph.

At the beach she slips off her shoes and socks and walks in her bare feet along the wide sloping strip of hard wet sand. She passes a young family searching for treasures in the rim of pebbles and shells and seaweed deposited by the receding sea. It is the moon that moves the tide, the father is saying.

She is surprised by the coldness of the sand and the freezing water washing over her feet. Not like the beaches at Lake Winnipeg, with that shallow warmer water that goes on forever. She remembers her father swimming out so far from where they were playing, that his head would be a tiny dot on the horizon. Sometimes she had wondered if he might never turn back, if that black dot would simply drop from view forever. If he might think of dropping from view forever.

This icy cold water reminds her more of Wood River in mid-May, when the local daredevils take the plunge off the town docks. One year, she and Beth and Paul had jumped in with them. Everyone was gathered at the hotel tavern, sharing in the excitement while the blue-lipped swimmers were wrapped in dry towels and blankets. Uncle Mickey had served up cocoa for the kids, steaming black tea laced with rum for the adults. A foolish thing to do, he'd scolded Cailey as the oldest of his own, his face stern, still hiding his returning grief. The three of them had sat there staring down at their cocoa, realizing.

It was always in those moments that Cailey would watch intently for any sign on her mother's face. A sign that she knew what Cailey had seen. But there was nothing.

"What are you staring at?" Her mother would sometimes hurl at her.

All that year Cailey scrutinized her mother this way. But not a flicker crossed her face, not a glimmer of awareness in her eyes.

There was nothing in the way she looked at her brother whenever Uncle Mickey came by for a visit, nothing in the way she spoke to Uncle Mickey of Becky, or of poor Val dying so soon after. Of a broken heart, everybody said. Cancer and a broken heart.

"And what would you know about a broken heart?" Cailey had wanted to scream at her mother, whenever Uncle Mickey left their supper table to go home alone.

Cailey crouches down on her heels now to peer through the shallow clear water. A large snail, its glutinous grey body stretching and contracting, stretching and contracting, hauls its weighty shell over the grainy surface.

Around a point she can see several fishing boats still idling at the wharf, their engines belching out fumes. A coastguard boat is moored at the far end of the wharf where there are clusters of people milling about, talking back and forth with the men on deck.

Cailey follows a path up the hill to the park store. She will enquire if something happened in the storm.

An hour later, back at her campsite, Cailey places a bottle of white wine in the cooler where it can swim around in the melting ice with Wendy's block of cheddar and a few plums. Dinner for one.

The woman at the store had apologized about the ice. "The power's still off," she'd explained, "but help yourself, we don't charge for bags of cold water." They both laughed.

"Yes," she confirmed, "it was a bad storm. But the boats got in all right, all but one that is. No radio contact all night. The coastguard picked them up early this morning, drifting, out of fuel. Well, they're safe in the harbour now," she said as she counted out Cailey's change.

Searching now through the back seat of the car, Cailey finds the tape she is looking for. "You might be surprised," Jennifer had insisted, "you might be ready to work on that series sooner than you think."

And so.

She is ready.

She opens the wine, checks the label on the bottle. Nothing but the best, eh Wendy? Blanc Plonk, Wendy always called it. She pours a small amount of the tepid wine into her enamel cup, and drops the bottle into the cooler of cold water.

In the bright sun, she sits with her grandmother's letter open on the table. It is held down from the evening breeze under a corner of her sketchbook. At the other corner, the amber pin. The evening sun glimmers over the flat water. She puts on the tape.

The opening bars are riveting, bold and firm. The deep voice of Jennifer's cello rises from the earth itself, it seems to Cailey.

She begins to draw a circle of stones.

CHAPTER

13

It is after midnight when Cailey pulls up in front of the Daniels' house. Her intention is to leave a note telling Jennifer about beginning the story of the amber pin, and that she'd be over with the car later the next day.

She is surprised to see all the lights burning on the ground floor, and cars in the driveway. They must have company. It is unlike them to be up this late, especially in the middle of the week. She backs the car up and parks it under a large maple tree in front of the neighbour's house. She turns off the lights and the ignition and stretches her arms back, pushing against the roof of the car. Her whole body hurts. Especially her head, which has been pounding ever since she ate at a roadside *casse-croute*. Hamburger, fries, coffee. A chocolate bar and more coffee along the way. And then that bag of rancid chips. *Well that'll do it, Cailey.* She grimaces and leans her head back, nauseated, every muscle taut from all day behind the wheel. She must have been insane to drive through in one day. What she needs now is twelve hours at home in her own bed, and Wendy to serve her fresh orange juice as soon as she wakes up. Perhaps she could just slip up to the back door and leave a note in the screen. That way, no one will see her.

She finds the note in her purse and is deciding what to do when she notices the front door opening. Someone is stepping out onto the steps. Andrew. Oh God. Just what she needs, a midnight chat with Erica and Andrew. She is about to start up the car again so she can back up the street, and wait for them to leave. But she stops when she notices Andrew is just standing there. Weaving slightly on the top step. He is alone. He is drunk. And he's leaving the door wide open.

Where is everybody, what is he doing? She leans over the steering wheel, trying to get a better look at him through the windshield. He's wiping his forehead with his handkerchief and then looking at it under the light. He does this several times.

Cailey doesn't quite trust her perceptions. Perhaps she's been alone too long, hypnotized by endless miles of highway. The air is heavy and close around her. Lifeless, no fragrance, or sound. She hears Andrew cough. He walks slowly down the steps. He trips at the bottom and catches himself on the railing. He stands still and looks around.

Cailey's head hurts.

The others must be inside. Andrew's stepped out for air. Nothing too unusual about that when Andrew's full of booze.

Or perhaps it's unbearably hot in there, he's cooling off and will go back in. Or he's waiting for Erica who's in there nattering away at poor Jenn about jam recipes.

Cailey's first instinct is to drive away. Andrew is too upsetting. It's not her problem. Most likely, it's not a problem at all. The family's at the cottage and Andrew, inebriated or not, is checking the house for them. Except that he's getting into his car without closing the front door of the house. He must be waiting for Erica in the car.

But no. Something is very wrong here.

Cailey slips across the front seat to the passenger side next to the curb. She hopes Andrew won't see her, or recognize the old car if he backs out of the drive.

She hears his car door slam and the engine roar much too loudly. She pushes herself into the corner against the window and drops the sun visor. He reverses at full speed, bouncing off the curb on the other side of the street and turning with a screech. He careens around the corner, out of sight. The headlights aren't even on.

Cailey sits in shock for a moment, staring at the empty street. Then she looks back at the house, the blazing lights, the open door. She looks at the other car in the drive. It is certainly not Cliff and Jenn's van.

She gets out of the car and walks up the drive, up the steps.

"Hello?" she sends nervously through the open door.

There is no reply. She does not ring the bell, she does not go in. She is not sure why, or what she is afraid of finding. Instead, she goes back down the steps and crouches along the front of the house, trying to look through the windows. The windowsills are too high up. All she can see are wall lamps and the tops of bookcases.

She looks out at the street. What if Andrew comes back? Maybe she should wake the neighbours, call the police? The thought makes her feel foolish, but her fear grows. *Don't be ridiculous, Cailey. The man was drunk. And he's gone.*

The thing to do is go back up those steps, turn off some lights, check that the latch is on, close the door. Go home to bed.

Then she remembers the other car. She turns to look at it. An old Honda. They must have bought another second hand car while she was away. Cliff loves working on old cars. She's been driving one of them. She peers into the backseat. There are papers and books everywhere. She walks around the car to get a closer look. Most of what she can see is not in English. Or French. She looks again. Spanish. That's Spanish.

Consuela.

Cailey takes the steps two at a time. In the front hall, she is frozen to the spot, listening, terrified. There is not a sound in the house.

She whispers Consuela's name, an inaudible whisper, afraid Consuela might answer, afraid she will not. She forces herself to call more loudly. There is no reply. She moves from room to room, holding on to doorways and chairs, her eyes searching out every corner.

In the kitchen there are ice cream bowls on the counter, dishes in the sink. Pots on the stove. She touches the kettle. It's warm. There are toys on the floor. Rob's space car, a Lego house with smiley figures at the windows.

She runs back to the front hall, looks up the stairs to a darkened second floor. Halfway up the stairs, she catches a different view of the playroom. She stops, stares straight through to the other side of the kitchen counter where she hadn't thought to check.

At the base of the counter. Just her dark head, face down on the floor.

"Consuela!"

She reaches her in a flash, puts her hands out helplessly, not knowing where to touch her, afraid to turn her over. She puts a hand on Consuela's forehead. Nudges her shoulder with the other.

"Consuela. It's Cailey."

A low moan.

Thank God.

Carefully, Cailey turns her over.

"Oh dear God Consuela, dear God, what has he done to you?"

"Shut... me up... shut me up..." Consuela eyes open wide, look directly into Cailey's, her face so pale, almost grey.

"What?"

Consuela's eyes close. She does not respond. Cailey's heart pounds; her head clears. She pulls a pillow and a blanket from the playroom couch and shifts Consuela from the floor onto the soft rug, the pillow under her head.

She picks up the blanket to cover Consuela. Cailey gasps. Her skirt is soaked in blood.

She glances over at the bare floor where she had been lying. Blood. There is a lot of blood.

Oh dear God. Now a prayer.

She touches Consuela's forehead. Clammy and cold. She speaks quietly, telling her what she is going to do. "Everything will be okay," she says, at this moment unable to believe her own words. She has no idea if Consuela can hear her.

She reaches for the phone next to the couch, calls the police emergency number; they are dispatching an ambulance.

She gets up, searches for a note on the fridge, for the number Jennifer always leaves when there's a sitter. It doesn't seem to be there.

She has no idea how to reach Gaetan.

She hurries to the front of the house, shuts the front door, then changes her mind and leaves it open for the stretcher to be wheeled in.

Hesitating a moment in the doorway, it dawns on her, and she whirls around.

What about... oh God, oh God, what was she thinking?

The kids.

Oh please, surely not...

She takes the stairs two at a time. On the landing, she gropes for the wall switch, turns on the hall light. At the far end of the hall the kids' doors are wide open.

Okay. That's okay. This is how they usually fall asleep.

She tiptoes into the first room. Trisha. Sound asleep. She lingers to hear Trisha's soft breath, to watch her clutching a wide-eyed doll with a bare cloth body.

On to the second room. Robbie. On his tummy. Breathing. A low snore. One arm flopped over the edge of the bed, his room strewn with Hot Wheels tracks.

She pulls their doors to. Something larger than relief floods over her, brings her to weeping.

Something about their innocence. The sweetest innocence.

Back in the kitchen, Cailey imagines she sees Consuela's eyelids flutter at the mention of Trisha and Robbie, and the reassurance that they are both safely sound asleep, that an ambulance is on its way.

She opens the cupboard where the coffee cups and Cliff's good whisky are kept. She resists the urge to take it straight from the bottle, instead pours herself one good stiff shot.

She lowers herself to the floor next to Consuela, holds a damp cold hand in hers, while they wait together for the ambulance to arrive.

The tears do not let up.

CHAPTER
14

Jennifer and Cailey stir packets of white sugar into chipped white cups steaming with muddy cafeteria coffee.

It is five in the morning. At the table next to them nurses are smoking and telling hospital jokes. There are loud eruptions of laughter, which seem to Cailey to be amplified somewhere inside her head.

A sour faced woman in a pink uniform and a hair net is drying trays at the back of the cafeteria. For the last half hour Cailey has watched her wipe one tray after another, drop each one with a clatter into a metal container, then go back to the kitchen for another pile, and begin wiping again. Tray after tray. Another waitress is leaning with her back against the counter reading a book. There is no one else in the cafeteria.

Out in the corridor someone is pushing a floor polisher back and forth. It has a low laboured hum. Like a moan.

"I think you should get home, Jenn. Take a taxi. I'll call you when Consuela wakes up."

"I'm okay, Cailey. Really. I want to wait a bit longer. In case I can see her. I slept all the way in from Magog. God this is terrible coffee. I think I'll get more milk. You want anything?"

"Actually, I could use a whole glass of milk. Let me get it, Jenn."

"Cailey, I'm not sick," Jennifer objects, getting up. "I'm pregnant. Believe it or not, it's quite good for me to move my body. "

Jennifer returns with two glasses of milk. "That is the grouchiest person I have ever met."

"The one on the cash? Yes, I noticed." Cailey empties her glass of milk in one go. "She's been drying and stacking trays ever since we got here. She probably wanted to hit you with one."

"Exactly." Jennifer finishes her milk slowly, drinking it through a straw, eyes closed, elbows propped on the table. She looks up. "My God it was a relief when Gaetan came in, Cailey, and Consuela opened her eyes at the sound of his voice."

"Yes. Yes." Cailey presses her fingers to her temples. "Could you understand what he was saying to the nurse? His French was way too fast for me."

"For me too a bit. He was in shock I guess, saying the same thing over and over. Mostly about how his buddy drove in him from Dorval, how the airport would only give him one hour off his regular shift."

"The poor guy. So scared and confused."

"He has strength though. I could see it." Jennifer is thoughtful. "I have to tell Cliff that Andrew was at the house when you got there at midnight. Maybe you could be there with me? Since you're the only one who saw him? Besides Consuela."

Cailey stops for a minute, stares at the table. "Maybe, but why not let the police tell him?"

"No, no, he has to know before the police get to him. I think before they arrest Andrew."

"Then you need to tell him as soon as you get home, Jenn. The police will be back early this morning they said, to talk to you both."

"Oh great." Jennifer fidgets with the buckle on her purse. "I have to tell you this other thing though. Cliff spoke to Andrew while you were in the Maritimes."

"About what?"

"Well, not long after you left, Cliff and I had this dreadfully strained exchange about Andrew and his harassment of Consuela. It was a confrontation really. We've never had one quite like that before! He tried to say there was no longer a problem because Consuela had already left their employ. When I told him how Andrew had also come on to you, about the threats he'd made about your business, and that we both feared that Erica herself was at risk, he seemed to get it. By the end of the conversation, I know he grasped that this was no longer a family issue of protecting his sister's marriage to Dr. Andrew Wilson. I'm still bothered though, by the fact that Cliff only saw a reason for taking action when Erica herself appeared to be at risk, but that he could continue to hold off when it was Consuela alone who was at risk. It makes me furious."

Cailey nods. "Of course. I guess we put it off too, Jenn."

"I know. I'm furious at all of us."

"Yes. So what happened when he took Andrew on directly?"

"He wouldn't give me details, except to say that Andrew was livid. Still, Cliff is sure that what he said to Andrew will put an end to the whole thing."

"Wow, that seems a bit naïve to me. To put it mildly."

"Of course. I certainly don't think that's an end to it." Jennifer pauses, a stricken expression coming over her face. "Andrew must have come to our house, Cailey, knowing we were out, to tell Consuela to keep her mouth shut. I mean, after his talk with Cliff, Andrew might have decided to... Why are you staring, Cailey?"

"Because that's what Consuela said to me, Jenn. That's exactly what Consuela said."

"What?"

"I told you this already, on the way over here. When I found Consuela on the floor, her eyes opened for a second, and she said something like 'shut me up, shut me up.'"

"Oh. Right. You did tell me. What a muddle my head is. Holy Mary Mother of Jesus." Jennifer puts her head down on her folded arms and sobs. "Oh God, Cailey." She looks up, tears spilling over. "My babies were at home sleeping? All this horror in our house? Our own home. That monster. Raping. Raping our beautiful Consuela. And what if you hadn't arrived when you did? What if Trish and Rob had come down in the morning and...."

The horror washes over Cailey and she does not try to hold back her tears. "Thank God they're safe, Jenn. They were meant to be safe. I believe that." Cailey rests her hand on her friend's arm. "Trish and Rob saw nothing. They never need to know. They're safe, sound asleep at home with their father."

"But Cailey, if only I…"

Cailey waits.

"If only I hadn't told Cliff, Cailey, or if he hadn't taken it on alone to confront Andrew…"

"We can't do this to ourselves, Jenn. None of us quite knew the beast that was lurking. We've made mistakes, but we do know what to do. Support each other. And also, we both know that Consuela's strength is very real, we'll see it grow again, and we'll stay close to her and Gaetan."

"Yes. Yes, okay." Jennifer's face begins to lighten. "Is it time to check back with the ward?"

"Yes, and then we both go home to sleep. And Jenn, you will stay home and look after yourself and be with your family. Wendy and I will come back to the hospital this afternoon."

Jennifer nods. "How about supper at our place tonight? Trish and Rob can have as much ice cream as they want before bed, and I'll never be cross with them again." Jennifer smiles through her tears. "And we'll all breathe."

Cailey laughs. "That could be a bit much for you, Jenn."

""Cailey.:

"Okay right. You're not sick." Cailey stands up, her arm around Jennifer's shoulders as they head for the elevator. "I could make something to bring over. I have no photo sessions tomorrow. Or we could order out."

"No. I need to cook. You know? I need to sleep, and then I need people in the house." Jennifer presses the button for the elevator. "Wendy's welcome for supper if she's not doing anything."

Cailey hesitates. "You know how brutal Wendy can be about stuff like this."

"That's the point."

They are almost laughing as the elevator doors slide open.

***

Cailey sits at the window staring out at the wonderful, dreary, wet rain that is not coming down on her tent. She has slept for six hours. She wonders about ringing the hospital for an update on Consuela's condition, but instead goes to the bathroom, turns on the water, stares at herself in the mirror. She is golden brown. Her long hair is sun-bleached at the temples. Except for the horror that so disturbingly registers in her eyes, she quite likes the face looking back at her.

Back in her room, she opens the closet and finds her terrycloth robe. She drops her clothes on the floor, wraps herself in the robe and slips her feet into warm slippers. The phone rings.

"Hello?"

"Have you checked the shelf under the telephone?" Click.

Very funny, Wendy. Cailey checks the shelf.

Steve. Another letter from Steve. She slips it into her bathrobe pocket.

She calls Wendy at work, tells her the latest about Consuela. Wendy will join them all for supper but can't make it over to the hospital. She'll find her way to Jennifer's as soon as she's off work.

Cailey phones the hospital line she was given, hears from the nurse in intensive care that Consuela's condition is stable and improving, and yes, she is still in and out of consciousness, which is why she's in intensive care with a major concussion, and no she doesn't know if Consuela read the notes from Cailey and Jennifer, nurses aren't paid to keep track of every Tom, Dick and Harry, and yes, there will be regular visiting hours when Consuela is moved up to the fourth floor, tomorrow if all goes well, and yes, in the meantime, Gaetan is with her.

Cailey slips into the bath and rests her head on the cool white rim. As soon as her eyes close, her cluttered mental landscape rises up with its repeating images from the last twenty-four hours: the blur of highway signs, the truck stops, warnings flashing neon, strangers in a coffee shop, Consuela's ashen face, Consuela over and over.

She slides further down in the water, wills herself back to her world by the sea. She is walking alone along the beach, her feet in cold water, she is brewing tea in early morning fog, savouring the salt sea air, the treasured days of full sun, she is drawing the story of the amber late into the night, a lantern glowing, the fire burning.

Becky burning, crumpled and hurled into the flames.

Becky. Her little face still warm and alive, dancing through Cailey's heart, even as the fire curls her image to ashes again.

Cailey sits up quickly, splashing water out of the tub, and reaches over to the towel rack, dries her hands, lifts Steve's letter from the pocket of her robe.

November. Steve will be here in November.

***

They sit by the fire, the four of them, trying out various bits of conversation. Cailey complains about trucks on New Brunswick highways, Cliff tells them of an interview he heard with Marie-Claire Blais on Radio Canada, they all agree the leaves are turning early, that Margaret Trudeau has come unhinged, that the Mounties should not be spying on the Parti Québécois. One by one, the topics trail off to the outer edge of their little circle, exhausted by the unnamed crisis at its centre.

Cailey tucks her feet under her and settles into her corner of the couch. She looks over at Cliff who is staring at the fire and sucking on an empty pipe. His glass of whisky sits untouched on the arm of his chair.

Beside her, Wendy remains unusually quiet, munching her way through handfuls of peanuts, tapping her fingers, apparently to something going on in her head. Jennifer is across from Cliff, watching him anxiously.

In the middle of the glass table in front of the fire, one large white candle burns with a low flame. Cailey notes that Jennifer is uncharacteristically oblivious to several small rivers of wax spreading out over the table. They are forming and reforming into unusual shapes, travelling between bottles of wine as if they had some purposeful destination. Cailey is tempted to press her fingers into the molten pools that travel her way, perhaps help them to blossom into a flower, or become this spindly figure that is apparently about to dance off the edge of the table.

Jennifer is laughing with Wendy about taking Trish and Robbie to see Star Wars for the third time as a bribe to get them into bed early. Wendy has seen it four times she says. Cailey is not sure she heard that right. She is escaping into the details of the room, her eyes instinctively needing the angles and light, framing a sketch in her mind. Off in the corner, behind Cliff's chair, Jennifer's cello sits propped on its stand. Next to the cello, on top of the piano, which is stacked high with books and papers and teacups, one soft shaded lamp drops its low light onto sheet music, onto the solid, silent, black and white keys. A few small candles burn on the windowsill.

Perhaps she will draw her way through to the other side of this moment. Consuela unconscious on the floor. Moments with Jenn at the hospital cafeteria. Confusion. Fear. This fire in front of her, that cannot quite warm these four stunned and heartsick friends.

At last Jennifer speaks of Consuela, of the Consuela who is completing her high school diploma, the Consuela who has learned both English and French in a few years, of the Consuela who now lives with Gaetan who adores her.

It is Wendy who asks about the Consuela who is barely conscious in a hospital bed.

It is Cliff who speaks up.

"Perhaps you already know, Wendy, that Consuela's concussion is quite severe," he takes a first sip of whisky, "and that it was sustained as a result of being struck on the back of the head and hitting the floor of our playroom while our children were asleep upstairs. Consuela has also suffered a miscarriage, a result, it appears, of being raped, very brutally raped, by my brother-in- law." He downs the rest of his drink in one tip of the glass.

Wendy nods and drops her handful of peanuts back into the bowl.

There is not a sound in the room. It is a profoundly shared silence, not an uncomfortable one.

At the sound of the timer bell in the kitchen, Jennifer smiles. "Food. Yes. Food."

"Shall I come and carve the roast?"

"It's not a roast, Cliff." Jennifer turns on her heel. "You watched me make lasagna when we came in from the movie."

"Of course. Sorry, my love. I'll get us another good bottle of wine from the basement then."

At that moment there is a voice from the hall.

"Hello? Anybody home?"

Jennifer's eyes grow large as she stares at Cliff. "Erica!"

"Oh here you are. Oh my. Isn't this cosy. What a nice little party. Do I know you all? No, no, I don't believe I do. Well, Cailey. Of course, hello dear. I could hardly see you with just the candles. How are the children, Jennifer? Do you mind if I turn on this light? Oh that's so much better. I don't like it too dark do you? Well, to tell you the truth, I just wanted to know what's happened to Connie, I mean to Consuela. She doesn't like being called Connie does she? Andrew came home an hour ago from his rounds at the hospital. He has some nasty scratches on his forehead, poor love. However would he get those? Something at the hospital I imagine. He said Consuela was in there in intensive care – well oh dear – I knew she was here with Trisha and Robbie last night wasn't she and Andrew didn't seem to know much about what had happened to her, a miscarriage he said, he's so busy you know with the new residents.

"It's not a very good group this year and he's tearing his hair out, and then the most astonishing thing just now Clifford, the police came, and Andrew left to go to the station and make a statement about Consuela, a formality they said, so, well, I asked our new girl to put the children to bed and I came right on over just to find out, you know... well, anything you can tell me, Cliff. Oh, hello, I think I know you. Should I know you?"

"Yes hi, I'm Wendy, Wendy Petersen. Cailey's friend. We met at the gallery I think."

"Oh of course what fun it was, you were playing the spoons weren't you? I was able to make it for the last half hour. Delightful, absolutely delightful. The children loved the dancing. Well then, Clifford, what's the occasion here, I mean for all of you, something to do with Consuela I suppose..."

"Stop Erica. Just stop it. Sit down." Cliff leans over pours a glass of whisky, places it in her hand, and sits on the arm of her chair with his hand firmly on her shoulder.

"Okay, thanks big brother, well I dare say I'm sounding a bit wound up. A busy day today with that committee, you know the one, Cliff. We're trying to get new traffic lights at the school crossings. It's altogether too dangerous, I worry constantly, all the mothers do; well you know what it's like don't you, Jennifer? And you too, Cliff. Oh well no, yours aren't in school yet are they, and with the new one coming along now – how are you feeling, Jennifer, three months is it? Four? Oh dear me here I am, barging in like this. Well now, Clifford, how perfect, this tastes wonderful, just... just... I... needed..."

The glass slips from her hand and smashes onto the hearth. Crystal shards scatter across the floor and hiss into the fire. Fine Scotch whisky rises in smoke into the air around them.

Nobody moves.

"Fine then. I know. I already know. He was here wasn't he?" Erica eyes each of them frantically, hoping for a signal, some sign of denial. "He was he was he was. I see it in your faces. I know all about this. Oh yes, I've always known. Always known. I..."

She turns to Cliff for reassurance only to see his eyes brimming with tears. He wraps his arms around his sister and holds her, stroking her head.

CHAPTER
15

COMFORT IN WAITING
MONTREAL
SEPTEMBER 1977

Consuela's colour is much better, they agree on the bus ride home from
the hospital.

"What a relief to laugh at Gaetan's really bad jokes." Cailey talks over
her shoulder as they make their way to a free seat at the back of the bus.
"And to see Consuela smiling at his imitations of all those accents they
both hear at work."

"Yes. I felt I was watching her come alive again," Wendy says as they sit
down, "but still there were those heart stopping moments when the panic
came flashing back into her eyes, and she gripped both Gaetan's hands."

"That look scares me, Wendy, and I worry so much for her, but there
was Gaetan calm and gentle, his voice so strong and reassuring. I have
to trust that Consuela's strength will come through in the end. It will,
I know it will." Cailey watches two boys running alongside the bus,

shaking their fists as the driver speeds by. "Consuela was so focused on Gaetan when we left, she didn't even notice us going out of the room."

Wendy nods. "Neither did Gaetan. They are sweet together. Not mushy sweet. Solid sweet."

Cailey laughs. "Yes, exactly. I still worry though, Wendy." Cailey adds as they step off the bus at their stop. "I mean even with me as a witness, and whatever evidence the police find in the house, they might still have to let Andrew go if Consuela doesn't press charges. I didn't see him do anything. Only Consuela did."

"But there are fingerprints."

"What if they can't determine if the fingerprints are from previous visits?"

"Right. I remember. Perry Mason. So then, Cailey what about Gaetan's role with Consuela? You can't blame the guy, or her for that matter, for worrying that pressing charges could put her at greater risk. Even without the supposed connections he's threatened her with, it's possible he'll find a way to interfere with her visa renewal. Say she stole things, was dishonest or something. Say she presses charges and he's acquitted? No consequences for him? The honourable citizen unjustly accused? No deterrent to his behaviour?"

"What a horrific thought."

"It happens, Cailey…"

"Yes."

For several blocks they walk, lost in their own thoughts.

"It can't happen in this case, Wens. It just can't."

"What can't happen?"

"Andrew being acquitted. It mustn't happen." Cailey pauses. "Another thing that worries me, is Consuela's inevitable suspicion of any sort of police investigation, or court trial, or whatever. It will be hard for her to trust the process here. Can you imagine struggling in the midst of the violent crackdown in the '73 coup, having to flee your own country, only to land in a safe place where you're threatened, attacked and brutally raped. At this point, why would Consuela trust any justice system?"

Wendy stops at the bottom of the stairs. "Consuela would know it's not just for her."

"Okay, yes, that's it isn't it? That's it exactly, Wendy." Cailey unlatches the front door and they climb the stairs to the second floor flat. "That has to be what will carry her through – that passion for social justice."

Wendy slips off her jacket, kicks off her shoes. "First she needs to feel safe again. I'd hate for the system to pressure her to take action before she's had time to heal, or rally a reliable support network."

"Right, but it would be too creepy if they don't keep Andrew in longer for questioning. I'd hate to think he's out there while charges are pending. Jennifer's going to call us as soon as she hears anything." Cailey sorts through a pile of newspapers on the floor and puts them out in the hall. "By the way, I think you said that Consuela has met your Chilean friends at the women's centre, Wendy?"

"Yes, of course, some of them are her good friends also. I was thinking about them today, but she's not ready to connect. Gaetan told me."

Cailey heads to the kitchen. "You for tea?"

"Not right now, twinkletoes." Wendy flops down on the couch.

Cailey grins as she puts on the kettle.

"There's beer in my plans tonight." Wendy stretches her legs up the back of the couch. "You know Cailey, that Chilean group is the most organized crew any of us have ever encountered at the centre. As a group they seem to have sorted out how to tap resources in no time at all; they've educated themselves on the law, bureaucracies and red tape hoops refugees have to jump through. And at least one of them's a lawyer. The whole centre's benefitting from it. I expect Consuela's been hearing lots about what they're doing."

"Well then, hopefully that will be her starting point."

"Yes, for sure."

The phone rings. Wendy sits up, suddenly alert. "Can you grab that? I'm avoiding Larry. He's after me for my half of the car rental."

"Ha! Good luck to him!" Cailey places her cup on the coffee table, reaches the phone by the third ring. "Oui allô? Oh hi, yes Gaetan, it's Cailey." She rubs her forehead. "Oh, oh Émile… sorry, yes I do remember you." She listens. "Steve? When?" Her eyes widen. "Tonight?" She turns to see Wendy fluttering her eyelids, patting her hand on her heart in mock hysteria. Cailey sticks out her tongue and repeats the flight number for Wendy to take down. "Yes I can meet him. Sure. Wow! Yes, okay Émile. Oui, merci, thanks. *Oui, oui, à bientôt, Émile.*"

Cailey stands transfixed, brushing an imaginary wisp of hair off her forehead.

"I thought he wasn't coming till November."

"He wasn't," Cailey answers.

"We'll share him okay? Shall I change the sheets?"

Cailey laughs with her hand over her mouth.

***

Cailey takes a quarter from her wallet for the parking meter. Sharp crystals of hail, like tiny arrows, blow at her face, making it difficult to see the coin slot. She fumbles at it with her fingers and finally pushes the quarter in. She kicks at the metal post when the meter won't start. As she turns to cross the road, she can barely make out the *Arrivées* sign above the glass doors. How can planes land in this? Surely they won't try to land in this.

Inside the terminal she checks at the information desk. "All air traffic is grounded. No, the flight is not cancelled, but it will be at least two hours late, possibly more." The attendant smiles brightly. "We would have informed you, madame," he smiles harder, "if you'd called ahead."

Cailey sits for a while in the cafeteria, nursing a coffee, wondering if she should ask the waitress if this would have been Consuela's shift. It's a sad thought, which she keeps to herself while she watches the blowing ice pellets streak across blackness on the other side of the airport windows. Periodically, headlights from a service truck cast a straight beam through the dark.

There is comfort in waiting, in being safely stranded in an isolated moment like this. She allows her deep feelings of apprehension about Steve's return, her deep love for him, her resistance to changing her life right now, her longing to be with him.

The cardboard rim of her coffee cup has gone soggy, and begins to peel off in her mouth. She rolls the bits between her fingers and drops them in an ashtray. She would smoke if she had a cigarette. A tired looking couple at the next table is enveloped in their own nicotine cloud. They talk quietly, as if there is danger, as if raised voices might somehow increase the turbulence outside. They wonder if they should just give up and go back home, rebook their flight.

A while later Cailey finds a vacated couch at the back of the lounge. She hangs her hat, which is dripping wet, on one arm of the couch, and lies on her back, her handbag held across her chest. With a nagging fear of missing Steve's arrival, she allows herself to fall asleep.

Two hours later, the excitement of arriving passengers wakes her with a start, and all at once she is standing at the bottom of an escalator, watching exhausted travellers appear one by one on the top step. Normally, she would take interest in the faces, create their lives from expressions she observes, from the various greetings and waves of waiting friends and relatives. Tonight though, she dismisses each face with a sort of breathless relief. It is not yet Steve, he is not quite here, she is not quite ready.

He is leaning to the side, talking to a group behind him on the escalator. They are laughing. They seem to know each other well. Like one does after a long flight. Halfway down he turns, still smiling, and adjusts his bag over his shoulder. The spotlights shine on his dark hair, fall over a tanned face as he searches for something in his jacket pocket. He finds it, his ticket folder, he looks up, and then he sees her.

Cailey. Without a sound he says her name, and the smile disappears from his face.

She understands. She raises her hand. Not so much as a greeting. More to reach out to him, to touch him. To be sure he's there, even before he reaches her.

***

He stands close besides her at the stove while she stirs a pot of simmering hot chocolate.

She glances at him, points to an open shelf above the stove.

"Marshmallows?"

"Absolutely." He smiles, but his eyes remain on the wooden spoon as it circles round and round the pot.

Cailey reaches in front of him, grabs the cello package from the shelf. She drops a marshmallow in each cup, pours in the chocolate, waits while they bob to the surface.

He leads the way to the living room with the slight limp she'd noticed at the airport. She places their cups on the coffee table, lowers herself to the floor opposite him on the couch.

There is greying hair at his temples; she leans back onto a pile of pillows; she sees a fresh scar on his cheek.

"Are you avoiding me, Cailey?"

"Not really." She smiles, sits up and inhales a sip of chocolate, scalding her tongue on the melting marshmallow. "It's just that I don't know you very well."

Steve holds her gaze. "Maybe on our second date then?"

Still those eyes. Everything in her stirs. She is incapable of a reply.

"So tell me all about yourself, then."

A few minutes pass. He is asleep.

She waits, noticing the shape of the scar, that it is wider, perhaps a little redder right under his left eye. In the dim light, she cannot tell if it's a shadow or a bruise that colours the back of his right hand an angry looking blue.

He wakes with a start, knocking the table with his knee, splashing hot chocolate in Cailey's direction.

He wipes the spilled chocolate with his sleeve. "Sorry, more tired than I realized Cailey, and quite probably brain dead." He grimaces as he lifts his mug, watching her intently, then puts it down without taking a sip. In a gesture of sheer helplessness, he drops his head into his hands.

"God I love you, Cailey."

"I know that. You're trying to get me onto the couch."

"That's right."

Cailey is nervous, tentative. In love completely.

"Did I put my bag down somewhere?"

"At the front door."

"There's that music I mentioned in the car. Would it wake Wendy do you think?"

"A brass band wouldn't wake Wendy."

He laughs softly. "Ah, I remember." He stands with difficulty, walks to the front door and rummages through his canvas bag until he finds a shoebox of cassette tapes.

"Why are you limping, Steve?"

"A bit of a sprain just before I left." He goes over to the light, sorts through his cassettes, selects one and inserts it into the player. "Here, listen to this."

"So really, Steve. Why are you limping?"

"There was trouble last week, a bit of a skirmish, nothing much for me, but there are general strikes going on, protests. Made it hard for me to leave."

He turns to her.

She catches her breath. His pain. His eyes linger a moment on her alarm.

"It's okay, Cailey. I'll tell you." He fiddles with the cassette player. "But not tonight, it will take me a while, where the hell's the volume on this thing… Okay then… here. Listen."

He is waiting, holding his hand out. "For God's sake Cailey, come and sit with me."

"Andean flute." She takes his hand, pulls herself up.

"You know this."

"Well not exactly this piece. But you left me some beautiful music, remember?"

He nods.

She plants herself at the far end of the couch. Where she always sits, she explains a little lamely, in the direction of his raised eyebrows.

"Right. So yes, Steve, everyone loves your tapes at parties, sometimes at exhibitions. And I wrote you about the street performers in the old city. They are spectacular. Their instruments, their songs. Some are from Ecuador. Also Bolivia. Some from Chile. Peru. The big favourite this summer has been our crazy/happy band, as Wendy calls them; no one sits still, the whole street turns into a dance floor."

She looks over expectantly at him. He smiles. His gaze is distant, but close, and she feels a deepened love, a great expanse of their years apart. He raises a finger to his lips to tell her to listen to the music.

She lets the music in, lets it calm her nervous chatter. "It's enchanted. This solo flute, the purest sound…"

"From the mountains."

For a moment, they are silent, inhabiting the music in different ways. She wonders where it takes him as she observes his eyes fixed in his own distance. She moves over to him. "I'd so love to take you back with me, Cailey." His eyes are closing again, his arm tightening around her shoulder. "Maybe next time we'll go together."

"You're going back?"

"I have to. Not right away, and only for a short time. I need to wrap things up at the school, pack stuff to bring home. Give the rest to my friend Apu. Can you put up with me for a couple of weeks?"

When she doesn't reply, his eyes open. "I'd assumed…"

She leans over, touches his lips with her fingers, and that is all that is needed for him to fall soundly asleep.

Cailey is fitfully awake. She fetches a blanket from the hall cupboard, nudges his shoulder, lifts his legs onto the couch; he shifts sideways, and she covers him with the blanket.

An hour later, after a soaking bath that has turned her skin alluringly prune-like, and with one dismissive glance at the drawing she's been working on, she curls up in her own bed. She reaches out, eyes closed, places her watch face down on the table.

She is swimming. Swimming alone in the night. The waters of the river swirl around her, enclosing her in darkness, just ahead there is a bridge, she is nearly there, she must not fall asleep until she gets to the bridge. In the darkness, she sees, all at once, the ribbon of light she needs to make her way.

She is awake.

The light shines from under the bathroom door. The shower. Wendy. No. Not Wendy. Never before seven. She waits. The light goes out, and she knows he will come to her. She longs for him in every moment it takes him to find his way across the room, to fold his sweet warm body into hers.

CHAPTER

16

Steve and Cailey stretch out at opposite ends of the couch. Coffee in hand, pajama legs intertwined, they've been trading bits of news from the weekend papers. Wendy is propped up on her elbows on the floor, chuckling her way through the comics section.

A scattering of breakfast leftovers covers the coffee table. There are small white plates with dollops of butter and jam, bits of cheddar, a few orange peels, crumpled paper napkins, buttery croissant crumbs, and four of Wendy's prized juice glasses with painted yellow lemons with smiling faces, bright red lips, and a speech bubble asking *'sour you doing?'* Wendy finds this is very funny. Every time.

"As far as I can see, Cailey," Steve drops his newspaper emphatically onto his lap, "in the whole of this useless bloody Montreal Gazette, there's only one article on Latin America."

Cailey glances across at him, jarred once again by the biting anger in his voice.

He taps a finger on a photo of Jimmy Carter. "There. That's all there is. One pathetic report about the shift in US policy on Nicaragua. Great news! But there's no analysis. It's headlines for Carter, it's not about Nicaragua."

"Ha! Had you forgotten, Steve?" Wendy rolls over on her back. "If it's not for the Yanks, it's not headlines."

"Yes." Steve groans. "Yes, I had forgotten that."

Cailey doesn't try to respond. All week, Steve's angry tone has set her nerves on edge. Often it's a tone set by Émile when he drops by after work. Even with music on her headphones, Cailey's focus can be ruined by Émile and Steve's strident voices sounding through the living room door while she's trying to sketch. She watches him anxiously as he returns to his paper, loving him too much, wishing she could find a way into his world.

"More coffee anyone?" Wendy stands with a grimace, massages her knees and waits for a response. "Fine then boys and girls," she straightens up, "I'll take that as a no."

Cailey begins reading out loud from an editorial about Quebec's new language bill. She knows no one is listening.

"Can't hear a word you're saying, Cailey." Wendy shouts from the kitchen. "By the way Steve, will you still be here next Saturday?" She pokes her head around the corner. "Hello? Stevie Boy?"

"What? Oh. Yes I will be. I don't leave till a week Monday."

"Perfect. So you can come to Cailey's party."

Silence.

Wendy returns to the living room with a full pot of coffee, fills her mug, and sits down cross-legged at the coffee table.

"What did you just say?" Cailey looks up with a laugh.

"A party. Next Saturday."

Cailey leans toward Wendy, pours herself more coffee. "A party. So what's brought this on?"

"Beats me. This waving brain I guess. It's just that Consuela's been home from the hospital for a while now, and with the evil doctor tucked away in his designer rehab, I thought it might be a great time for a get together, have a few people over. Like normal life. Remember? It would lift our spirits."

"Yes, I think it's a great idea." Cailey glances at Steve. "You Steve?"

"Yes, sure. You're thinking small and casual?"

"Absolutely, Steve." Wendy grins at Cailey. "That's exactly what I was thinking. Small and casual."

"Ha! Believe small when you see it, Steve." Cailey gets up to choose some music. "Where's the tape I bought at the Gilles Vigneault concert? Ah, of course, right here at the bottom of all things Andean."

Steve seems amused. "Are you complaining, my darling Cailey?"

"Probably." She turns the volume up. "It's just that you and Émile seem to have taken over our tape deck."

"Not really. Everything's right there."

"I know." Cailey turns to Wendy. "Shouldn't we run the party idea past Consuela and Gaetan first?"

"I already did." Wendy follows Steve's eyes to her lengthening list of invitees. "Don't you worry darlin' Stevie boy. It's just the usual suspects. I'm only adding a few of Consuela's Chilean friends. Émile and the boys of course. Oh, wait, Patrick and Marie-Claude." She leans over to jot more names on the list. "And that's it, you see? Only a few others from my gang." Wendy sticks her pencil behind her ear. "By the way, Consuela's been asking us lately if she'd see you again before you head back."

"Well good. Talking to Consuela is a tonic. Girl power, that's what she's got," Steve teases, "you girls have it too."

"Aw gee, thanks, Stevie boy."

"Consuela has the most interesting take on IMF policies, especially their effect on Peru right now and the causes of the general strikes. I wonder if she has training in economics somewhere along the line."

"Yes, I think she does," Cailey speaks from the other side of the room, "but she hasn't felt much like struggling with language on that topic. With you she can relax and be herself completely."

"Yes, I suppose that's true," Steve replies.

"I do wish we could understand when you and Consuela are trading stories." Wendy shakes her head. "When you're talking up a storm in Spanish, I've no idea what the hell you're talking about."

"Me neither," Cailey agrees, nudging Steve's foot as she sits down again.

"Maybe we'll be able to grab some time with Consuela and Gaetan on their own. I could translate. I'd get her to talk more about her experiences in the '73 coup. What she's been through is pretty amazing. She and I just got started on those stories last time they were over here. She makes me feel right back home."

There it is again. Cailey hears Steve's words, 'right back home...' Even Wendy picked up on Steve's habit of referring to Peru as 'home'.

It's natural enough, Wendy had dismissed Cailey's irritation, he also calls Winnipeg back home.

True enough, Cailey is thinking now, but it still makes her uneasy considering his growing anger at Canadian news coverage. In the past few days she's been wondering how he'll ever navigate his way back to a Canadian reality he can live with. Wanting to be with her can't be enough to ground him in the long term, or her, for that matter.

As she listens to him banter with Wendy, she's wishing for time with just him, so they can talk more about their plans before he goes back. Steve, unlike Cailey, is assuming that sorting out future living arrangements will fall into place of its own accord.

"Okay, here's an idea," Wendy offers, "this week, I'll learn Spanish. Then, come next Saturday, I'll be fluent."

"Of course you will, Wens. You can translate for me." Cailey closes her eyes and hums to the song she's put on for Steve to hear. '*Gens du pays, c'est votre tour, de vous laisser parler d'amour.*' "Listen, Steve. Have you heard this?" She looks over at him. "Maybe Émile has played it for you."

"I don't think so." Steve hesitates. "No, no, definitely not, I'd remember if I'd heard this before." He listens with intensity, repeating one line several times when the song has ended: '*Le temps de vivre leurs espoirs*'.

Cailey waits, knowing that all the connections are there for him to make.

"That song is heart stopping, Cailey. The music is so different from the music of Peru, but it expresses the same longing, doesn't it, the longing of a people. It's almost like an anthem."

"Exactly," Wendy agrees.

Cailey nods. "We're already hearing it these days as the anthem of a sovereign Quebec."

"The first time," Wendy adds, "was this year at Saint Jean Baptiste Day with everyone..." Wendy checks her watch. "Oh yikes you guys. I'm being picked up for skiing in a few..."

The door bell rings.

"...minutes."

Cailey sits up. "It's October, Wendy." She hopes she's not looking altogether thrilled that Wendy's leaving. "Where's the snow?"

"Up at Saint Sauveur. Two inches, just enough for them to make snow for one hill. We'll grab a burger and stay up for night skiing. I so hope you'll survive without me."

"I say lucky you, Wendy." Steve pulls a section of La Presse out from under Cailey's pile of newspapers. "It seems forever since I was bombing down a hill on a pair of skis. Makes me feel ancient."

"Ahh Steve, our decrepit old elder," Wendy rushes off to the bedroom to get ready.

In a matter of minutes she's into ski clothes and clattering down the stairs with boots and skis from the front hall. She leaves them with the sound of laughing regrets about deserting them for a whole day.

***

"Mon Dieu, Marie, you can't move an inch in this place." Patrick stands immobilized in the crowd, one arm draped casually over Marie-Claude's shoulder, the other raising a beer above his head. A bedraggled young couple is pushing their way past him through to the kitchen. "Okay, so tell me, Cailey, who was that?"

"Beats me," Cailey mouths at Patrick with a resigned shrug. She presses herself against the wall, surveys her personal sanctuary now transformed into a throbbing smoke-filled dance floor. She is not one bit surprised by Wendy's idea of a small and casual gathering.

Wendy herself has been working non stop in the kitchen for hours; she is finally busy spooning out large bowls of her homemade chili.

"I don't know half the people here," Cailey laughs. "Wendy found them somewhere."

"Before you know it, she'll be opening a soup kitchen," Patrick suggests.

"Don't even whisper such an idea, Patrick!"

Marie-Claude points to the invading couple now arrived with hands outstretched at the chili pot. "Those two were right behind us on the stairs, Patrick." She glances up at him. "The ones going on about free food and beer."

"Ah yes." Cailey sends Marie-Claude an appreciative smile. She stands up on her tiptoes, trying to spot Steve across a sea of bobbing heads. Émile is there of course, on the far side of the living room, his *Gitane* dangling as always, dropping ashes into that bushy beard and onto the floor. He is leaning over the tape player. The room jumps when the volume goes up.

Drums. Andean flute. All at once turned into noise. Émile is grinning. Cailey presses her palms to her temples, closes her eyes until someone, she hopes it is Steve, turns it down. She catches sight of him then, enjoying the joke with Émile.

There's a group gathered around Consuela and Gaetan: a few of Consuela's Chilean friends, Émile's girlfriend Jeanne, Jennifer and Francine. Consuela's hands animate the story she and her friends are telling; Gaetan listens, tapping his beer glass to the beat of the drums.

The music slows, the haunting strains of a solo flute fill the room; conversations settle into the movement of the music.

Patrick follows Cailey's eyes with amusement. "Here we go, Marie-Claude, time to make our way over to that Steve guy we've been hearing about."

"*Tout à fait,*" she grins at Cailey, takes her hand, and winds the three of them adeptly through the crowd.

"… 'scusez… 'scusez," she inches along. "Aha, here we are, and this might be Steve, *n'est-ce pas?*" Marie-Claude tilts her head coyly in Steve's direction.

"This might be Steve, *oui.*" Cailey slides her arm around his waist, presses against him.

"I am making some fun now." Marie squeezes Cailey's hand. "My turn, yes?"

"Touché, Marie. Your turn, yes!" Cailey feels Steve's arm around her shoulders, pulling her close without interrupting his conversation. She relaxes into him, knowing the colour is rising in her cheeks. Marie spares her the teasing, offering little more than her famous cheeky smile as she and Patrick join the French conversation with Steve and the others.

Cailey finds her way over to Jennifer, rests a hand on her arm. "I didn't see you come in, Jenn."

"Francine and I came a while ago. With Consuela and Gaetan." Jennifer supports the small of her back with her hands, takes the opportunity to leave the group and rest up against the back of the couch. "I'd hoped Cliff might be here by now." She keeps one hand protectively over a rounding belly.

"He's coming after all?"

"Wendy took the message. She asked him to bring more bowls."

"Of course she did. She's made enough chili to feed half of Montreal."

"This is half of Montreal." Jennifer's laughter turns into a dry cough. "I thought," she catches her breath, "that Wendy had asked people not to smoke."

"She did. I'm so sorry, Jenn." Cailey reaches past her. "Just a sec. The window right here behind you opens." Cailey pulls the latch, and they both welcome the cool fresh air from the balcony.

"Better. Much better. So did I tell you Cliff is bringing Erica?"

"No, you didn't. Well that should be interesting."

"The thing is, it's her first day back at home with the new *au pair*. A lot of changes in that woman. She seems a different person with Andrew away at rehab, Cailey. Cliff was wondering if you'd mind."

"Mind what?"

"If he brings Erica."

"No, of course not. She's more than welcome. Not exactly her kind of party though."

They both laugh.

"Exactly," Jennifer says, "but I was thinking maybe your friends might get her stoned. Cliff too. That would be good. Don't let them in till they've shared a joint."

"I'll get Patrick right on it, Jenn."

"Perfect."

"They'll fit right in."

Jenn smiles weakly. "Seriously though, Cailey, those two are driving me nuts. Brother and sister solidarity. They're joined at the hip. But I need my mate right now, which might seem obvious to some, but apparently not to him. I've lost him to our wretched Andrew fiasco."

"You know that won't last, Jenn. I'm betting things return to normal now with Erica and the kids no longer under foot at your place. I can't imagine how you've managed all this time."

"I haven't managed at all. I'm a beast to Cliff whenever he fusses over the weeping high society sister. Call me heartless. I don't even care." Jenn looks embarrassed. "At least Trish and Robbie know how to ignore me. They shuffle off and talk quietly under the kitchen counter! I heard them plotting the other day what they'll do with the new baby when Mommy is grumpy!"

"Oh wow, those little kids are something else."

"No doubt you're right about all this working out Cailey, but Cliff and I are not in the best place at the moment."

"I think I've seen it. I mean a certain strain showing between you two. I doubt any couple could get through such heartbreak without huge tensions building up. You're only human."

"Yes, it's good to be reminded of that! But we're inhabiting a foreign territory right now, and neither of us is any good at it."

Cailey is not surprised to see tears in Jennifer's eyes. "And the baby? Monthly check-ups for you both are good?"

"Yes yes, absolutely." Jennifer dabs the tears with a finger. "Much to look forward to, and I'm being neurotic."

"You're allowed."

"That's me. Neurotic little woman with baby," Jennifer's green eyes widen in amusement. "You know, it's strange," she pauses, "but Consuela herself is a point of sanity for me. Look at her. She's radiant. How can she be radiant after all she's endured? Talking to her just now, I had to feel foolish for being so woebegone."

"She is radiant, I agree, but I'm frightened for her still. There's a sudden terror I see flash across her face without warning."

"I think I'm seeing less of that as the days go by." Jennifer stands up. "I hope I am at least." Jennifer takes Cailey's arm and they move to rejoin Consuela.

As they approach the group, Émile lights up another cigarette.

"Maybe stay away from Émile and his *Gitane,* Jenn.*"*

"It likely makes no difference at this point, Cailey. Sorry to say but right now your flat is as polluted as Los Angeles. I might as well be smoking myself."

Cailey grimaces. "If Cliff doesn't show up soon, I'm calling you a cab."

Standing next to Consuela and Gaetan, Cailey tries to pick up Émile's discourse on the new language law. From what she grasps of the French flying back and forth, he's making a certain sense about preserving culture. It's Gaetan who seems most at odds with Émile's position, opposing him quite heatedly. Cailey is pleased to see this side of Gaetan, although much to her own surprise, she's inclined to agree with Émile.

When she feels Steve watching her, she returns the love in his eyes, many times over. She wonders how well he reads her distress about Émile and his buddies landing in the midst of both their lives. He certainly couldn't have missed her clumsy backhands aimed at smokers and loud meetings. So far, he's offered very little in response. 'Hand Émile over to me,' Wendy had suggested the other day along with a string of lewd suggestions intended to make them laugh.

To Cailey's relief, the conversation now shifts from Émile's lecture and takes up Consuela's concern about a journalist in Nicaragua covering the Sandinistas. This particular journalist is someone who, according to Émile, doesn't know his Ortegas from his Colonel Saunders.

Cailey notices that Consuela is laughing with Émile about this. Unlike Gaetan, she seems to be enjoying Émile immensely, regardless of falling cigarette ashes, scruffy beard, moth eaten sweater and all.

Gaetan is moving with Steve over to the tape player. They chuckle at a shared joke as they sort through the pile of cassettes. With a glance at Cailey, Steve waves the cassette he's been looking for, and slips the tape into the player.

"Yes, this is the one." She returns Steve's wave. "Here's the piece I told you about, Jenn. Remember Steve promised to play it for you? It made me think we could work with it, if we ever get to an exhibition using Steve's photos."

"His photos. And your drawings, I hope."

"Maybe. A bit presumptuous though, since I've never visited the Andes, or witnessed such festivals."

"Not knowing your subject didn't stop you with the Consuela study you did.

"Sore point, Jenn. Maybe we could drop that. Consuela was right here I could see her, I could be in touch with her, talk to her."

"Right you are. Point taken." Jennifer pauses, listening hard. "Oh yes, this is special, Cailey. I'd love to work with this. I always feel we land in a shared space when we join in music like this; deep roots, no borders; a mystery that lifts us all high."

"An inspired description, Jenn! I so agree with you."

"A tad romantic, but no apologies. I'd be happy to play around with some arrangements, find out more about the musical tradition." She hesitates. "You realize, of course, that we have way too many plans!"

"I do, but I don't want to miss anything."

"You could go to Peru. I keep wondering why you're not joining Steve for the month. He wants you to. He told me. You and your sketchbook would give us a more authentic blend of story and music."

Jennifer stops for a moment, craning her neck to see if Cliff has come in yet.

"I know, but I've told you Jenn. And him. I'd love to go some time. Right now I've too many unfinished contracts with the schools. And I'm late developing my commercial photo shoots. Not to mention that the dynamics would be impossible. Think about it. Me and my trusty sketchbook trotting along behind Steve as he makes the rounds to bid farewell to the dearest of friends and colleagues. Can you imagine? I'd be saying, 'oh hi there Peruvian people, I'm Cailey, the other girlfriend, and I offer you my best 'buenos dias.' There's just no way, Jenn."

"Okay, got it." Jennifer nods with a smile.

"No way what?" Steve appears beside them, plants a chaste kiss on Cailey's cheek.

"No way I'll come with you to Peru this time, no way I'll follow ten paces behind while you wind things up."

"It wouldn't be like that. I'd make sure it wouldn't be."

Jenn watches them affectionately. "Much as I might trust your reassurance, Steve, if I were Cailey, I'd feel like a fifth wheel. I wouldn't touch it this time around!"

"Next trip, Jenn," Cailey says, "we'll both go. How about that?"

"Don't joke, I'd be there with you in a flash!" Jenn exclaims. "Two hips, two arms, three kids. I'll balance it all. Or get Cliff to." She turns to Steve. "By the way, I'm hoping you'll bring this recording to brunch tomorrow. We want to hear about the Festival of the Condor. I know it's gruesome, but Robbie loves gruesome, particularly if it scares Trisha. Bring some slides if you feel like it." Jennifer looks back at Cailey. "That is if you're really coming for brunch tomorrow."

"Of course we're coming," Steve and Cailey confirm in unison.

"We'll bring chili," Cailey jokes.

"Speaking of chili, I'm famished." Steve makes a gesture toward the kitchen. "How about we make our way over there before all the chili's devoured by the riffraff."

"Yes please," Jenn responds. "Oh look over there, there's my riffraff guy Cliff, arriving with his riffraff sister."

Cailey and Steve wait while Jennifer edges along the wall to Cliff, then they make their way through the various clutches of dancers, slowing here and there to chat with people they know, along with several they've never laid eyes on.

Minutes later they are watching Jennifer emerge from the kitchen with three bowls of chili balanced between two hands. She is concentrating very hard on her manoeuvre; she looks up at them sheepishly.

"Lazy man's load. My mother warned me."

"Here, let me help with those." Cailey reaches for one of the bowls.

"You know it's probably better if I just..." Jenn stops, her eyes fixed wide-eyed over Cailey's shoulder. "Oh shit *la merde*..." Jennifer's exclamation carries loudly through the room.

Three bowls of chili smash onto the floor.

Cailey turns to see Andrew Wilson weaving his way from the front hall into the living room.

"Oh no, don't let him." Cailey's voice trails off as the party chatter dies to a murmur.

Appearing at Jennifer's side in an instant, Cliff steers her back to the kitchen. Someone – Wendy –begins cleaning up the mess underfoot. Bits of broken china clunk into a plastic pail.

"And that would be…" Steve whispers to Cailey.

"Andrew. Dr. Wilson."

"Apparently not at the rehab centre."

"Apparently not." Cailey slips over next to Erica who is motionless up against the wall where Cliff has left her. Her face is frozen in an unsmiling smile. She jumps at Cailey's touch on her shoulder.

Cailey searches the room for Consuela and Gaetan. They are with Émile. They have not yet seen the reason for the hush that has fallen.

Andrew takes off his hat and coat. He seems to be moving in slow motion. He is drunk. Or medicated. More likely both. He's not dressed right. Cailey takes in details. Checked shirt. Pinstripe suit jacket. Sweat pants. Buttons askew. Shirt open.

"Hang this up for me, there's a good man." He hands his coat to the person beside him who laughs and lets it drop on the floor. More laughter. Andrew's eyes dart about the room in confusion.

"I have just come from a meeting." he announces.

Cailey watches as a tear slips down Erica's cheek.

"And yes indeed, indeed, I've straightened everything out." He moves toward Erica, but stops suddenly as his eyes rest on Cailey. He seems, for a moment, unable to absorb her presence.

"Oh I see. Yes I see. You're intent on ruining this party too, are you? After Erica's gone to all this trouble. Can you not see how upset you're making her?" He raises his voice. "Just when she'd stopped all that crying."

Steve takes a step forward, but Cailey shakes her head. Her eyes are riveted on Consuela who has moved in to the right just out of Andrew's sight. A few guests behind them in the hall, pick up their coats, leave quietly.

"This is my party, Dr. Wilson." Cailey hears her own steady voice. "This is my home." Her heart is pounding.

He leers at her, his head moving mechanically, mockingly, from side to side, "my party, my house.".

"Andrew, no. Please." Only Cailey hears Erica's whispered plea as it is drowned out by a single clear voice.

"Señor Wilson."

He whirls in Consuela's direction, steadies himself against the bookcase.

"Well, well, well." He gestures toward Cailey. "Of course you two would be in this together wouldn't you?" He gathers himself to his full height, swaying slightly and gazing out at the gathering as if to deliver an address. People turn away, embarrassed, talk quietly amongst themselves. There is no more laughter.

Cailey catches Émile's eye, points to the tape player. He nods, switches the music back on.

"You're all the same, you lot." Andrew shouts above the music. "You'll never learn." His eyes narrow in the direction of an unflinching Consuela. "But you learned something didn't you, you little Latino tart."

At that, there is a turning of heads and an audible gasp from those within earshot.

"Yes, well we fired her you know," his hand comes up, points at Consuela, "we had to, of course, for not doing her job, not doing as she was told. And now we have a nice new girl, haven't we Erica," he faces his wife. "And you'll be happy to know, my dear, that our new girl was extremely helpful when I told her I'd lost the address for the party. Not like this one here," he wags a silly looking finger at Consuela. "You never were the cooperative type, were you?"

All at once he slaps his hand hard against the side of the bookcase. "I'm talking to you! I'm warning you what the authorities will do. I told you. I told you what I'd have to do if you weren't cooperative with your Canadian employers." Émile turns up the volume. "Well? Didn't I?"

Erica lets out an agonized groan. Steve and Gaetan and Cliff move at once from different points in the room, about to restrain Andrew who appears on the verge of a physical attack. Instinctively, they hold back.

It is Consuela's eyes, her searing voice, that fire at Andrew, immediately diminishing him, as if her fierceness could drill right through him. In an instant he shrinks under that furious gaze, and she moves to confront him.

"*Cállate!*" Consuela's exclamation is strangely quiet. Also loud.

"You, Señor Andrew, you will do nothing at all. You will do nothing! Never again! Not to any woman. Not to anyone." Her words become careful, slow, perfectly formed. "Never again," she repeats softly, "never again."

Consuela turns her back on Andrew. The only sound in the room at that moment is the Andean flute, the slow rhythm of the drums. She holds her hands out to Gaetan. He reaches her as the tears well up and spill out of those gentle fiery eyes.

Andrew opens his mouth to speak, but his face is crumbling. There are visible twitches; words do not come. With his coat still on the floor, he turns and flees.

Erica holds tightly to Cailey's offered hand and goes with her to the stairs, calls goodbye with an unhinged buoyancy as Cliff races after Andrew. Jennifer appears beside them and leads Erica to the nearest chair.

***

An hour later, a call from the rehab facility confirms Andrew's safe return. The attendant on duty regrets the incident, but with Dr. Wilson disrupting the terms of a voluntary recovery, Erica will be encouraged by medical staff to obtain a committal order so he can continue in the programme.

For the briefest moment Erica looks blankly into her brother's face, the trace of a small sad smile turning the corners of her mouth. She asks Cliff to take her home, home to her children, she whispers in a soft weary voice.

In the kitchen, Cailey spoons coffee into the filter. Consuela rinses out cups at the sink. In the living room, a window is open wide. Émile guiltily, if begrudgingly, agrees not to smoke inside. Jennifer is relaxing at last, her feet up on the couch. Steve stands in front of them all, attempting to tell a joke in French. The laughter that erupts has little to do with the joke, and everything to do with his rusty French, which keeps getting muddled in with his Spanish. She can hear Gaetan nudging him along on to a punch line that Cailey doesn't get.

Consuela fills the pot with water and pours it into the coffee maker. "When Steve will be back with you Cailey, for all of you my friends, you will come please for a feast by Gaetan and myself Consuela! That will be when I tell you so much things." Consuela leans against the counter. "I can say then how I am too afraid for trouble in this country, how so much frightened maybe to press charges. I will say stories of family in Chile. My mother. In pictures you will meet. And sweet brother. How forever search for brother. Mine brother. My brother. I know in Steve his understanding, he knows our struggle, and you are my sister. You have stayed beside me."

"Yes." Cailey looks up into Consuela's eyes, she cannot find the words, she can only put her arms around her, hold her close.

Wendy appears balancing a tray littered with beer bottles and ash-trays, half-eaten bowls of chili and bits of baguette. She reports that the others are cleaning up the living room, although so far they are proceed-ing while lying down.

"And," Wendy slides the tray onto the counter, "they've made a pact in there not to talk about Andrew. Jennifer's request."

"Good for Jennifer," Consuela agrees.

"You okay?" Wendy looks anxiously at Consuela.

"*Sí chiquita*, I am okay."

"You amaze me, Consuela." Wendy holds a hand out to her, wraps one arm around Consuela's shoulders. "I don't believe in heroes," she tells her, fighting back tears, "but you, *ma chère amie,* you will have to be the exception."

Exhausted women, all three, seem to be of one breath in an easy silence, of one mind in their unspoken awareness of domestic service to the very wealthy; together they relax into the slow drip drip of aromatic coffee rising to the top of the pot.

When the coffee's done Cailey lifts the glass pot, carries it to the living room. Wendy and Consuela bring cups, spoons, cream and sugar. A current of fresh air from the open window is clearing out the smoky haze. Gaetan and Patrick are bagging up the mess of paper cups, plates, crumpled paper napkins. Francine and Jeanne and Marie-Claude fetch damp cloths from the kitchen, and with paper towels in hand, they wipe tables and tops of bookcases while discussing the many political obstacles to daycare funding. They share their outrage that even Levesque is break-ing his promises.

Émile switches on the vacuum but doesn't move. Instead, with nozzle in hand, he continues a talking with Steve about some ongoing union action. Something about mining, challenging Noranda investments. The two of them shout at each other over the idle whirring vacuum.

Cailey heads back to the kitchen, happy all of a sudden, about such an insane collection of friends gathered in her home. She fills the sink with hot water and dumps the first stack of bowls into the suds.

Consuela is behind her, drying as Cailey washes. Consuela places each bowl as she dries it, in front of Wendy. Wendy sits at the kitchen table with pencil and paper, attempting a list of whose bowls might be whose.

"*Merde,* I have no idea about these ones. Cailey look, are these Jenn's bowls, do you recognize them? Do you Consuela? This is driving me nuts."

Consuela checks the bowl Wendy is holding up. "No. I never saw it at Jennifer's."

Cailey looks up from the sink. "Why don't you just wait for people to come and claim them?"

"Because. I don't want those people back in our house. I don't like them. I only invited them for their bowls."

"You're ridiculous." Cailey is too tired to think of a witty rejoinder. It's Consuela who starts to laugh. She sits down across from Wendy and surveys the stacks of bowls that are now nearly covering the surface of the table.

"How many did you ask to bring bowls?"

Wendy stares at Consuela for a moment, smiling idiotically, as though the answer required higher mathematics.

"I don't know. Everyone."

Cailey drops her head over the sink, convulsed with laughter, her hair falling into the warm sudsy water. They laugh together luxuriously, until the tears roll down their cheeks. Cailey slides onto the floor with her back against the kitchen cabinet. They are holding their sides, trying to catch their breath when Steve and Émile and Gaetan appear at the door with the vacuum cleaner still running.

"What's going on in here?"

"Back to work, slaves," Wendy chokes out. "This is a cabinet meeting." And they are off again, laughing until it hurts.

Minutes later, Cailey stumbles into the living room, collapses breathless into the easy chair by the front window.

"Don't let that mad woman near me." Cailey waves to Steve who is talking to Émile on the other side of the room. "I'm serious. I need protection."

Steve has clearly been enjoying himself; he rushes to her side, and in a gesture of mock gallantry, raises her hand to his lips, then lands rather unsteadily on the arm of her chair.

"Can you die from laughing?" She looks up at him.

"Yes, you can," he grins and messes her hair, then slides into the chair with her. His face is flushed with the pleasure of good company, and a few too many beers; it's the most relaxed she's seen him since his arrival.

"Dear God what a night," she drops her head onto his shoulder; in an instant her eyes are closed, and she feels his hand gentle on her face, the deep warmth of a kiss that seems to linger forever between them.

A round of whistling, which they cannot ignore for long, sets off around the room.

"Émile," Steve whispers in her ear. Cailey leans forward and laughs over at Émile and Jeanne who look altogether pleased with their school yard heckling.

"If anyone in the scullery out there is up to making a second pot of coffee," Cailey calls out in a hoarse voice, "this one's already empty. Do please bring a couple more cups. Do not bring Wendy."

More laughter from the kitchen.

Finally, whatever burst of dishwashing and vacuuming energy they'd come up with gives way to fatigue; they become part of one another in the quiet, haunted still by a residual violence hanging in the air.

Cliff, just returned from taking Erica home, appears stressed but relieved to be talking quietly with Jennifer and Francine in the armchairs near the door. Consuela is curled up with Gaetan on the couch, and Wendy, cross- legged as always, is on the floor by the bookcase where she has apparently wrested control of the tape deck from Émile. Francine, Émile, and Jeanne are stretched out on the floor next to her. Kitchen chairs complete complete the circle, with Patrick and Marie occupying all four, two of which serve as footstools.

It is Consuela who first breaks the silence.

"Wendy," she asks, lifting her head from Gaetan's shoulder, "that one again, yes please."

"That one what?"

"That one music. Steve will tell story of the Condor. How he went in festival of the Inca in a beautiful mountain, yes?" Her laughter rolls on gently as she burrows further into her corner with Gaetan, "I am ready please! We listen now. Canada Condor story! Señor Steve!"

There is a smattering of uncertain applause, but it's a few minutes before Consuela's request registers with Steve. He finds Cailey's eyes. She nods, the longing and love between them seeming to her for the moment, to make all things possible.

Steve says nothing for several minutes.

Consuela is watching him. "I'm here, *chico*, so if you say silly *gringo* thing, I tell you!" The music of the flute and the drums rise up again, and Consuela's laughter softens into half sleep. "No, I am not sleeping," she insists, "I am listening."

"It's not so easy, Consuela. This is your story."

"You tell your learning of my story Señor Steve, of Apu's story. Is important to hear what happens to my fiesta on your tongue."

Steve laughs, not sure if he should be reassured. He keeps his eyes on Consuela as he begins.

"Well okay," he leans forward in his chair, "some of you may have heard of this festival, it shows up in the news sometimes, the Festival of the Condor?"

Several people shake their heads.

"It's a very dramatic ritual of the Andean peoples. Festive for sure, but also pretty gruesome, just as their own history of conquest has been; it carries deep symbolic meaning. The condor, this largest of vultures, lives high in the mountains, where the oxygen is thin. It can survive on very little; it feeds on carrion. It's wingspan can be more than ten feet. The sight of it soaring is absolutely startling to someone like me, who's never witnessed anything larger than an eagle."

"*Wingspan*. New word!" Consuela leans against Gaetan, spreads her arms to their full length. "From here," she waves one hand at the other, "to here." Gaetan is laughing at her.

"Exactly," Steve continues with an affectionate smile. "It was Apu who taught me about the great Andean Condor that is sacred to his culture, and how it symbolizes the power of the Inca to survive and return, to at last defeat the Spanish *conquistadores*. Apu," Steve gazes into the distance, as if calling his friend's spirit to his side, "Apu, I should explain, is my *compañero* back in Peru. I'll see him next week. It's with him that I experienced the *Yawar Fiesta*, the Festival of the Condor. I saw, side by side with him and his family at their own village festival, how still today the men trek high into the mountains to capture just one condor for their village. Often it's days before the men return triumphant. Once they've trapped the condor, they will give it just enough strong drink to calm it for the descent to the village. They thread a string through its nostrils, its beak is tied shut so they can lead it down safely. On this day, with everyone waiting in anticipation, word of the men's success reached the village hours before their return. The feast that was being prepared for days was laid brought out from many houses, the colourful bands, with flutes and drums and fiddles, lined the streets. Singing and drinking and dancing reached a frenzied pitch."

Steve pauses a moment, and raises a finger to the sound of the flute that has just begun to play. "Not soft like this beautiful piece," he laughs, "this is much too peaceful, not wild enough for the raucous celebration!"

"*El Cóndor pasa!*" Consuela sits up. "It is when the condor soars home to his mountain. Original on flute Steve, I love, not Simon Garfunkel."

"Me too. Would you take over, Consuela?" Steve asks. "Continue about the festival?"

"Better I will interrupt you."

"Thanks a lot." Steve joins in the laughter, then picks up the story where he'd left off. "Okay, so when the condor was led into the village, its long wing feathers were decorated with brightly coloured ribbons as a prayer for the coming harvest. It was paraded in front of us all, then strapped to the back of the bull that was chosen to represent the aggressive virility of the Spanish *conquistadore*. The bull had to be defeated by this great Andean Condor, invested now with the power of the Inca to triumph over their conqueror. The condor displayed its furious power, embedding its talons into the back of the bull; it was horrifying to witness it gouging fiercely into the bull's flesh with its beak. The wounded bull raged through the village, charging at anything in its path while the bands were weaving their way around the streets, the villagers dancing and singing along the side of the road. When it was clear that the bull was about to collapse from exhaustion, the victory cheer went up, and the bull was corralled by the men and stopped from rolling over on top of the sacred bird. Finally, the condor was led away by its wings to a precipice where there was enough air current, and then, after several failed attempts, it lifted off, much to the relief of onlookers, I'd add, since the condor must survive, or there will be death and destruction instead of victory and prosperity."

The room is silent as Steve finishes and eases back, with a long sigh, into the chair with Cailey. "I guess I'm running out of words for this, although there's more to tell," he concludes. "Words wouldn't capture the impact of this experience, how awe inspiring for me to be standing just behind Apu, to witness that great Andean Condor liberated after battle, banking back and forth over the valley, as if in a blessing, then watch it soar high once again, back to its mountain home where the Inca hold power."

"*El Cóndor pasa!*" Consuela claps her hands. "Condor by Señor Steve! Not so bad for English tongue," she says softly, smiling over at him. Then slowly, she looks around the room, searching for responses. When there are none, she begins to speak. "Is gruesome ritual, I know my dear *amigos*, cruel like my people's history, like all violent conquest. I and my people we hold our belief of condor as spirit of the Inca, as messenger soaring between earth and heaven, who still holds returning power of our Inca kings, a power to pull the sun across the sky, bring seeds to rise from the land. That bless us. Our gruesome story is of great love. It is the longing of my people."

CHAPTER
17

SPEAKING PHOTOGRAPHY
MONTREAL
OCTOBER 1977

They move furniture, water plants, pick off dead leaves, throw out news-papers, clean the fridge. They change sheets, scrub the bathroom. They impose an essential external order on their lives.

Wendy takes a quick phone message from Jennifer: she'll meet Cailey tomorrow to work on the exhibition.

Cailey thinks about Steve as she fries up mushrooms for a chicken stew. She was only with him for a few weeks. What if there's nothing more to say? What if that was nothing more than a week long affair of passion and confusion.

"I'm having lunch with Cliff this week, Wendy," she calls out as she tips the frying pan over the stew pot. "He's still pushing this idea for a book." The buttery mushrooms sizzle into the chicken gravy.

"A book?"

"My photo essays. Why is no one remembering this? Yes, a book. Cliff was going through portfolios with a colleague this summer, and they thought there might be a book in a collection of my photo essays. The lives of women in Montreal. This guy knows a local publisher who might be interested."

Wendy appears at the kitchen door, filing a broken thumbnail. "But those are the photos you don't even like, remember? One reviewer made nasty noises about romanticizing women's oppression. And so did you, if I"m not mistaken."

"I know. Cliff was impatient with me about that as always. He told me not to be a fool. That photography is my living. And this is fine artistic work with a message that matters."

Wendy opens the fridge, closes it again. "I agree with him. We're talking success here. Why do you always steer yourself toward problems?'

"I didn't know I did."

"Well, you do."

Cailey laughs, grateful to feel things back to normal. "Well, thank you very much, it's nice to know these details."

"Any time, *chica*."

"If I do the book though, I don't want to lose the inspiration I had going when I returned from out east. There's new stuff I'd started that I'd rather be doing."

"Well how much would you have to do for a book like this? Really, you've already finished your part. Wouldn't you simply hand the photos over to an editor, they'd do a layout, and someone would write up a few blurbs?"

"Well not quite. Cliff thinks I'm the one who should write the text. I'd have to spend quite a lot of time on that."

"We both know you can't write to save your life, Cailey."

"Exactly."

"But you could easily find a writer to work with. I know a ton of people. You could go through each shot so they'd get the gist of how to describe your subject, the intent or impact or whatever. Hell even I could do that."

Cailey turns to Wendy while the spoon drips gravy on the floor. "Wendy! Why don't *you* do it?"

"Why don't I do what?"

"Work with me to write the copy for the photographs."

"No way. I wasn't serious. It's not my thing. I mean, is anyone wearing lingerie in your photos? I only do bras and girdles."

"Of course I'm serious. You've been working on your play, which I've been trying to convince you is actually quite excellent and insane in an avant garde kind of way."

"You want an insane text then? Besides, I don't speak photography."

"Come here, I'll show you." Cailey wipes her hands on the dishtowel and goes into the living room. "Where's the Dorothea Lange book?"

"You're asking me?"

"Just wait." Cailey moves things around on top of the bookcase, finds the book, flips quickly through the pages. "Here. Check this out. See what's written under the photo? It's just the story of that woman. No one is speaking photography."

As Wendy reads, her expression changes. "Oh. Yes. The Depression, dustbowl in the midwest. Wow. And this piece about the mother, living in a truck with two kids." Wendy sits down on the couch, runs her hand over the page.

"You know you could do that, Wendy. A short text, a story, about each of the women. You know so many of them personally now."

"I think I could figure something out. What about interviewing them? Put each story in their own words."

"Perfect. Exactly what's needed. You see? Come with me for lunch with Cliff and this publisher friend of his. He's bringing some of the prints. We could talk about what we want."

"Or what Cliff and his buddy want. What makes you think they'll go for the idea of someone like me writing the text for their book?"

"Well, I can't write it myself. They'll want someone who understands my work."

"Okay, I'm interested. But by the way, I thought I heard Steve trying to talk you out of giving up photography entirely."

"Not the business side. I wouldn't give up the portraits and school photos. That's my living. Maybe this book will boost my income, who knows. But the thing is, I have to follow my passion to focus on drawing and painting. I know I have to do that."

Wendy stares at her, puzzled. "Well, you've lost me a bit. Your photos seem such a key part of your art. They are original, moving, and full of emotion. Humour. They engage the viewer. Issues come to life."

"There now. You see? This is why you should do the text for the book. You understand my photos better than I do. And you like them better than I do!"

"Probably." Wendy is still leafing through the Dorothea Lange book.

"So you'll join us then, to discuss it?" Cailey can see Wendy wants to do it.

"You and me girl," she slaps the book closed, "we'll give it a try."

CHAPTER
18

THERE IS SOMETHING ELSE
MONTREAL
NOVEMBER 1977

"Hello? Anybody here?" Cailey slides her camera bags from her shoulders onto the floor inside the front door. She has just come from three family portrait sessions, one easy one at the studio, two in private homes with screeching kids.

She is surprised to find the apartment in darkness. She rests her tripod in the corner, hangs up her coat, and sits for moment on the arm of the couch listening to the radio left on, the traffic report, the weather, more snow tomorrow, the usual idle chatter filling spaces before the six o'clock news. She switches on the standing lamp behind the couch.

In the bedroom, she goes on her daily hunt for slippers. One under the bed, one behind the open closet door.

Steve's notes and papers are scattered over the bedspread. He must have left in a particular hurry this morning. She frowns at the mess with a mix of affection and annoyance.

"So now what?" she asks out loud. That question, she realizes, is as much about her life, as about whether to have tea or wine.

Tea. When seeking comfort, drink tea.

She grabs her tattered sweater from behind the door, slips it over her head, welcoming its familiar warm embrace as it falls to her knees. 'You'll grow into it,' her gran had laughed, watching the new sweater drop all the way to Cailey's ankles.

She jumps when the phone rings. Steve. The relief she feels when she hears Wendy's voice come on the line surprises her. She's in a rush to a movie, Wendy says with no opening for response, she'll be out late, she hopes Cailey and Steve will think of something to do without her there for supper. Cailey wishes there'd been time to talk, to ask Wendy's advice about ongoing disagreements with Steve, the various stresses since his return.

In the kitchen, she savours her first sip of hot tea on this cold night. It transports her to precious moments alone by the sea, wrapped in this same sweater, her sleeping bag over her legs and feet as she sits at the picnic table. The sun had been disappearing behind a bank of retreating clouds. All afternoon she'd sat there sketching, littering the table with drawings of Gran's amber pin, of Becky down on the rocks, of Wood River flowing under the bridge.

Now with tea in hand, she wanders aimlessly about the living room. She leans over to check newspaper headlines, arranges throw pillows on the couch, brushes crumbs from the coffee table to the floor. She lingers at the front window.

She wants that to be Steve coming down the street.

She wants to be alone.

An hour later, she is at her drawing table. The sound of Jennifer's cello is filling the apartment. There is still no sign of Steve. She has lit the two kerosene lanterns she bought last week, and adjusted the light; she likes the familiar smell of burning fuel, coal oil they call it back home. For her, it becomes the magical aroma of precious times gone by. She fingers the amber pin under the light, imagining a young girl crouched in the tall grass outside a circle of standing stones. Above the circle, the moon is high.

Cailey's pencil moves quickly. The girl is Becky. She is drawing Becky into the story of the amber, drawing her to the river, to her death, she is drawing the river deep and turbulent, the river is a passageway…

Next to her on the floor, on top of her pile of discarded sketches, is Gran's *Story of the Amber*. She retrieves it, rereads it slowly. She moves everything aside, places the large drawing of her grandmother in the centre. She stands up, examines it carefully from every angle, shifting the lanterns this way, than that. She chooses the pencils she needs. It surprises her to see so many changes from the earlier sketches on the floor spread on the floor, the transformation she's given her grandmother's face, the warm glow from the amber at her throat.

In this sketch, Cailey is giving her grandmother an expression that startles her, something darker, more inaccessible, a deepening, anxious love. It is no longer the face of a grandmother; it is the face of knowing, and not knowing, the face of all questions whose answers lie on the other side of this mystery, of any mystery.

She walks a few more times around the drawing, shifts the lamps, sits down again. Her pencil is moving swiftly as she makes her decisions. Maybe she will finish it next week after all. She wonders what music Jennifer will compose, if some inspiration will rise from this drawing. The two of them have already made a pact not to talk about their separate creations for a while. There's been too much talk, and not enough creating, they'd agreed. Soon though, Cailey is sure, there will be a meeting point.

She is totally engrossed when she realizes that she has heard the key turn in the lock, the door open.

"Steve?"

"Hi."

Something in his voice. Reluctantly, she puts her pencil down. She turns off the tape, lowers the lantern wicks and quickly blows them out. In the hall she finds him leaning against the closed front door. He makes no move to take off his jacket. His face is so stricken, so hollow, she hardly recognizes him.

"Cailey..."

"My God, what is it?" She follows him to the couch. He sits for the longest time in silence, his elbows on his knees, his head bowed. She waits in the armchair across from him, until at last he looks up at her.

"Beautiful Cailey. I've been walking for hours. I should have come back here right away. Apu has died. The family contacted Émile to let me know. I can't absorb it. I can't. I don't even know where I've been walking."

Cailey is frightened at the sight of such panic in his face. She is afraid of his anguish. Afraid for him. She has the most dreadful instinct to shake him, anything to bring him back to her, to shake out of him everything he has not told her since he arrived back last week. Apart from the story of the Condor Festival, she doesn't even know who Apu is. Right now, she hardly knows who Steve is.

"Oh Steve, I am so sorry." Cailey doesn't know what to do. At the moment his posture warns off physical contact. "Have you eaten anything?"

"No. A drink would be good."

"Wine. And some food. Okay?"

"Anything."

"There's not a lot in the fridge. I'll do scrambled eggs."

"Sure." He doesn't move.

She pours two glasses, takes him one, leaves while she begins clattering about in the kitchen. Mixes eggs, chops onions and pepper. She gulps her wine. The shower goes on while she is slicing bread. She slices it unevenly and the fat end gets stuck at the top of the toaster and burns. Butter is burning in the pan.

It is too much. She gives up. She sits down at the kitchen table with the rest of the bottle of wine.

Steve is in the shower a long time. Finally he appears at the kitchen door.

"I'm driving you to drink."

"Yes." She looks around the kitchen. Everything is half-made on the counters and on top of the stove.

"I'm not really hungry, anyway."

"Just as well."

"Cailey."

She looks up at him.

"I was just noticing the drawing of your grandmother." He waits. "Can you tell me about it?"

For the moment, Cailey cannot bring herself to respond.

"Well, that drawing got me thinking. Or maybe your grandmother did. Thinking about your life going on here. Your work."

"And?" Cailey is trying, without little success, to resist her impatience with this stranger named Apu. Now dead.

"Okay, so I guess I'm taking a long time to land this time, Cailey. Especially with the news of Apu. I know we've hardly talked. I want to hear everything, I want to tell you everything. I don't know where to begin."

"At the beginning I guess."

"I'll begin at the end." He focuses past Cailey the wall out the kitchen window. "Last week in Peru of course, the protests escalated, with the general strike going on for days. My friend Apu. He was shot. Apu was shot not far from where I was standing. It didn't seem such a bad wound at the time. Just on his arm." He holds his own arm, as though he can feel the pain. "Up here close to his shoulder."

He pauses, doesn't continue for several minutes.

"He was in the hospital. His wife was reassured. The doctors said not to change my plans. I left him there at the hospital. That night I had to fly to California, to settle a few things with Anne, before I came home. To you." He turns to find her eyes. "I had to leave that night, I couldn't change my ticket. I couldn't have stayed with him. I couldn't have."

He stops. "The strikes..." He stops again. "There's too much Cailey. I can't work it out yet. There's pressure from outside the country. The IMF, the US, increases in prices being imposed. Did you read about it? It's impossible to live. Infrastructure is collapsing. Émile says there was actually coverage in Le Devoir. I was hoping you wouldn't see it."

"I didn't. I go for days without reading the papers."

Steve smiles. "Well anyway, that all transpired just last week. I was there, with Apu, he had come down to the capital with me from the village, he was meeting someone from the ministry, about the co-op he runs, to tell him the price increases will be impossible. He's... he was the manager, amazing guy really. He's... from the region where the university is... where I taught... where the festival was I told you about. Anyway, today there was this call to Émile from Peru. From a teacher, a friend of mine at the university." Steve reaches out, touches Cailey's face. "Apu died there in the hospital. He died the day I left him, that afternoon, all these days I didn't know. I don't believe for a minute that he died from that wound. There's no way it was enough to kill him. The doctors told me, his wife, he would be okay. I think they knew what was going to happen. I think that's what's going on. They got rid of Apu."

"Oh dear God." Cailey goes to him.

***

There is a bustle of waiters, a mellow energy of late evening chatter, steamy wafts of Giorgio's sauces mingling with aromas of rich Italian wine. There are low lights, candles on every table, commotion in the kitchen.

The waiter pours wine from a carafe, nods his recognition with a smile for both of them. They order their pasta; they barely glance at each other.

Cailey holds her palms against an impending headache. "I know my timing is atrocious," she looks up at him apologetically, "but I just couldn't stand one more minute in the apartment, in all that darkness. With your grief. And me so irritable. Sorry, you must think I'm heartless."

"Not heartless. Maybe overwhelmed though." Steve studies her face. "This was a good idea, Cailey. It's better being here."

"Good." His response is a relief. "Better for both of us then."

For a while, neither of them tries to fill the silence that settles in. Eventually Steve reaches for her hand. "Today, Cailey after learning that Apu was dead, all I could think of was renewing my contract for two more years if—"

"Steve." Cailey is stunned. She finds his eyes.

He realizes quickly. "If you would come with me."

"Oh."

"Oh?" He watches her closely. "For God's sake, Cailey, do you think I'd drop in on you, and then... Oh my God, don't you realize?"

She is silent.

"Cailey..."

She presses her fingers to her temples. "It's okay. I understand. There's so much we aren't saying to each other, Steve."

"I know. I wanted to tell you that today the thought had crossed my mind. That you might consider coming back with me. I'd never go without you."

"But also Steve, you shouldn't be stopping what you really want to do because of me. I feel we know so little of each other's lives. You have no idea what I'd be giving up to make that kind of a move. I've an exhibition on the go with Jennifer. A book in the works. A photography business to run. I've no intention of being a tag along in Peru."

He lifts his wineglass, replaces it on the table without taking a drink, he turns the glass round and round at the base. He doesn't look up. "That's a bit harsh, don't you think? I'd hardly expect you to be a tag along, Cailey. But okay, let's put an end to this. I am not renewing my contract. I'm staying here. In more ways than one, this is the only place I want to be." At last he looks up. "I guess I'm floundering here."

"I think we both are."

"Well, I'm sorry to have come so unstuck with the news of Apu's death. Honestly though, I'm not surprised my first instinct is to head straight back to Peru. Taking you with me. In so many ways I'm still there, Cailey. Surely that's to be expected. But I think we both know this is where I belong. Even Apu told me my work was back in Canada. So being here, in a way it honours his memory, you know?" Steve's voice breaks.

Cailey holds back tears. She plays with her fork. She knows he's right. Besides, she thinks, as she swallows her tears with a long sip of wine, when he's right here in front of her, opening up like this, there is no room for anything but this love she has fallen back into.

"I'm too much in love with you, Steve. Seems you can have your way with me. Can't you do something about this?"

Steve looks at her with relief. "In front of all these people?"

"Very funny. Seriously though, what I think we both need more than anything right now, is to find time away from the whirlwind." She leans over to smell the sauce that has just arrived atop a mountain of spaghetti. "I really do want my life back Steve. Right after I've devoured this insane amount of spaghetti."

For a time over dinner, they take refuge in more general topics. They talk about the new citizens' coalition, with Cailey arguing that it overlooks women's issues; nothing new in that, Steve insists. Which is not okay, Cailey responds, and he agrees.

They talk about mutual friends in Winnipeg, make a plan to walk up the mountain tomorrow, maybe go to a movie.

"What time do you have to be at the studio?" Steve's eyes seem troubled again as he pushes his plate away.

"I should be in there by eight-thirty." Cailey puts her fork down, leaves half her plate of spaghetti. "I think I'll have a cup of coffee before we go. Nothing could keep me awake tonight."

"I could."

"No, you couldn't." She knows he could.

"There is something else, Cailey."

"What do you mean?"

"Something important to tell you. I'm sorry, but even on top of everything else, this can't wait."

"Oh great."

He is staring at the wall of wine bottles behind her, avoiding her eyes.

He stirs sugar into his coffee. "Remember I told you I had to see Anne in California on my way back here?"

"Yes." She waits.

"When Anne left Peru with Greg, this American guy she'd shacked up with after she and I broke up, she was pregnant. I'd never seen her content like that, Cailey. I never could meet her needs. And mostly I didn't want to. Greg seemed a good resolution. For them. For her. Certainly for me."

"But it wasn't?"

"Well, in one important way, Cailey, it's no resolution at all."

"Can you just spit this out, Steve?"

He hesitates. "Okay. A couple of months ago, we got a letter announcing that Greg and Anne had had a baby girl. They felt very grateful, they said, because the baby had been three months premature, but had still arrived in perfect health."

"So…" Cailey has a vague inkling.

"It was Paulina who came to me with the letter."

"Who's Paulina?"

"Apu's wife. The letter from Anne, it was to all of us, it was passed around, Paulina returned it to me, tears streaming down her face. She was crying, señor, señor, I must tell you. I must, forgive me. She told me Anne's baby was not premature. It seems Anne had confided in Paulina just before she left for California. Paulina knew, she knew it was a full nine month pregnancy."

"And… that means…"

"Greg is not the father."

"And you are."

"Yes." There are tears in his eyes. "What I thought I was doing, Cailey, was going to see them to make practical arrangements. But then I saw her. Last week. I was transported from a violent world of death in the streets, all that hatred, Apu in the hospital, and I saw this… tiny *innocente*…" he searches Cailey's eyes for some sign of reassurance, "… my own baby daughter."

"What's her name?"

"Kim."

"Kim." Cailey tries it on. Kim. Steve's daughter Kim.

"It is the hardest thing, Cailey. To tell you this. Does it have to make such a difference?"

"You thought it wouldn't?" Cailey tries rearranging her outrage, a feeling uncomfortably close to jealousy. "What should I say, Steve? I mean, surely there's nothing more intimate than having a child with someone."

"There's nothing between Anne and me, if that's what you're thinking."

"There's a baby between you and Anne! What if I were sitting here telling you I had a kid, with, say Patrick, and that kid would be part of our life… and…"

"And…?"

"And… I'm just saying what if I'd had a child with my friend Patrick, and then sprung the news on you. Just try it out. You know. Imagine. Imagine me saying, 'oh Steve I've been meaning to tell you, my old lover

Patrick's dropping our little baby off for a visit, and I really hope it won't make a difference.'"

He shakes his head, laughing. "Okay okay. But it's not so much the idea of a kid Cailey. The problem's with this fellow Patrick. Were you in love with him?"

"What? That's really nothing to do with this."

Steve raises his eyebrows.

"Okay no, I wasn't in love with him. But I love him."

"Still?

"Still. You're jealous."

"So are you."

"Okay."

"I know I'm asking a lot of you. Too much happening all at once. Can I hope that the only difference for us, will be to have Kim visiting from time to time?"

"Oh wow, Steve, the difference is way bigger than casual visits each year. This is your own daughter you're talking about. Your child whose mother is Anne."

"Yes."

"I gather you and Anne have worked out some arrangement."

Sort of. Greg and Anne were almost too glad when I showed up; they seem to have been holding on to some idea of communal parenting. I made it clear that was not an arrangement I could take on. To be honest, Cailey, I thought I'd be going to see a baby, their baby in my mind, and find out what the three of us could work out in a purely financial arrangement. Then I'd get on a plane back here to be with you."

"You really thought that you...?"

"... that I wouldn't be moved?"

"I can't imagine how anyone wouldn't realize."

"Ouch." Steve looks away. "I was numb. I was following a plan. A straight line. I didn't grasp what it would mean for me until I held that little girl in my arms."

"What about the time you'll have with her? Travel back and forth?"

"It's possible Kim will come to Montreal for a month each year when Anne visits her family. Summer would work for me if I could line up a teaching job, juggle my time around her visits. I'll grab chances to visit her in California."

"Not exactly commuting distance from Montreal, Steve."

"I know that."

"Okay, so go on."

"There's nothing more to say really, there's no easy way to absorb it all."

"No. There isn't."

"Cailey," he holds her eyes, "can you accept that this is where I belong, I belong with you, I belong back in Canada for every reason I can think of. I'll work something out how to spend time with Kim. I'm not asking you to participate in that part of my life, unless it's natural for you. I'd love her to know you, to know how much I love you, I'd love her to grow up knowing us together."

Cailey softens. "It'll take time."

"Of course it will." Steve catches the glimmer of hope he's been hoping for. He exhales, leans back in his chair.

"It's a whole hell of a lot to get used to." She knows she is stating the obvious. "Right now though, I've got one of those wicked headaches coming on. I need to go home."

"It's pretty smoky in here."

"And pretty stressful."

"Right you are." Steve stands up. "Let's go. I'm not saying another word."

"Not until we get home, not until I'm lying down." Cailey slips on her coat. "Let's walk back. In the fresh air."

They stand side by side at the cash, waiting for their change. Cailey nibbles from the dish of revolting pastel mints. She pockets all the pink cinnamon ones. Just the thing for a headache.

They welcome the burst of cold air that greets them when they open the door head out onto the busy street.

CHAPTER
19

Cailey and Wendy arrive home to find Steve right where they left him in the living room, still two finger pecking at his portable typewriter.

He rolls the paper out of the carriage. "Okay, girls, *terminado*!" He looks up with a satisfied smile. "This wretched proposal is finally finished." He clasps his hands behind his head and leans back on the couch. "Only thing missing is Émile to edit the whole damn thing, of course. So how was supper with Lucie?"

Cailey notices the sandwiches they'd made together that morning remain untouched. He looks exhausted, and happy, and inviting, sitting there with tousled hair in his mess of papers. Even as her heart melts, she is sure of her decision. Live together, but separately. Another flat nearby. She's been on the lookout for rental signs at the laundromat, and up and down their street. The best solution, she will tell him. No loud meetings for her while she works in the evening. No pressure on him to tone down the boys on cigarettes and noise. She can hardly imagine, as she watches him now, that she'll ever be able to broach the idea with him.

"Supper was fun. Lucie's a riot. Her kids made the meal! And Wendy's interview with Lucie was superb. And by the way, Steve, Lucie wants to check you out. Soon she said. Before it's too late. Make sure you're good enough for me." Cailey curls up on the couch beside him.

"And am I?"

"We'll see. Lucie has the final word." She returns his kiss. "Wendy's making coffee, aren't you Wendy?" Wendy comes out of her bedroom, already in her pajamas.

"I'd rather have hot chocolate."

"Even after Lucie's sugar pie?"

"No, no, silly girl, with the sugar pie. I have the rest of it right here." She belches loudly on her way to the kitchen. Cailey knows this is for Steve's benefit.

"Wendy, you are highly skilled." Steve speaks with appreciation.

Cailey has been enjoying the irreverent banter between the two of them, though she knows it disguises a few tensions under the surface.

Cailey is about to turn the TV on when the doorbell rings. "Who's at the door at this hour?"

Steve looks apologetic. "Sorry. I'm afraid it's Émile. This is the last night, the thing is done. It's just the editing, it shouldn't be more than an hour. We have to present tomorrow. Someone else will retype it in the morning."

She knows he'll be up into the wee small hours. "No worries, Steve. We'll put on the coffee for you two and leave you to your own devices."

"Yes indeedie, follow me Cailey." Wendy heads toward her bedroom with a tray of hot chocolate and the bag of sugar pie. "And you, my sugah pie," she grins over her shoulder at Steve, "you can kiss your sugah pie goodbye."

***

A groggy-voiced Cliff answers the phone. "Jesus, Cailey. It's Sunday morning. The baby just fell asleep."

Oh God, Cailey realizes, *how could I forget?* "Sorry Cliff, I'm not thinking straight."

"Never mind. Here's Jennifer."

"Thanks." She'd forgotten about the baby. How could she forget about the baby?

"Cailey? What's wrong?"

"Oh . I'm sorry to wake you Jenn, I don't know what I was thinking. I must be driving you nuts. You have enough on your mind."

She hears Jennifer's long sigh on the other end of the line. "My problem, Cailey, is that I have nothing on my mind except babies."

"I won't keep you, just that I've been worrying about how bitchy I've been with Steve about his constant meetings, having Émile around here smoking up the apartment. We had a very upsetting fight about me wanting him to get his own place. He was over at Émile's all night last night."

"Okay Cailey, just come with me to the *boite à chanson* this afternoon. I'm getting out of here. Rehearsing with Francine for a couple of hours. Leaving Cliff with a bottle and three kids. I mean a milk bottle."

Cailey hears Cliff chuckling in the background.

"So we'll have a chance to chat, and you give some feedback on the pieces I'm rehearsing with Francine. It would actually be very helpful, since it's for your next exhibition."

"Perfect. Thank you thank you, Jenn. What time should I be there?"

"I'll pick you up. Best chats will be in the car! I'm picking Francine up at two, we'll be at your place little after that. Between us, we'll knock some sense into you!"

"I do believe you will. Sorry to Cliff."

"Don't worry about it, Cailey."

As she hangs up the phone, Cailey is horrified at herself. How could she have been that stupid.

She decides to take herself out for a coffee. She'll read the Sunday papers in that new café she and had Wendy checked out last week. She slips on her coat, pulls on her boots. She won't come back to the flat until Jenn comes by for her on the street in front. She'll enjoy the rehearsal. Steve will phone and she won't be home. She is thinking like a teenager.

At the rehearsal, the music goes, as always, straight to the heart. None of the group who usually show up to jam at the converted garage have shown up. With just the three of them, drinking strong black tea at their breaks, discussing their harmonies, changes Jenn might make to a few bars here and there. The afternoon flies by, and at last takes Cailey out of herself and into the creative sanctuary she has learned to rely on.

By the time Jennifer and Francine drop her back at her front door, she is restored to some semblance state of normal maturity.

"Thanks for the music you two. And the heart to hearts! Best thing…"

"Clouds clear tomorrow," Francine predicts. "It's always like that with men. Sun again. No explanation needed!"

"Ahh so true," Jenn agrees. "I'll call you tomorrow, Cailey."

They wave as the car pulls away from the curb.

She walks slowly up the stairs to the apartment, she is not tired, but her heart is pounding as she turns the key in the latch. She is afraid he won't be there, she is afraid he will be.

"Where were you?"

She doesn't answer for a minute, she doesn't trust herself. She hangs up her coat, pulls off her boots. He is sitting on the couch, reading. Pretending to read. A part of her wants to tell him that it's none of his business where she was.

"I went to a rehearsal with Jenn."

"A rehearsal?"

"At the *boite à chanson* where the band plays. The group Jennifer plays in with Francine." She knows she is sounding impatient. "You heard them over at Jenn and Cliff's, Steve. They're doing the music for my exhibition."

"So it was good? The rehearsal?"

"No." She sits down at the other end of the couch. "It wasn't."

He closes his book and puts it on the floor beside him.

She waits.

"And so?" he asks.

"You're asking me?" she responds.

"Okay, sorry. I do understand that it might work to live separately but nearby. I'd just never considered the possibility."

Finally she looks over at him. She sees it all then, everything she needs to know, the love in his eyes as he watches her.

"Steve, I love you."

He reaches for her. "I know."

She silences him with her fingers on his lips. She wants him in the most urgent way.

***

"You got the tickets?" Wendy barges into the living room opening the envelope Cailey had left on her bed the night before. "How many. Six. So who's coming? What do I owe you?"

"It can be whoever you want, Wendy. It's a present from me and Steve."

"Come on, since when did you two hit the big time? These are fifteen bucks a piece."

"It's your going away present."

"Holy shit *la merde*." Wendy looks down at the tickets in her hand. "So." For once, Wendy's snappy humour fails her. "A going away present. I guess that makes it official." She does not look up. She is leaving in three weeks for a position in Winnipeg as editor of a new women's magazine, a result, in part, of her success writing and editing Cailey's book of photo essays.

"Who are you inviting, Wens?" Cailey braids her hair absent-mindedly, understanding for the first time, that in three weeks, her dear Wendy will no longer be here. The thought does not sit well.

Wendy drops into the big armchair and stares out the window. "It will be you two. Consuela and Gaetan. And Lucie."

"Perfect!"

"Yes." Wendy turns to go back to her room. "So now, I must sort out some of the crap in my room. I'll yell at you if I need immediate service."

"Wait a sec, Wendy." Steve folds his newspaper. "I want to tell you both about this idea I have. I want to tell you about next week."

Wendy sits down across from Cailey. "We already know about next week, Steve. You're moving to your new apartment and you're having separation anxiety."

"In fact," he goes on, "I'm asking you two to come on an outing with me next weekend. I'm thinking of buying a cabin."

"What? A cabin?" Cailey stares at him, astonished. "Where?" It's the first she's heard of it.

"I've been thinking about this for a while. Don't look so surprised, Cailey. I've talked to you about a place Kim might be with us in the summer, out of the city."

"Okay, go on." She had successfully put Kim right out of her mind.

"A couple of days ago I heard from a friend whose family is in Huntsville, at the edge of Algonquin Park. He says there's an old cabin for sale near his folks' cottage."

"How far?"

"Maybe six hours. No, come on Cailey, hear me out. I know it's probably too far. It may not be the right place. But it's on a lake. There's really no harm in looking, is there? And it's a good deal. Anything around here is way too pricey for us, even with the separatism scare bringing prices down. I want to go and look. It's an old log cabin on four rocky acres. It could be beyond repair. I couldn't really tell by talking to this guy.

The thing is, though, I think we could buy it on time, with no down payment, if we agree to operate the outfitters store for their canoe trips each summer. We could pay it off in a few years, Cailey. You could never get a deal like that around here."

"We're going to drive six hours on Friday? Next Friday? In winter?" Cailey is incredulous. "So we can set things up to work in a store all summer?"

"For this weekend, there's a ski lodge nearby. We can rent cross country skis. I made reservations." He glances at Cailey, then at Wendy. "I mean just in case you two liked the idea." He laughs at her expression. "I just thought it would be fun, Cailey, before Wendy goes, even if we don't like the cabin."

"Well now hear this," Wendy exclaims, "this is a fabulous idea. I mean the weekend away. And this cabin. I love it!"

"Wendy, cross country skiing bores the hell out of you, to use your words of many years, and besides," she turns to Steve, "if Steve got this cabin, how could he afford to be away from Montreal for so long?"

"I'm taking that high school job. I told you I'd had an offer, Cailey. That means I'll have time for Kim in the summer. I could do most of my work up there. My union contract with Émile is finished in June. Then there'll be nothing until I start teaching in September. I've got enough saved up. I'd spend most of the summer fixing the cabin up. And still get courses ready. And make sure, Cailey, that you'd have a place to work."

"Dream on, Stevie boy," Wendy quips. "But hey, I'm all for the weekend. It's just what I need right now. So let's at least do that part."

"Let me get this right, Steve. We'd both work in this store? And you'd look after Kim? She's still a baby."

"I know."

Cailey holds Wendy's gaze for a moment. "Am I being railroaded here, Wendy?"

"Absolutely."

"Wait a minute, Cailey, Kim won't be coming this year. Probably not for a couple of years. She's too little. If I can afford it, I'll go out to California for a week or so at the end of June." He rests his hand on the back of Cailey's neck. "And then we could go up to the cabin for the rest of the summer. And work on it. Well, you wouldn't have to work on it. We won't have to work in the store until the second year. Apparently it may have space for a studio. You could even have time there on your own, once we get it fixed up, you could go up before I finish teaching each spring, it could be like the time you had in the Maritimes last summer, every year you could have that."

"I see. I believe you've just tricked me, Steve."

"Correct." He grins.

"Also it's a tad closer to Winnipeg," Wendy chimes in. "I will arrive every summer to save you from your boredom. Maybe Beth and Paul could visit."

Cailey raises her eyebrows and ignores the second suggestion. "You realize we'd have three places then Steve. Two apartments empty for three months every summer?"

"Maybe one month for me. Émile says they'd rent it for union people coming in for meetings."

"I wouldn't want anybody in my place, though, not with all my work around, although I suppose I could pack it up and leave it at Jenn's."

Wendy stretches out on the floor and begins her routine of sit-ups. "What about someone you know who could come and stay? Nine ten eleven... like another artist... fifteen sixteen seventeen..." She puffs out the words. "What if... twenty, twenty-one... what if, say Patrick and Marie-Claude rented it for part of the time... and... twenty-four, twenty-five, twenty six... came down from Quebec City?"

"Something like that might work out, Wendy. Okay, I'm in. No commitments though. Let's just have a look."

In the kitchen, Cailey cuts oranges and presses the dripping halves, one at a time, onto the juicer.

Steve puts the dishes away. "You're very quiet."

"Just thinking." She pours juice into the pitcher, cuts more oranges. The familiar task relaxes her. "I'm thinking, in three weeks Wendy leaves for good. You're moving on Tuesday. I'll be living alone. You have a daughter I've never met. We'll spend summers with her in a cabin we haven't seen yet. Your head's still half in Peru."

"It is a bit much, isn't it?"

"Yes."

"You realize I'm trying to fix things so you'll have to live with me for part of the year."

"Yes." Cailey continues twisting the oranges onto the juicer. "And I like it."

She is aware of his smile as he puts cutlery away in the drawer beside her. She is feeling only slightly off balance, teetering only slightly on the last crossing stone in a fast stream, still anticipating the outcome of the final leap.

CHAPTER
20

DO NOT RUN FROM MAGIC (REPRISE)
NORTHERN ONTARIO
AUGUST 1985

"I still don't get it, Cailey."

"Don't get what?"

Beth props their two paddles up in the corner of the porch, "Why you won't come back with me." She turns to look directly at Cailey. "And help find Paul."

"But you think he's headed up here, or to Montreal. Maybe we'll hear from him."

"And if we don't?"

"Well maybe. I'm not sure what I could do." Cailey hears the falseness in her voice, the foolish words.

The phone rings. "Could you grab that Beth, while I get this backpack off?"

Beth pushes open the screen door, letting it slam loudly behind her as she picks up the phone. Cailey receives the sound as a slap, an intended reprimand.

"Hello? Wendy! Hi! No, it's Beth. How are you? What? Sure she's right here."

Cailey takes the phone. "I hope you're calling to say you're you coming next week."

"I am. And I'm bringing that cute brother of yours."

Cailey looks straight into Beth's eyes. "Don't joke Wendy, we've been worried sick about him."

"I'm not joking. I'm calling because Paul just found out from your Uncle Mickey where Beth is. He's okay. There's nothing to worry about."

"Beth, it's okay, Paul is fine." She watches Beth sink onto a kitchen chair. "So tell us, where is he?"

"Well the weird thing is, he's been right under my nose all week and I didn't even know it. He's working in the coffee shop downstairs. But we've been so busy here, someone else has been doing the coffee run. Anyway, I just went down for the first time this week, and there he was. Tanned and healthy and gorgeous."

"Don't you dare, Wendy. He's too young for you. You're a fallen woman."

Beth laughs quietly, gives Cailey the thumbs up.

"So go on."

"Well, we just went out for lunch, and he told me this horrendous story Cailey. Did Beth tell you about the accident on the river?"

"Yes of course."

"And, oh shit."

"What?"

Cailey hears a long sigh on the other end of the line. "I guess your Dad really flipped out on him. And everyone in town was freaked out because it was right where Becky drowned. Mickey was the most upset. He wants to talk to you, Cailey. This incident with Paul has got your mother, in her drunken way, blathering something about the letter she sent you with the story of the amber."

"Oh no."

"And Paul says he'll never go back."

"To Wood River?"

"That's right. Ever heard that before?"

"Ha."

"Anyway, I'll see Paul tonight. I've offered him my couch till he finds a place he can afford. He's been in a sort of flop house downtown."

"You're an angel, Wendy."

"I thought I was a fallen woman."

"That too. A fallen angel."

"In any event, I'm not playing saviour here. I'm doing this because I like him. And because he's your brother. He's a very special person Cailey. You should meet him sometime yourself."

"Yes, I know. Shut up, Wendy."

"He knows I'm calling you. He actually tried calling Montreal himself, but someone else answered. So he hung up."

"Consuela and Gaetan are staying there right now, at my place. But anyway Wendy, why don't we call you back tonight, when Paul's there with you?"

"I was going to suggest that. It will have to be late though, he doesn't get off until ten. So maybe if you call around twelve your time."

"Sure. We'll do that. Is he really planning to come out here with you? Beth will have to go back before then."

"He's apparently seen Beth once or twice in the last fifteen years. I got this feeling he might be coming to see you, Cailey."

Cailey does not respond.

"You still there?"

"Tell him I really want so very much to see him." She looks over at Beth and all at once it is clear what she will do. She knew it would come someday.

"How's Steve, Cailey? And Kim?"

"Good. They're both having a great summer so far. Some might say I've been a tad irritable about getting to my work for the exhibition. But it's wonderful having Beth here. There's a lot of catching up to do, we haven't even begun really. How's work?"

"Very challenging at the moment. Speaking of which, I'd better go. We're about to lose funding for the magazine, but we have a big campaign right now, so we might last another year. A special interest group we're called. We're women for God's sake. Oh don't get me started. I'd better go. I'll talk to you tonight."

"Give Paul a hug from me. And one from Beth."

"That means he'll get at least three."

"He's too young for you."

Wendy is chuckling as the line goes dead.

***

"Steve? Are you awake?" The only response Cailey gets is the creaking of the bed as Steve rolls over in his sleep. She slips quietly in under the warm covers. Tonight the air has an unmistakable autumn chill, and a light breeze rustles up from the woods and sweeps across the porch, playing gently on the wind chimes, cooling her flushed face. For a moment, as she lies perfectly still, she is aware only of her rapid heartbeat, of her shallow breath, of the light of the full moon filtering down through the tops of the tallest trees. It is the one moment of solitude she's had in a day that she could measure in years rather than hours. She sits up again. Maybe she'll go to the back room and work on her drawings.

"Cailey." Steve squeezes her hand. "Come on, come on back to bed."

"I thought you were asleep."

"I am."

She turns to him. "I was going to work on that drawing."

"I know." He folds his arms around her. "You need to be here right now."

She doesn't protest. "We talked to Paul."

"I heard the first part. Tell me."

"You won't remember if I tell you."

"I will. I'm wide awake now. So what did he have to say?"

"I could hardly keep up with him. He didn't stop talking for half an hour. First to Beth, then to me. I found it strange at first. Well I mean in a way he is a stranger to me. Those short calls for his birthdays were always such a strain, which was my fault. But tonight he seemed completely open. And the most surprising thing, under the circumstances, is that he was so funny. Making fun of himself, mostly."

"But was he upset?"

"Oh I think so. Beth says he always jokes about the serious stuff, and then gets freaked out by something trivial in a friendly hockey game or something. That doesn't sound like the Paul I knew, but then of course... I don't know him." Cailey stops.

"Has he been in touch with your parents?"

"No. Just Uncle Mickey. Wendy can't get him to call Mum and Dad. He knows Beth will call them now, but he doesn't want them to know where he is."

"That makes things a bit hard for Beth."

"Yes it does."

"Is she going to stay for Wendy and Paul's visit?"

"No, now that she knows Paul's safe, I think she wants to get home to Andy Mac."

***

It's not until late the next afternoon that Cailey notices the amber pin is not in its place.

"Beth!" Cailey removes the headphones and turns off the tape. She looks more closely at the drawing she's working on, rubs out one line, reworks it.

Cailey turns to see Beth already standing in the doorway, stirring a bowl of cookie batter held in the crook of her arm. Kim stands just behind her, licking the egg beater. "We're making chocolate ones, you wanna lick?" Kim holds the beater out for Cailey.

"No thanks, Kim." Kim's face is covered in chocolate. "Where did you put the amber pin, Beth?"

"I gave it back to you yesterday. On the way up the path."

"No you didn't. I would have put it right back in the dish if you'd given it to me."

"Cailey, I watched you put it in the back pocket of your jeans."

"Oh." Cailey remembers. She is embarrassed by her irritation. "Okay, sorry Beth."

"Let's get out of here, Kim, she's an old grouch today, isn't she?"

"Yeah, let's eat all her cookies."

"Good idea."

Cailey puts her head down on the drawing board. She doesn't know whether to laugh or cry. She goes to look for the amber pin.

"Can we cook out down at the lake tonight, Cailey? Dad said we could cook out." Kim is at the kitchen table spooning the cookies onto the cookie sheet. The tablecloth is covered in flour, eggshells, smears of butter.

"He said maybe, Kim. We'll see when he comes up from the store. It looks like it might rain."

"He said," an entire raw cookie disappears into Kim's mouth and she continues to talk through the dough, "he said it would be all starry tonight."

Cailey smiles on her way out to the porch. Muffled giggles come from behind her and she can only guess what faces are being made behind her back. What a pair, she is thinking, as she searches under the swinging bed for her jeans, what an absolutely wonderful pair. Pajamas, socks, underwear, what a mess. She pulls everything out and stuffs it into the laundry bag inside the kitchen door.

"Where did I put my jeans?"

Beth calls to her from the kitchen. "They're hanging on the back of the bathroom door."

"Oh that's right," Cailey mumbles to herself as she walks back through the kitchen. "Thanks Beth, I guess I'm just losing my mind, that's all, nothing serious really."

Beth comes to find her just as she takes the amber pin from the pocket of her jeans.

"Ease up Cailey, chocolate is good for the soul."

"I know." Cailey fingers the pin for a minute. "So I'm coming to eat cookies and help you finish up in the kitchen, then we'll figure out supper."

"Good. Okay Kim, the old grouch is coming to try your cookies."

Cailey goes into the kitchen. "Beth, would you wear this for a while?"

"What? Why?"

"Just wear it for a bit." Cailey fastens the amber pin onto Beth's shirt. "I'll explain tonight. I'm going to draw you some pictures."

There is an indignant cry of protest from out on the porch. "Oh no! It's raining."

"Never mind, Kim," Cailey pushes open the screen door. "We'll cook out down at the lake tomorrow."

"That's what always happens, it always happens if I say I want to cook out. I'm never saying it again. I'll just sneak the food down there tomorrow in an old box." Kim stands watching the sky, her bottom lip curled, her palms turned up to catch the rain, which is beginning to blow hard against the front of the cabin.

"Okay Kim, but don't just stand there. We need to bring your hammock and sleeping bag inside, you can sleep on the sofa tonight if it's still raining."

"With the fire on. I like to sleep by the fire, we can roast marshmallows. Hey, I know. We'll cook out, right in the living room. We'll do our hot dogs on sticks, and then marshmallows." She looks up at Cailey, blinking through the rain in her face. "Okay Cailey? Please?"

A sudden realization. A yes somewhere in Cailey's mind.

"Yes, Kim, that'd be fun. We better hurry with that sleeping bag though, before it's drenched."

"Maybe this will be even better than cooking out at the lake!"

Kim races inside with the sleeping bag. Beth rolls up the hammock while Cailey drops the awnings on the screened side of the porch and clips their hooks to fasteners on the wooden floor. She lifts Kim's suitcase and a few books and comics up onto the swinging bed. Down below, she can hear cars pulling out of the parking lot. She hopes none of the canoes is caught out on the lake. They hadn't expected the wind to pick up like this today.

***

"That tree came down right across the path," Steve says, jogging up the steps in the pouring rain. "Barely missed the corner of the cabin." The sound of it falling, a prolonged thunderous crack, had startled Beth who'd been reading in front of the fire, but Kim, already asleep at the other end of the sofa, had made only one small murmur of protest, having no reason to distrust the world around her.

"Everything's okay at the store as far as I can see. At least the power's still on. I haven't seen a wind like that in all the summers we've been here." Steve is out of breath as he hangs his dripping poncho on the hook just inside the door. "Have there been any calls?"

"No, nothing so far. There must be some pretty drenched campers out there." Cailey shivers in the cold draft as she latches the door.

"Drenched is okay. It's that wind that worries me." Steve reaches into his pocket. "I forgot to bring the mail up earlier. There's something from Jennifer. Another tape probably." He hands a pile of letters to Cailey. Jenn's latest composition, Cailey guesses as she pushes the mail to the back of the counter. The last thing she wants right now is a reminder of how late she is with the exhibition drawings.

"I love this kind of storm, don't you, Cailey?" Beth pulls a plate of cookies from the top shelf of the cupboard where she'd hidden them from Kim. She takes two and puts the plate on the table. "Remember Granddad that time, trying to get the motor off the boat, the wind blew him over into the river."

"Yes." Cailey senses that the memory is different for her. "You and Paul thought it was pretty funny."

Beth's expression is amused, but slightly defensive. "Well it was funny," she stifles a giggle. "Anyway Granddad thought so. He came in laughing and cursing at the same time about going ass-over-teakettle." She looks directly at Cailey. "You didn't always have to be so grown-up you know."

"I guess... that's probably true. What do you feel like doing now, Beth?"

"Don't know. Have a beer maybe."

"How about bringing it to the back room. I want to show you some other sketches of Wood River." Cailey's stomach tightens into a painful knot as she catches Steve's eye.

"Sure," Beth opens the fridge, "I don't mind. Anyone else for a beer?"

"I'll make some tea." Cailey puts the kettle on and lights the burner.

"And a good dose of rum for me." Steve reaches under the sink, pulls out the bottle of dark rum.

Beth is opening her beer, wiping the lip of the bottle on the corner of her shirt.

"What if I move Kim to the bedroom for now, and you two can build up the fire in the living room?" Steve washes his hands at the sink. "It could get pretty cold out in the back room."

"Okay. Then maybe I'll just sleep on the sofa. Just let me get a few things before you move her." Beth disappears into the bedroom.

"Steve." Cailey puts her hand out stop to him. "Where are you going?"

He looks surprised. "To move Kim, then to bed. With my tea." He checks out the kitchen window. "The wind seems to be dying down now. It'll be fine on the porch." He smiles at her anxious expression. "I'll warm the bed for you."

"You know what?"

"What?"

"I need you to be with me. The drawing I have to do. Well, you need to be there. For the drawing. And for me."

"Really? You're sure?"

"Very sure."

Cailey goes to the back room with a candle. She quickly selects a few sketches. She has done this over and over in her mind. A few she takes from the wall. Then she piles them up inside the front cover of her sketchbook and slides a few charcoals into her shirt pocket. She picks up the tape player and several tapes, tucks the drawings under her arm and blows out the candle. For a moment, in the dark, she does not move. She listens only to the sound of her own breathing. Her heart beats so hard, she can feel it in her ears.

Back in the living room, Cailey fidgets absently with the top of the teapot, she forgets how long it's been steeping, but it looks dark and strong enough; she fills two cups to the brim.

Beth comes in and sits down, bends over her book, flips through pages till she finds her place. The amber pin on her shirt glows warm and golden in the light from the kerosene lamp behind the sofa.

Cailey waits, observing the progress of hungry flames as they leap around the logs that Steve piles on the grate. He settles in beside her and she curls up against him in the corner of the sofa.

Around them in this room, Cailey senses the mingling of stories, old and new. Newer stories like Beth's, and hers, and Steve's, woven into the silenced voices of an old cabin. The idea evokes for her the eerie presence of those who came before, those who may have sat side by side on this sofa, taking comfort around this fireplace.

She glances up at a row of small framed photos propped on the mantel just above the silly dangling marionette. A couple of summers ago, one of the old timers from down the lake had presented Steve with these yellowed prints of the young trapper and his wife who had opened the first portage store back in the twenties. In one photo they stand together in front of their horse drawn stoneboat, ready for their next haul through the woods and up the rocky hill. With their own hands, the two of them had built the fireplace, and constructed their cabin around it. In another snapshot, the trapper's wife is seen stirring a blackened pot hanging from its hook in the fireplace. Their life must have suited them, for they'd lived to a ripe old age and died within days of each other; that year someone, a dealer most likely, had come from the city with a wagon, in the thick of winter, and cleaned out every piece of the valuable hand made furniture. The one item left behind had been the immoveable horsehair sofa where Steve and Cailey and Beth now sit together, their stories weaving their way into its history.

Cailey finishes her tea and looks down at the sketches that lie on the floor next to her feet. She leans over finally, and reorders them in a particular way, the way she has planned. At this moment, the images are not separate from her, her fingers find the emotional current. Tentatively, she offers the first sketch to Beth.

Beth closes her book and takes the drawing from Cailey's hands. "I've seen this one. It's from your wall."

"That's right."

"Maybe I didn't look all that closely." Beth holds the sketch closer to the lamp. "Okay, sure. I remember Gran like that, leaning over me just like that. Just like that. And the pin. I do remember the pin." Beth puts her hand on the amber still fastened to the pocket of her shirt. She loosens the clasp and holds it to the light of the flickering fire. "That's the colour, Cailey. It's beautiful. It glows like that in your drawing."

Steve pours more tea, adds rum to both their cups. Cailey sips, welcoming the sweet burning at the back of her throat, the strong spirits making her eyes water.

She reaches over and picks out Jennifer's composition, *The Amber Suite*.

"Okay, Beth, here's some music I want to play. My friend Jennifer composed this. It's inspired by Gran and the story of the amber pin as Gran told it in the letter you and I were reading this afternoon. Here. Let's hold up one of the sketches." Cailey props the sketch against the raised hearth.

"I thought you were going to draw."

"I am. But listen just for a sec."

Cailey presses play. The first sound, the cello, slow, haunting.

"Well now, that's cheerful Cailey, just what I feel like."

"I know. Sorry. Maybe I should turn it off." Cailey glances back at Steve. "No wait." She changes her mind, turns up the volume. "Wait, listen to this part."

"Bagpipes?" Beth is wide-eyed as she listens, a smile spreading across her face.

"Francine and her bagpipes." Steve laughs at Beth's expression. "That was the big surprise for everyone, Beth."

"Weird." Beth leans forward. "And we're listening to this because...?"

"I just hoped you'd enjoy it with me. For some reason, it makes it easier to draw this story out of the shadows. Weird or not, for me it goes with what happened. This is the only way I know to get there." Cailey takes Beth's hand and opens it, palm up, to expose the amber to the light of the fire. She places her sketchpad on her lap, and begins to draw. "Imagine," she whispers as Beth and Steve move closer to watch the images taking shape, "imagine the amber as our witness through time, imagine the dark forests fallen, the deep deep heavy earth, pressing down, and then," Cailey's charcoal moves quickly, "there is amber, and here, the great *menhirs,* the mysterious standing stones, rising from that ancient earth, yearning skyward. And in this music, Beth, the dance, a healing circle, the mystery that is ancient, but not old."

Cailey lifts the amber from the palm of Beth's hand, holds it in her own, and turns it over to expose the rough surface on the underside where the markings have been preserved. She points to the faint pattern of criss cross lines scratched into the stone.

"Look closely Beth, there, do you see the markings?"

"Yes, yes, I do." All at once Beth is engaged, Cailey can see it. She's drawn to this magical source, the source of Gran's story.

Word for word, the final lines of their grandmother's letter run through Cailey's mind. "Remember the last part of Gran's letter Beth, when she's talking about her own mother, our great grandmother?"

Beth is watching Cailey closely. "I'm not sure, Cailey," she replies, tilting her head to one side.

"Okay then, here's what Gran's own mum told her about the amber pin," Cailey looks at the fire, while she recites the lines from memory:

"It was not until just before I came out to Canada that my mother called me to her room."

"So that would be our great great grandmother," Beth comments wryly, "calling our great grandmother to her room."

"Exactly." Cailey smiles at her sister, continues reciting.

"She unclasped the pin from her own collar and put it in my hand. Turn it over, she said, and look closely at the markings under the setting, where it has not been polished. You see these brush strokes, she pointed with her finger, they are worn down by the centuries, but they do not lose their meaning. When my mother closed my fingers around the pin, she told me that the markings were an ancient symbol of energy, and they signified the healing power given to the amber by the heat of the sun."

"Your healing amber, Cailey."

"And yours."

Beth nods.

In a hushed voice, Cailey recites again, more to herself than to Beth or to Steve, *"...the healing power given to the amber by the heat of the sun."* She closes her fingers around the amber pin, and turns to the next blank sheet in her sketchbook.

She draws quickly, the sweep of a wide river, the outline of a bridge, the suggestion of a current swirling around piers, figures gathered around a bonfire, kids running around. She sketches her dad, Uncle Mickey, Auntie Val, a few friends, talking with their backs to the bridge. Beth beside their father; herself where she'd stood that night, at the edge of the circle, her head turned toward Becky, the lone figure of her mother at the rocky ledge near the bridge.

Cailey puts her charcoal pencil down. She closes her eyes for a moment, relaxes into the feel of Steve's hand on her neck. He massages slowly, deeply, into the tightest muscles. His hand is warm, gentle, sure.

In this one brief pause, Cailey's sudden flash of clarity. Becky's joyful laughter sounding out to Cailey as clearly as if she were running in the door to greet them. And startling her, the call of the cuckoo, a distant call, somewhere high above a circle of standing stones. It is almost too real. For a moment Cailey cannot breathe. The amber grows warmer in her hand.

All this, a confusion of lives, come to life in Cailey's mind.

Becky is running around the bonfire. Wanting marshmallows, 'now,' she insists. 'No hon,' says Auntie Val, 'not yet, they're for later.' Becky hanging around for a bit, still whining, pulling on her father's hand. 'You heard your mother,' Uncle Mickey is saying, lifting her up in his arms, holding her there, laughing at her. Becky's face golden and sulky in the light from the fire. That auburn in her curly hair. The love on Uncle Mickey's face. He is setting her down. She is leaning into his legs, she is scampering off to grab the whole bag of marshmallows and present it proudly to the other kids. Uncle Mickey speaks in low tones to Cailey's dad, Cailey hears him clearly. 'Come on, Jim, Ellen's had enough,' Mickey warns, glancing anxiously over his shoulder at Cailey's mother, 'someone needs to take that beer from her.' 'You know it never does any good, Jim,' Cailey's dad is replying, 'she'll only find another.' Gran's songs picking up speed, everyone joining in, moonlight rippling across the river behind them.

It is only a moment later that Cailey catches sight of a movement near her mother. It is only in that one moment that Becky is standing there, grabbing at the beer bottle in Ellen's hand.

Cailey stares at Beth who nods. She knows. Cailey picks up her charcoal.

She draws the figure of her mother. She draws one arm raised up, the arm that has yanked the bottle from those two small hands. She draws the other arm, the arm that is landing hard against the side of Becky's head, the small body landing on the rock with a crack that only Cailey has heard, the small body sliding away into the fast current.

That small body. Pushed. Taken by the river.

Printed in Canada